PRAISE FOR
THE WHITE CITY

"A delightful debut! Bursting with intrigue, romance, and historical tidbits that bring Chicago during the Gilded Age to vivid life, *The White City* is a story that's certainly destined for the keeper shelf."

–Jen Turano, *USA Today* bestselling author

"From the first sentence until the last, Hitchcock has crafted a tale that weaves in and out and all around, keeping me guessing until the final page was turned. *The White City* is a story I won't soon forget!"

–Kathleen Y'Barbo, author of *The Alamo Bride*, *The Pirate Bride*, and *My Heart Belongs in Galveston, Texas*

the WHITE CITY

GRACE HITCHCOCK

BARBOUR BOOKS
An Imprint of Barbour Publishing, Inc.

Print ISBN 978-1-68322-868-4

eBook Editions:
Adobe Digital Edition (.epub) 978-1-68322-870-7
Kindle and MobiPocket Edition (.prc) 978-1-68322-869-1

All scripture quotations are taken from the King James Version of the Bible.

This book is a work of fiction. Names, characters, places, and incidents are either products of the author's imagination or used fictitiously. Any similarity to actual people, organizations, and/or events is purely coincidental.

Cover Image: Holly Leedham/Trevillion Images

Published by Barbour Books, an imprint of Barbour Publishing, Inc., 1810 Barbour Drive, Uhrichsville, Ohio 44683, www.barbourbooks.com

Our mission is to inspire the world with the life-changing message of the Bible.

 Member of the
Evangelical Christian
Publishers Association

Printed in the United States of America

Dedication

To the one who holds my heart.

The LORD is my light and my salvation; whom shall I fear? The LORD is the strength of my life; of whom shall I be afraid? When the wicked, even mine enemies and my foes, came upon me to eat up my flesh, they stumbled and fell.

PSALM 27:1–2 KJV

Chapter One

*"If adventures will not befall a young lady in her
own village, she must seek them abroad."*
~Jane Austen, *Northanger Abbey*

Chicago, July 1893

Winnifred Wylde concentrated on his forehead, nodding, trying to respond appropriately, but it was so difficult with his nose hair escaping and retreating into his left nostril with every breath. Clutching the gold-rimmed china teacup, she averted her gaze to the front entrance of the Ceylon Teahouse, envying the rest of the fairgoers passing by, free from listening to Mr. Saunders drone on and on.

I cannot believe Aunt Lillian made me set aside my novel for this. She promised me a day at the world's fair, not a never-ending monologue. Winnifred thought of the poor heroine that she had left in the clutches of danger and longed to return to her chapter. *Rowena might not even get to marry her love, Lord Francis! She may end up with the villain!* She swallowed, trying not to resent Mr. Saunders for keeping her from her reading. *Why does Aunt Lillian insist on bringing me suitors? I keep telling her I don't want a man "brought." I want him to ride through the meadows and sweep me off my feet. I want adventure. I want—*Mr. Saunders snorted at his own joke, sending the dreaded nose hair twirling in the air as he chomped down on his scone, strawberry jam smearing on his pale chin.

Not him, that's for sure. She pasted on a smile. *You must endure as Rowena did when she was captured by her father's evil business partner, Aloysius. Endure.*

A flake of scone caught in his thick mustache.

But I am no heroine. I cannot endure this any longer. "I can't."

"Pardon me, Miss Wylde?" His thick brows rose at her interruption.

Her eyes grew wide as she barely refrained from slapping her hand over her mouth. *Did I say that out loud?* "I am so sorry. I meant to say—" A flash of green drew her gaze to behind her suitor's shoulder and into the shadows of an exhibit where a lean man with a thick mustache seized the wrist of a woman in an emerald day dress as he reached for her dangling reticule. The woman's mouth twisted in pain, and she attempted to wrench herself from his grasp, but she stilled when the man pulled what appeared to be a small revolver from his pocket and pressed it to her corseted waist.

Thinking of the numerous disappearances of young women lately and the countless stories she had read of ruffians ransoming young women, Winnifred dropped her napkin and in her haste to rise, jarred the table, setting the teapot to rattling. She picked up her white skirt and rushed out, leaving Mr. Saunders calling out for her as she ducked under and around the booths in the Woman's Building, knocking loose her pink chapeau as she raced to the main entrance in pursuit of the couple. But the sea of fairgoers outside had already swallowed them. Her gaze flew from white building to blinding white building, her stomach churning at the thought that she was this woman's only hope if this man was indeed the devil behind the White City disappearances.

"Miss Wylde! There you are." Mr. Saunders's cheeks puffed with the effort it took him to follow her. "Whatever drew you away?"

Righting her hat, Winnifred turned to him with her hands on her hips. "Would you be so kind as to take me to the police station? I need to report a kidnapping."

His eyes widened as he clutched his brocade-embroidered waistcoat. "Wh–whatever do you mean?"

"I witnessed a man forcing some poor woman to comply with his will under threat of death." Winnifred twisted around, searching for an exit sign. In the event of a kidnapping, every second counted. "We need to leave *now*."

He swept off his hat and fanned his face. "I can hardly believe it. We were only feet from a crime. I mean, you read about these things in the paper, but you never imagine that they could happen to y—"

Spying a sign for the nearest grip car station, Winnifred dug into her reticule for fare. "Mr. Saunders, I'm afraid we have no time to waste. We must be off at once."

"But our luncheon?" he protested.

"Will have to end prematurely." *Thank the Lord.* Winnifred set off at a brisk walk, attempting to keep an obtainable pace for Mr. Saunders, but he soon flagged behind, collapsing into a chair at one of the many outdoor restaurants as he muttered for her to wait. But time was of the essence. She wove through the crowds, desperately trying to reach the line before the next grip car departed. Paying for a ticket, she slipped inside the car only moments before the copper bell rang and the car lurched forward. Gripping the pole, she sat perched on the wooden seat, her knee bouncing as she counted the stops until she reached her father's station.

The woman next to Winnifred looked her up and down with a pinched expression before turning to her companion, whispering away.

Let them gossip. She lifted her head, knowing that her hair must look a fright after her chase, but she didn't have time to stop at home for a comb and an escort. This was an emergency.

The car jerked to a halt a block from the police station, and without even a departing glance at the women, Winnifred strode down the sidewalk, her skirt slapping against her calves in a raucous manner that would have appalled her Aunt Lillian. Taking the steps two at a time, she let herself into the police station and, with a wave to the front desk officer, she hurried through to the stairs, climbing them to the second floor. She marched toward her father's office, but before she could reach for the door, one of the officers called out to her.

"Miss Wylde, good to see you. Inspector Wylde stepped out for a cup of coffee, but he should be back any minute." Officer Baxter grinned, crossing the room to greet her. "Found any more criminals for us to lock up today?"

She laughed without mirth. "Very funny. As a matter of fact, I did." She crossed her arms, waiting for him to exclaim over her declaration, but much to her chagrin, he merely laughed at her, shaking his head as if her announcement was the most amusing thing he'd heard in a while.

"Never a dull day when you brighten our doors, Miss Wylde." The gangly officer sat on the corner of a nearby desk, crossing his arms as if to further mock her. "Can you tell me about this criminal? Was he tall, dark, and handsome, with a knife? I believe it was a knife last time, wasn't it? So maybe today he should be wielding, perhaps, a revolver?" He stroked his auburn mustache with two fingers.

Winnifred pressed her lips into a firm line as she turned her back to him. *Father will listen to me.* Letting herself into his office, she left the door open and sank into his large, worn leather chair behind his desk and ran her finger over the silver frame that rested on top. She lifted the picture and gazed into the face of the woman of whom she was told she was an exact replica. She traced the faint dimple in her mother's wide smile before traveling over the curled locks that, had the picture captured her coloring, would have been the same golden hue as her own. Winnifred tucked an escaped wisp of hair behind her ear and sighed. Never a day went by that she didn't long for another moment with her mother. She was only ten years of age when Mother fell ill, but Father spoke of her as if she were still living, though it had been nearly a decade since her passing. It was through his vivid memories Winnifred grew to know her mother more, but it was in Mother's library where she felt as though they would have been fast friends.

"And to what do I owe this pleasure, Daughter?" Her strapping father filled the doorframe, his presence commanding every officer in the precinct. "I thought you would still be on your outing to the exposition? Is Saunders waiting for you in the carriage?"

"Saunders was nothing like Aunt Lillian's description." She hopped up from the chair, giving her father a peck on the cheek. If she hadn't known that he was almost fifty, she would have guessed his age was nearer to the late thirties. She would have to try to match her father again, though he always dismissed her selections in favor of her mother's memory. If her selections were anything like Aunt Lillian's choices, she now understood his determination to remain single. "I left him behind because I have some time-sensitive news."

He removed his navy coat, hanging it on the back of his chair. He shook his head as if he knew what was coming. "Winnie..."

"Now, I know what you're going to say, but hear me out." She lifted her hand to stay his protests. Her past mistakes had done little to earn the respect from her father that she so desperately craved, but this was more important than her pride. A woman's life was at stake. "I'm sure I'm right this time. This kidnapper had a firearm! I've found the devil who has been stealing women at the fair and ransoming them!"

"You were certain last time, and you remember what happened with that poor fruit vendor." He rubbed the back of his neck. "I'm sure you *think* you have stronger evidence, but your overactive imagination has sent my men on more rabbit trails than I'd care to admit. And now that I've been promoted to inspector, I can't be responsible for such a waste of resources. I'm sorry, but I cannot jeopardize my career and reputation for another of your suspected crimes." He reached out and stroked her cheek in a rare show of affection. "Your mother had a fondness for those novels as well. Now, tell me, which one are you reading now?"

Her cheeks flamed at the thought of the stack of penny novels on the cane-back chair beside her bed. Winnifred had long since blazed through her mother's more refined novels of Austen,

Dickens, and Alcott before devouring her collection of romantic poetry by Tennyson, Browning, and Dickinson. Atop the current pile on the chair was *His Secret Wife*, the latest work of Winnifred's favorite author, Percival Valentine. "That is of little consequence."

He laughed and shifted through the stack of files on his over-sized desk. "I'm sorry, Winnie, but I have to get back to work. I have several cases I need to tend to personally, and I'm afraid I don't have any time to spare. I'll see you at dinner?"

Rather than saying something puerile that would confirm his analysis that she was just an overgrown schoolgirl spinning wild tales for the sake of garnering her father's attention, she nodded, gave him a kiss on the cheek, and slipped out of his office and shut the door before he could ask one of the policemen to escort her home. Feeling her hat was about to tumble, she paused and pinned her chapeau into place, her focus drifting to the corner of the room to a towering detective with thick, wavy brown hair whom she had never seen before. He leaned over his desk, supporting his weight on his knuckles, his shirt pulling against his broad chest and accentuating his muscular arms. Mesmerized, she watched as he raked his hands through his hair.

"Noticing our latest addition from New York, are you?" Officer Baxter chuckled from behind her. "I would have introduced you sooner, but he was digging around in the archive room when you arrived. That's Detective Jude Thorpe."

At his name, Detective Thorpe glanced up from his disorganized desk, his gaze meeting hers, sending her cheeks into flames. Winnifred gripped her gloves in her fist, muttered her goodbye to the officer, and hurried for the stairs, desperate to escape the new detective's amber eyes. His desk was so close to her father's office, she was sure that he'd overheard her father's reaction to her request. Her feet dragged the pavement as her cheeks tinted with the shame of being humiliated in front of not only Officer Baxter, but also the handsome new detective.

And yet, Winnifred couldn't get the image of that revolver out of her mind. At least, she thought it was a revolver. *I know I'm right. My instincts can't be that far off, can they?* She allowed her fingers to trail the black fence rails surrounding the red-brick prison on the first floor of her father's precinct, not caring that she was soiling her fingertips. *I could be that woman's only hope. What if I give up and her family is forced to pay an outrageous ransom? They would become destitute, and their ruin would be on my hands.*

She leaned against a brick column, keeping her gaze on the second floor of the station as determination to prove her father wrong grew within her. Like Rowena, she felt destined not to be the damsel in distress, waiting on a man to save her, but the heroine. She would find the evidence her father needed, with or without his help.

"Thorpe! Get in here." The inspector's voice cracked over the din of the precinct, sending the officers by the water station scattering to their desks.

Dropping his paperwork, Jude tugged on his coat and adjusted his cuffs and collar, eager to impress his new captain. He stood in front of Inspector Wylde's desk and clasped his hands behind his back. "Sir?"

The inspector lifted the open file in his left hand as he tapped it with his right. "Judging from your records, you were one of the best in New York. Says here that you single-handedly captured one of the leading criminals in the city." His brows rose as his lips pressed into a line. "Pretty impressive for an officer only twenty-four years old."

"Thank you, sir." Jude tipped his head, pleased that he was being recognized on his first day.

"So, I want you to follow my daughter." He dropped the file on the desk and, setting his elbows on it, pressed his fingers together into a steeple point.

"Your *daughter*?" Jude repeated tentatively, unsure if he had heard the inspector correctly.

"My daughter has a tendency to exaggerate because she reads too many of those penny novels by that Valentine author, but she is observant. If she did indeed happen to see a man out there with a revolver kidnapping a woman for ransom, I want her protected."

"Pardon my asking, but if she is so observant, won't she notice me trailing her?"

Inspector Wylde chuckled. "That's why I've chosen you to do the job. If you are as good as your records indicate, it shouldn't be a problem."

Is this some sort of test? "No sir, it is not. I'll keep an eye on her."

"I want you to protect her privacy. I trust my daughter and only need to hear a report from you if you find her in a potentially dangerous situation. I only wish for her to be safe and distracted until I have the real devil of the White City behind bars." He set aside Jude's file and reached for another, effectively dismissing him without another word.

With a bow, Jude retrieved his hat and headed for the street, the sticky, warm breeze greeting him. He scowled as he pulled his hat over his brows. It was far too hot to be running around Chicago playing nanny, but if this was what it took to get on Inspector Wylde's good side, he would do it.

Spying Miss Wylde down the sidewalk, he stepped behind a street vendor who was selling baked potatoes. *How does the man expect to make a living in this heat?* He watched as she slapped her gloves in her palm before marching down the walkway with determination in her strides.

Here we go. He ducked his head and strode after her, vigilant to keep an inconspicuous distance between them as he observed her hail a carriage and direct the driver to take her back to the fair.

He lifted his arm, silently signaling to a nearby cab and, climbing in, instructed the driver to follow Miss Wylde's carriage. When her carriage halted at the fair entrance on 59th Street, he waited in his cab for a moment as Winnifred followed the path to one of the ticket booths, presented what seemed to be a season pass, and hurried along before he stepped out and purchased a general admission ticket for a half dollar.

Tucking the decorative ticket into his pocket, Jude made his way through the energetic crowds, scanning his surroundings. He had heard tales of the grandeur of the world's exposition from passengers on the train bound for Chicago, but seeing it for himself was quite another thing entirely. Following the flash of Miss Wylde's white gown that practically glowed in a sea of navy skirts and suits, he wove through the maze of exhibits.

She walked with such purpose that he knew she must be retracing her steps from this morning, possibly attempting to recreate the scene as she searched the ground for any clues. All he could see were the thousands of footprints, with little to no hope of finding anything useful. Miss Wylde paused by a building where he could see couples enjoying some refreshments through the window. Crossing her arms, she tapped her finger to her lips much like he had seen her father do.

Miss Wylde seemed so engrossed in thought that she fairly jumped when a man approached her. She pressed her hand to her chest, her eyes wide, as if she were afraid. Jude reached for his holster hidden under his civilian's coat and tried to resist the urge to rush in without cause. He didn't want to expose himself if the man was not the suspect. But the man had a thick mustache and was rather skinny, much like the man she described to Baxter. Grasping his revolver, Jude approached the couple from behind.

Chapter Two

"Facts are such horrid things!"
~ Jane Austen, *Lady Susan*

Winnifred had been so distracted keeping an eye on the tall man following her that she did not even realize who was in her path until it was too late. "Mr. Saunders!" She gasped, stepping backward into a brawny man who bumped her shoulder, crushing one of the perfectly puffed sleeves of her gown. Sidestepping her, the man gruffly bid her to mind where she was walking. Winnifred righted her sleeve and turned her attention back to her would-be suitor. "You are still here."

"Well, since I took today off from work and you abandoned me without so much as a by-your-leave, I figured I might as well return to my tea and scones and see a bit of the fair," he replied, the evidence of said tea clumping the ends of his bushy mustache into two moist peaks as he held out her lace-trimmed parasol to her. "You left this at the restaurant."

"Thank you." She fought back a grimace as she grasped it by the carved handle. "I'm so sorry for running off, but—"

"But you've returned, and so, all is forgiven." Mr. Saunders grinned, reaching for her elbow. "However, I think you at least owe me a stroll around the exposition. Now, since we've already seen the Woman's Building, let's go to the States exhibits."

Winnifred withdrew her arm and licked her dry lips, trying to find the words to politely inform him that she wished never to spend one more second in his company. But, glancing over her shoulder, she found that the man following her had paused by a vendor, perusing the chocolate-covered fruit. She inwardly groaned as she forced herself to admit that it would be much safer to roam the fair with Mr. Saunders at her side to defend her if the man trailing her decided to make a move. Opening her parasol, she gave Mr. Saunders a demure smile and a stiff nod.

Mr. Saunders slid his hand under her elbow again and gave her a guiding tug. "I saw the most astounding thing on the way in to meet you. There is a display of a tower of oranges. Oranges! Can you believe it? One would think the fruit would have rotted in the process of assembling the exhibit, but there they are, as lovely as the day they were picked!"

"Oranges?" She bit her lip at his overwhelming enthusiasm. *Hold it together, Winnifred Rose Wylde. You can do this. Politely refuse, and guide him to where the man was last seen with the woman in green.* "While that does sound tempting, I—"

"If that doesn't strike your fancy, I heard there is a lovely exhibit of roses by the Horticultural Building that I think you would find most—"

She jerked away as the man who had been following her tackled Mr. Saunders to the ground. The nearby fairgoers paused and watched the spectacle unfold as if the grappling men were merely part of an exhibit. It was up to her to save Saunders. Dropping her open parasol, she used her reticule as a mace, whacking the man over the head again and again as he wrestled Mr. Saunders into submission, which didn't take much effort.

The offender lifted his arm to block her whirling purse, but her next blow knocked off his black hat, revealing him as the dark-haired man from her father's precinct. "Miss Wylde, stop! I'm with the police."

She halted her pummeling, the bag swinging in her iron grip. "Detective Thorpe? Why were you following me?"

"You saw me?" His brow wrinkled as he adjusted his hold on his prey.

She rolled her eyes, lifting a hand skyward. "You've been following me since I left the station. A child could have picked you out of a crowd with all of your veiled glances." Realizing that Mr. Saunders was still under the detective's grasp, she flicked her wrist, motioning for him to let go. "And Detective, please release Mr. Saunders at once. He is a friend of the family." Winnifred fluffed her reticule, attempting to return it to its former glory before retrieving her parasol, which was dangerously close to blowing into a mud puddle. Aunt Lillian was not going to be pleased, since she had purchased the ensemble especially for Winnifred's outing with Saunders.

Mr. Saunders brushed off his coat, straightening his shoulders as he gave Detective Thorpe a well-deserved sneer. "I say. First Miss Wylde sees a man pull a revolver on a woman. Then, I'm tackled to the ground by a—a nincompoop! Your superior will hear of this, Thorpe." He jabbed his finger into Thorpe's chest, his finger crumpling against the sturdiness of the broad surface.

Unmoved, Detective Thorpe retrieved his bowler hat and whacked it against his thigh, shaking loose the dust. "My apologies, sir, but it was my superior who asked me to look after Miss Wylde."

"Father sent you?" She rubbed her hand over her eyes and laughed. "While he might dismiss my claims, I should have known he would send somebody to watch me until he was certain I was safe. He may be too busy to listen to me, but not too busy to protect me." She dipped into a shallow curtsy. "I'm Miss Winnifred Wylde, which you already knew."

He returned her greeting with a stiff bow of his own, as if he was not used to such formality. "The pleasure is mine, Miss Wylde."

Mr. Saunders cleared his throat and stepped between them. "Miss Wylde, shall we continue as we were before we were so rudely interrupted?"

With the danger subsided, she grimaced at the task before her. If she did not turn Mr. Saunders away now, he would come calling again. Winnifred took his arm, gently pulling him away from Detective Thorpe's side to afford them a bit of privacy.

"Ah, I take it from our direction that you wish to see the tower of oranges." He lifted his finger. "Interesting fact about oranges—"

Enough with the oranges! She gritted her teeth and halted. "Mr. Saunders. I do apologize for the physical trauma you have experienced today from the hand of one of my father's own detectives, but I'm afraid this isn't going to work out."

"Pardon me?" Mr. Saunders scowled, his mustache dipping to his chin as his Adam's apple bobbed.

"I don't think we are well suited to one another," she whispered, in an attempt to maintain discretion.

"Any woman would be happy for me to pursue her." His nasally voice rose an octave. "I don't need to put up with being manhandled for a mere inspector's daughter, no matter how pretty she is."

Detective Thorpe placed a hand on Mr. Saunders's arm. "The fault was mine. There is no need to be rude, sir. Report me to Inspector Wylde if you will, but take care what you say about Miss Wylde. She is a gentlewoman's daughter and is to be treated as such."

Winnifred could have handled Mr. Saunders on her own, but she quite enjoyed the authority in Detective Thorpe's voice and had to admit to herself that it was nice to have someone handle the awkwardness of dismissing a suitor for her.

With a sneer, Mr. Saunders picked up his straw boater hat, swiped the grosgrain band with his wrist, and muttered something about incompetence as he strode away.

Winnifred looked up to her would-be-rescuer and smiled. "I guess that is one way to rid oneself of a suitor."

The detective shoved his hands into his pockets, his ears turning red. "I sincerely apologize for the confusion, Miss Wylde."

She waved her hand. "Please, don't think anything of it. Now, my father doesn't believe what I saw today, but I do, and I must keep searching for any clues to help us in finding the woman in green. I'm afraid we don't have much time."

"Please, carry on as if I am not here." Detective Thorpe nodded, falling behind her by several paces.

Winnifred smothered her laughter and waved him to her side. "It would be silly for you to follow me since I know you are there. Come on, you can help me look."

Jude walked beside her in silent mortification. Thankfully, Miss Wylde seemed so caught up in her search that she didn't appear to notice his discomfort. Here he was priding himself on his stealth and practically boasting to the inspector over his file, and this spritely young woman discovered his presence in a matter of minutes. If he didn't feel so chastened, he would laugh at the memory of her pummeling him. He straightened his shoulders and focused on his task at hand, protecting Miss Wylde. "So, where are we heading?" he asked as they paused under a directional sign.

"I don't think our suspect would return to the scene of his crime right away, so I'm not sure where to begin searching for him." She planted her hands on her hips. "He could be anywhere by now. He may not even be on the fairgrounds, but I have to start somewhere. I last spotted him leaving the Woman's Building, heading toward"—she turned, pointing down the Midway—"that direction."

I just need to keep her busy and away from this man, if he is indeed dangerous, until she loses interest. "How about the Ferris wheel? It's on the Midway and could give us a good layout of the whole fair." *And far above any threat lingering on the ground.*

Her countenance brightened. "Oh, that's true. I have been wanting to ride on it. The sign says it's this way." She lifted her impractical ruffled skirt to avoid a well-trodden muddy patch and stepped lightly around puddles until they reached a dry path.

Spying a gathering crowd to their left, Jude read a sign for lions on horseback and tigers on velocipedes featured in Hagenbeck's Arena. His jaw dropped as he stopped in his tracks at the ridiculous notion. "A tiger on a velocipede. Are they serious?"

"I haven't watched the show yet, but my friend Danielle, I mean,

Miss Montgomery, said it was positively thrilling. But I'm afraid we cannot linger," she said, tilting her head for him to continue down the Midway.

"Of course." He clasped his hands behind his back and walked beside her, stealing glances at her out of the corner of his eye. When he had first seen her enter the precinct, her ethereal beauty disarmed him. Even though he didn't wish to admit it, Jude was glad to have the opportunity to be near her and soon found himself captivated by her lilting voice as she told him which exhibits to avoid and which were to be seen at once.

She paused and turned to him, expectance in her brilliant blue-green eyes. "Detective Thorpe?"

He blinked and leaned toward her, brows rising as he chastened himself for growing distracted yet again. He would have to work on paying closer attention, lest she inadvertently give him a poor report to her father. Jude already had one mark against him, with her spotting him following her, and he could not afford another. "I'm sorry, did you ask a question?"

"I asked why you started working at my father's precinct," she replied, continuing down the wide path.

Jude knew that question was bound to come up, but he couldn't rightly tell the truth, that he had moved to investigate the so-called "accidental" death of his brother-in-law, Victor. Victor had been too alert to have stepped out in front of that grip car, and while the autopsy had uncovered a blow to the head, it had been ruled as the car striking him and not manslaughter.

Jude was one of the few people outside of Victor's department who knew that Victor had been working undercover on a fraud case. No, he would keep the secret close to his chest. He could not risk the murderer being warned and having any trail left behind growing cold, so he settled on telling only half of his reasoning. "I moved here from New York to be with my mother and sister Mary after my brother-in-law passed in the spring. I wanted to be here for them and my nephew should they need anything."

"I'm so very sorry to hear of your family's loss." She gently touched his coat sleeve, genuine sadness in her every feature. "A life taken too soon is too great a sorrow to bear on our own."

Jude nodded, knowing that she was speaking from experience. He had heard from the officers of the untimely, unexpected death of her lovely mother. "And I am thankful that we are not left alone to bear it. It was only by the hand of the Lord that I was able to be offered a position so quickly here in Chicago at your father's precinct." He grinned, hoping to distill the sadness settling about them like a cloud. "I'm eager to prove my worth to your father and show him that hiring me was not a mistake."

"Well, my father was excited to hire a seasoned detective with such an impressive record from New York, but it seems that since I found you out, *I* must be the best detective New York has seen." She turned sparkling eyes on him, a teasing light in her smile and voice.

Despite the twinge her words brought, Jude enjoyed her banter. "It would seem that way, yes. So shall you be going by Detective Wylde, or are you aiming for your father's position as inspector?"

"Of course. We Wyldes only want the best. I will answer to Inspector Wylde or Captain Wylde." She laughed. "But if I'm honest, I think you were only sloppy because you didn't think that playing nanny to the inspector's silly daughter warranted much stealth."

Jude dropped his gaze to the ground. The inspector had been right. She was very observant. He would have to be careful. "Miss Wylde, I would never call you silly." *Beautiful, disarming. But never silly.*

"So how long did Father assign you to my post?" She looked toward the bustling crowd that was gathering in front of the Street in Cairo exhibit as a vendor exclaimed in Jude's ear the marvel of his wares, nearly deafening him.

He pressed his hand over his ear and sent the man a glare before taking her arm, pulling her away from the screaming vendor. "Until your father feels that it is safe for you to wander about the city alone," he replied, studying her reaction as they continued down the Midway.

She sucked in her breath through her teeth and sidestepped a freshly dropped ice cream cone, sending the wailing boy a sympathetic glance. "With all the crime that the exposition has brought to our city, that could take *months*. If you want to get back to what you've been trained to do, help me solve this case. Let's find the proof we need together and capture this rogue before it's too late."

Only hours ago, her proposal would have sounded appealing, but now that he'd met her, Jude wasn't so sure that he wished to expedite his time with the charming Miss Wylde after all. "I don't know. Your father assigned me to keep you out of danger, not intentionally place you in harm's way by tracking a potentially violent criminal."

"Think of it this way," she said as he purchased their tickets, and she pulled him into the massive, winding line for the Ferris wheel ride. "If you hadn't discovered me, or rather if *I* hadn't discovered you"—she poked at him again—"I would still be doing what I'm doing, so you might as well help me. I'll be far safer with you by my side." She looked up to him, her blue-green irises pulling him in as her golden curls caressed a tan face, which told him that, even though she may look the part of a young socialite, she had an adventurous soul.

He bit back his laughter at this breeze of fresh air in the form of the inspector's daughter. "Come along, Miss Wylde." He extended his arm to her, escorted her to the front of the line, and flashed his badge to the engineer. "Police business."

The man gave them a wink. "Looks like mighty pleasant police business to me."

Jude felt Winnifred stiffen, but he ignored the man and led them inside the overcrowded car.

The air pulsed with the excitement of the fairgoers as Winnifred followed Detective Thorpe onto the crowded Ferris wheel car that carried about fifty other passengers. The doors closed behind them and the odor of warm bodies filled the air, but she refused to give Detective Thorpe the impression that she was a delicate flower and refrained from pressing her handkerchief to her nose as the fine ladies did behind her. As the Ferris wheel jerked to life and began its slow and steady climb, the passengers in the middle pressed toward the windows, jostling her. She grabbed at her hat and bit her lip as a man on her right stood a little too close for comfort. She turned to reprimand him, but caught him grinning at her in a most disconcerting way as he moved even closer.

Detective Thorpe reached for her wrist and guided her between the window and himself, spreading his arms on either side of her shoulders and splaying his fingers against the glass, creating a safe haven for her before narrowing his gaze at the offender. "Step back or you'll see naught but stars on this trip."

The man, eyeing Detective Thorpe's massive build, stepped away without an argument.

Winnifred nearly sagged with relief. Not wanting to reveal how much his action touched her, she kept her back to Detective Thorpe's chest and gazed out the window, breathless with the sight before her. Facing the east fairgrounds, the dome of the Moorish Palace rose up to her right and, beyond it, the brilliant white of the buildings gleamed in the light of the late afternoon sun. The crowds below didn't seem as overwhelming from this vantage point, and she felt certain that such a brilliant emerald-green gown would show as a beacon amongst the mostly dark-clad crowd. But the young maid and the man with the revolver were long gone.

"You were right to think we could see for miles up here, Detective Thorpe. I think that between the two of us, we can cover the places he would most likely visit this week to claim more victims."

She risked a glance at him over her shoulder. His golden-brown eyes met hers and she felt her knees weaken. Never had a man outside her novels affected her so. She returned her gaze to the fairgrounds below and tried to continue as if her heart hadn't just experienced an earthquake. "Now. . ." She paused at the tremor in her voice and, clearing her throat, began again. "Since I first saw the suspect outside the Ceylon Tearoom in the Woman's Building, and judging from the reports that the kidnapper tends to only take women, I think we should visit the places where women would feel comfortable without their husbands or escorts. So maybe we can start with the Rose Garden exhibit?"

His brows rose with what she hoped was approval and not scorn.

Clearing her throat, she pressed onward. "And I think after that, if we still don't find him, we should try looking over at the Fine Arts exhibit and then return to the Woman's Building." She gave a nervous laugh and wished she had a lemonade to cool her nerves. "I'm just trying to think of places where he could have an opportunity to abduct a woman."

"I think those are brilliant suggestions. Have you ever considered becoming a detective, Miss Wylde?" Detective Thorpe asked as the car began its descent, all teasing gone from his tone.

She dipped her head at the unexpected compliment. "There aren't any female detectives at my father's precinct, and besides, my father would never allow me to become one if there were. While I do enjoy the thrill of the chase, I can achieve that thrill safely from a settee, reading, and not on the street, flirting with life-and-death, according to my father."

"So, reading is your favorite pastime? Besides going to the fair to chase after criminals, what else do you enjoy?"

"I enjoy a great many things, but my aunt usually has me quite busy with social events. My family wishes for me to be safely married and tucked away in a nice, neat mansion." She swept her gloved hands together. "Of course, there's nothing wrong with being tucked away in a mansion, and all but one of my friends have husbands of their own, but I want to do something first before I settle down, something grand. Something that would change the course of history."

Realizing she had said too much, she ducked her head again. "I'm sorry. I don't know what came over me. It must be the thrill of the Ferris wheel." She turned to him, the closeness of him dizzying. "Please don't tell anyone what I said or what I plan to do about the incident. I would hate to worry my father over nothing."

"I'm not entirely sure I can do that, Miss Wylde. . ."

The doors of the ride opened, and fresh, cool air flooded the chamber as the tight space emptied of people, leaving them the last to disembark. "Also, if you promise to help me and stay silent about it, I will keep your stellar record intact by refraining from telling anyone at the precinct that I caught you tailing me within a matter of minutes." She held out her gloved hand, waiting for him to accept.

With a sigh, Detective Thorpe gripped her hand in his. "You've got me there. You have yourself a deal, Miss Wylde."

Chapter Three

"Something between a dream and a miracle."
~ Elizabeth Barrett Browning

And after your morning call to Miss Montgomery, we have. . ." Aunt Lillian flipped through her scheduling book. "The afternoon free?" Her voice rose in surprise as she scanned her little book a second and third time. "That can't be. . . ." Aunt Lillian rubbed her temples. "I was certain we had afternoon tea plans with the Andrews family."

"Oh no, how awful," Winnifred murmured absentmindedly as she peeked through the lace curtains of her small cottage dining room out onto Lakeshore Drive to find it overcast and threatening rain. Her heart thudded at the sight of a man in a straw hat leaning against a lamppost with his hands in his pockets and his gaze following a passing buggy. She knew he would be there, but the very sight of Detective Thorpe was enough to relive the memory of his closeness in the Ferris wheel, a memory she longed to repeat. Her stomach rumbled, bringing her back to the present. She would need a full breakfast for the day she had planned.

"Yes. Yes, it is," Aunt Lillian murmured.

"Pardon?" Winnifred blinked.

"It's a shame that I failed to plan for our afternoon. I suppose since I am leaving to visit my cousin in the morning, I must have forgotten to set the date with Mrs. Andrews." She sighed, shaking her head as she tapped her spoon on her three-minute egg, cracking the shell.

Winnifred set down her empty cup and reached for the silver coffeepot. "I suppose I have time to go to the fair today then?"

"By yourself?" Father asked, joining them in the breakfast room with his *Chicago Tribune* tucked under his arm. He gave his sister-in-law a peck on the cheek. "Over so early, Lillian? I know you live in the big house next door, but I'm always surprised by how early you rise."

"I wanted to discuss the summer plans with Winnifred before I depart tomorrow." Sipping her tea, she pursed her lips. "Honestly, I don't know if I should leave you two for the whole summer. With Winnifred turning twenty this year, we need to put all our efforts into finding her a spouse by the end of the summer, else people will declare her an old maid and she will be destined to be a wallflower at every social gathering."

A bubble of panic rose in Winnifred's throat. The summertime was her refuge from the strict regimen of social calls her aunt scheduled throughout the remainder of the year. "You deserve a respite, Auntie. You take such good care of us that you need to take a moment for yourself." Before Aunt Lillian could protest, Winnifred twisted in her chair to look at her father. "Now, back to the fair." Not wanting to admit to her father that she had already discovered Detective Thorpe, so of course she wouldn't be alone, she grabbed a raspberry muffin to take with her and answered, "I'll ask Danielle. I'm sure she could use a break from planning her wedding."

"Have a good day, my dear," Father replied as he too tucked a muffin into his pocket.

Pressing a kiss atop Aunt Lillian's head and on her father's cheek, Winnifred slipped upstairs and changed out of her pink visiting gown and into a simple navy gown paired with a muted gray hat with minimal frippery. The color didn't flatter her as well as pastels, but today she dressed for blending in to her surroundings while she searched for the man with the revolver. She could at least take comfort that her hair was arranged in a fetching manner with her golden curls framing her face. Winnifred finished her toilet before rushing to the window, disappointed to find Detective Thorpe walking with her father away from the cottage. *Perhaps Father found something else for him to do today since he thought I'd be chaperoned all day.*

With a shrug, Winnifred grabbed her Percival Valentine book from under her pillow to read on the walk only to step outside and find it had begun drizzling. Undeterred, she ducked inside for her black umbrella. Opening it and propping it on her shoulder, she devoured her breakfast muffin and flipped to her place in the novel, losing herself in the love story of Lord Francis, so much so that she didn't notice when the drizzling stopped. She almost walked beyond her friend's house and would have if Danielle's dog had not spotted her from the front parlor window and raised a ruckus.

"Thank goodness you've come," Danielle whispered as she slipped through the door, hat in hand. "It's not even nine o'clock in the morning, and Mother has me neck deep in wedding planning."

"Oh, then I suppose you won't have time to go to the fair with me today instead of our walk to Banning's Bookshop?" Winnifred drummed her fingers on her book, a mischievous smile spreading over her face.

"Now, I didn't say that." Danielle grinned as she pinned on her red chapeau, not quite the color Winnifred was hoping she would select for a covert trip to the fair. But then again, she had not mentioned her plan to her friend, so she could hardly blame Danielle for wishing to wear the daring hat. "One moment while I tell the maid." She slipped the book from Winnifred's hand.

"Excuse you, I'm not finished with it yet," Winnifred protested, reaching for it, but Danielle was already opening her door.

"Consider my borrowing it for two days as payment for incurring my mother's wrath for going with you to the fair." She poked her head inside and waved one of the servants over, whispering, "Put this upstairs on my nightstand. Then, wait an hour and tell Mother that I'm taking the day to help a friend, but will be back in time for dinner."

The maid groaned. "Oh Miss Montgomery, that's not fair. Your mother is going to—"

"I know, Joanna, and I'm sorry," Danielle closed the door with a giggle then slipped her hand around Winnifred's umbrella handle and propelled them down the sidewalk.

"I want my book back," Winnifred mumbled under her breath.

"The bookshop sold out of Percival Valentine's latest works, and I desperately need a distraction that only *His Secret Wife* can bring. My sister has been taunting me with little details, but will not loan it to me until she is finished." Danielle leaned her head on Winnie's shoulder. "And she is such an abominably slow reader."

"So, the wedding plans are a little more work than you anticipated?" Winnifred ventured as they climbed into the grip car.

Danielle grunted, curling her fingers in a show of frustration. "I can't handle one more minute of wedding planning. When I agreed to marry Edward, I thought the endless social calls would end, but"—she looked heavenward and crossed her eyes—"my mother and grandmother have only gotten three times worse. With the wedding only two weeks away, I'm counting down the minutes until I'm Edward's wife and am in control of my own destiny." Danielle sighed and told Winnifred of the dress fittings, calls, teas, parties, and planning that made even Aunt Lillian's regimented scheduling sound palatable.

By the time they arrived at the fair, the threatening clouds had blown away, but Winnifred sensed her friend's frazzled nerves would only dissipate with a sweet. Spotting Danielle's favorite baked good in a vendor's cart, she purchased two sticky cinnamon rolls dripping with vanilla icing.

Danielle took a bite and pressed her hand to her mouth. "This is divine. Did you know that Mother has taken away my dessert privileges too? She wants me to lose three inches on my waistline by next Saturday. Three inches."

"At least you have someone at the end of all this," Winnifred said between nibbles, still full from her breakfast. "I, however, seem to be blazing through an endless roster of potential suitors with nothing to show for it."

"I keep meaning to ask, how was your call with Saunders?" Danielle wiggled her brows before finishing off her cinnamon roll. "Is he as handsome as I've heard Lord Francis is, or perhaps as mysterious and aloof as Aloysius, the business partner?"

"Neither. Our time was wretched. The man is nothing like Aunt Lillian described." She rolled her eyes as Danielle gazed longingly at Winnifred's nearly untouched cinnamon roll. Winnifred handed it over to her friend and licked her fingers clean, almost hearing Aunt Lillian's screech. "It shouldn't be this hard for me to find my forever love."

Danielle pulled off a piece of the bun and lifted it to the sunlight as if examining it before popping it into her mouth with a groan. "Selecting a husband isn't like it is in books. It's not all moonlight and knights and furtive glances at dinner and fluttering hearts. It's more like discovering who has the biggest pocketbook and is tolerably handsome."

Winnifred rested her hand on Danielle's forearm. "You've never told me you were marrying Edward for his money. I thought you cared for him."

Danielle shrugged, handing back half the roll to Winnifred. "He's nice, and I'm quite fond of him."

Only fond? Winnifred stared at her friend. "And you are still going to marry him?"

"I have two younger sisters already out in society. Mother says I'm fortunate that he did not pick one of them, as Elizabeth is far prettier and Fanny has, to put it delicately, better assets. She says she has no idea why he prefers me, but that she is thankful to have me out of the way at long last." She wiped her handkerchief over her mouth, removing any trace of the treat. "Edward will be a good provider, so my bookshelves will never be in want."

"How awful of her to say such things!" Winnifred's heart ached for her friend. She couldn't fathom how on earth someone could live with another for all of eternity if they didn't truly love them.

"Enough of that. What shall we see and do first?"

Winnifred drew Danielle close and lowered her voice. "Well, I may have had ulterior motives for us coming today. During my tea with Mr. Saunders, I witnessed a kidnapping."

Danielle gave her an incredulous look. "Are you certain? Because last time you were in the middle of reading Percival Valentine's *A Ransom for a Bride* and you—"

"I know. I made one little mistake, but I'm sure of what I saw this time." She filled Danielle in on the events yesterday, ending with Detective Thorpe tackling Mr. Saunders and their conversation afterward about finding proof for her father to open an investigation.

"And is this Detective Thorpe handsome?" Danielle asked, eyes sparkling. "Is he the reason you are so keen on this scheme? To have the excuse to spend time with a dashing fellow?"

"Of course not. Well, he is dashing, very much so, but I believe what I witnessed."

"I knew it. Do tell me about him, Winnie." Danielle squeezed Winnifred's elbow.

Winnifred blushed, remembering the energy in the air as his arms encircled her, protecting her on the Ferris wheel. "Let's just say that if one of my heroines had to have a guardian angel, he would be perfect."

Danielle giggled behind her hand. "An angel? My, my, he does sound intriguing. Too bad he's only a detective." Spying a coffee vendor, she halted their promenade on the Midway. "I'm parched, and since you bought the rolls, the coffee is my treat."

Winnifred popped the last bite of the cinnamon roll into her mouth and caught a man staring at her from a nearby bench, a grin spreading under his thick mustache. *The nerve of that scoundrel! How dare he—*

"So I'm an angel, am I?" His deep voice startled her.

Realizing who he was, she choked and began coughing uncontrollably. Detective Thorpe closed the distance between them and patted her on the back.

"You heard me? I didn't even see you following us. How long were you behind me?" She couldn't help her shock from ebbing into her voice.

"Your father gave me instructions to watch you, so I was out front before the maid opened your curtains this morning, waiting for you to leave the house. I noticed you spotted me, so I took a stroll around the block with your father to throw you off my trail."

"That's hardly fair." She pointed to his mustache.

He peeled it off and tucked the disguise into his pocket. "After yesterday, I wanted to make sure you didn't catch me again. I also wanted to prove to you and myself that I can tail even the most observant person without getting caught."

Danielle joined them with two cups of hot coffee, her eyes on him, sparking with interest. "And who do we have here? Is this your guardian angel?"

Winnifred sighed in exasperation at her friend's teasing. "Yes. Yes, he is. Miss Danielle Montgomery, please allow me to present Detective Jude Thorpe, the angel."

Even though they didn't catch the suspect, it was not an unpleasant way to spend the afternoon, Jude thought as he escorted Winnifred to her cottage on Lakeshore Drive, catching glimpses of Lake Michigan behind the mansions lining the street. "If you don't mind me asking, why do you live—"

"In the guest cottage of my aunt's estate?" She laughed. "Before my grandfather died, he gave the cottage to my parents as a wedding present. When my mother passed away, and later my grandmother,

Aunt Lillian returned home from her European travels to stay with us for a year and care for me. Then Grandfather died and left the rest of the estate to his one remaining child, Aunt Lillian. Ever since she moved into the big house, she makes it her mission to visit us nearly every day to ensure that we are well looked after and my social schedule stays full."

"That is kind of her, but wouldn't it be simpler if you two moved in with her?"

"She offered years ago, but at the time, Father thought it would be too much change for me, so we stayed in our small cottage, and I quite prefer it that way." She smiled at him, pausing at her gate and nodding toward the man in a bowler hat across the street. "Seems like your relief has arrived. Until tomorrow?"

"Tomorrow," he replied with a small bow to her and tip of his hat to the undercover officer. Jude strolled back to the office feeling happier than he had in a very long time. Whistling, he made his way to his desk and riffled through a drawer. He retrieved a small black leather book for notes on Winnifred's case, along with the sobering file he had found the other day on insurance and loan frauds that Victor had been working on before the fair opened. The officers were spread so thin that the case had been shoved to the side for now in the chaos of the hundreds of criminals that flocked to the fair.

"You don't look as exhausted as you should for a man who was out on assignment all day in this oppressive heat. It has to be over a hundred degrees out there today," Officer Baxter commented as he packed up for the day, his brows rising with suspicion.

Jude shoved the file into his leather satchel to study tonight and gave the officer a wry grin. He would have to be careful not to reveal his assignment to the men or that he was looking into the fraud case that he was certain had led to Victor's death. In the eyes of the law, Victor's case had been solved, but the law did not know Victor as he had. "If you haven't noticed, the day is over and it is time for dinner, which my sister invited me over to her house to enjoy. No cheap pub food for me tonight!"

Officer Baxter nodded with understanding that if a home-cooked meal was involved, it would explain why any man would be coming into the office whistling after a long day. "Lucky. All I've got waiting for me is a cold turkey sandwich." He gave Jude a sideways glance.

Jude slapped Baxter on the shoulder. "I'll ask and see if I can't get an invitation for you sometime soon."

Baxter shook his head, dropping his gaze to the floor. "Cold, cold turkey. Probably a week old. I'm bound to get sick, but it's all I got in my icebox."

Rolling his eyes, Jude waved him along. "Fine, but don't blame me if Mary gets upset over an unexpected guest at her table."

Baxter grinned, grabbed his hat, and lightly punched Jude in the shoulder. "See now? I knew you were the friendly sort. What better way for two associates to get to know one another than over dinner?"

Jude returned his smile, having missed the camaraderie of his old precinct. He would have to be very careful about what he confided. If word got out about his assignment, he'd never hear the end of his so-called duty with the lovely Miss Wylde.

Chapter Four

"Run mad as often as you choose, but do not faint."
~Jane Austen, *Love and Friendship*

The sun was oppressive as Winnifred stalked the fair for the fifth day in a row, but this time she dressed in a fetching lavender skirt paired with an ivory shirtwaist with billowing sleeves, hoping to catch the eye of the suspect with Detective Thorpe hiding nearby. She was determined to use herself as bait to find the lean man with the dark mustache, along with the proof that her father required to open an investigation against him. Not having much luck at the Fine Arts exhibit, she signaled to Detective Thorpe to join her.

"I think we should return to the Ceylon exhibit," she suggested, already making her way in that direction. Winnifred shook out her flimsy, lace-trimmed handkerchief and blotted her neck, wondering why on earth she wore a high collar on such an extraordinarily hot day. But she kept walking, not wanting Detective Thorpe to stop on her account. They were almost to the Woman's Building when she felt herself sway, her vision dotting with black blossoms.

"Miss Wylde?" Detective Thorpe's hand hovered by her elbow as if he were unsure whether or not to touch her. "Do you need me to fetch you some water?"

"I don't want to make you do that. I only need a moment to catch my breath." She pulled the decorative pin out of her lavender hat and fanned herself, the ostentatious ostrich feather tickling her chin, momentarily distracting her from the corset stays pinching her waist. Why did she allow Clara to lace her so tightly when she knew she would be out in the heat all day? The black blossoms grew into a garden in her vision and with a sway, she gripped his navy sleeve. "Pardon me," she whispered, and forced herself to take a deep breath despite the corset.

Detective Thorpe drew his arm around her waist and led her to the side of a building where the roof extended, offering her shade as he leaned her against the white wall. Tentatively, he cupped her chin in his hand and examined her overheated cheeks, concern lighting his eyes. "Will you be well enough to stay here while I find some water? I can't have you passing out and have to report to your father that I neglected to look out for your well-being."

"Water does sound rather lovely." She gave him a weak smile. "Would you mind fetching me some? No need to tell Father our secret quite yet."

"I'll be right back." Detective Thorpe left her side, heading toward the Ceylon Teahouse in search of refreshments.

In the shadow of the building, her temperature lowered below the inferno she had felt only moments before. Feeling a mite foolish for allowing herself to grow faint, Winnifred mopped her forehead with her already damp handkerchief when she spied *him* by one of the tea vendors right outside the teahouse. *I can't believe it.* Even though she felt unsteady, she channeled the strength of the heroines she'd read about for years and stood upright. Tilting her hatless head, she sauntered past him, her hips swaying with every step before she paused at the stall, seemingly absorbed in a tea sample booth as she skimmed her fingers over the tea trinkets.

"Would you like to smell a sample, miss?" The vendor behind the booth extended a small china dish containing a handful of tea leaves. "This is our most popular tea with the ladies, called Pai Mu Tan, or White Peony."

Praying that she didn't appear as flustered as she felt, Winnifred accepted the dish and inhaled the sweet nectar of the tea, her neck bristling as she felt his presence gravitate toward her. "Very lovely. I'll take eight ounces, please."

"If you enjoy that scent, miss, may I recommend this sample?"

The man with the bushy dark mustache lifted a dish to her and gave her a smile, his left eye crossing back and forth as he attempted to make eye contact with her.

Hesitant, she looked to him and then back at the dish. *Do I dare? He could have swapped out the leaves with some malodorous poison.* She checked over her shoulder at the vendor who was busy with another fairgoer. Deciding to take a chance, she breathed in the scent. "Such a lovely hint of peach."

"It is one of my favorites." He bowed to her, tucking his bowler hat under his arm. "Please excuse my manners. My name is Doctor Henry Howard Holmes, but as that is rather a mouthful and I don't practice medicine at the present, please call me Mr. Holmes." With a flourish, he produced a business card and gave her a grin as if he expected her to be charmed.

"Thank you." She accepted his card and pretended to read it to disguise her rising panic at the thought of introducing herself.

"And may I have the pleasure of learning your name?"

Even though it was against all propriety to allow a man to introduce himself without a proper introduction from a friend, Winnifred knew she had to break the rules if she wanted to keep him around until Detective Thorpe returned. She gave Mr. Holmes what she hoped was an alluring smile and rattled off her favorite name paired with the first surname she could think of from her latest novel. "Miss Swan. Miss Cordelia Swan."

"A charming name for a charming young woman." He gave her another slight bow. "Tell me, Miss Swan, what brings you to the fair?"

What brings me? Oh dear. Why haven't I composed a story yet? She had been so preoccupied with finding him, she never once thought of what she'd say when she finally did. While she may not have considered it, surely Detective Thorpe had. Perhaps he didn't bother to mention it because he never believed they would actually find the man in question. Thinking quickly, Winnifred fiddled with the brim of her hat that she had yet to refasten and cleared her throat. "I'm actually looking for a job. I heard that the fair was a good place to find a position."

Mr. Holmes's brows rose. "Really? I'd say that it was providence that brought you to this exhibit, for you see, I'm looking for a new secretary. Someone bright and"—he eyed her—"young. My last secretary, a Miss Minnie Williams, left me, and I need someone soon to help me with the records at my new hotel business. Can you read? Possibly type?"

She nodded. "I'm an avid reader, and while I'm no stenographer, I am a fast notetaker and can type a little, but I'm sure I can pick up speed as I gain practice."

"Well then, if you'd like to stop by my office in Englewood on Monday around eleven o'clock, I'd love to interview you for the position." He tapped the card still in her hand, nearly sending her scurrying backward. "My address is directly below my name."

Monday. . .that leaves me only tomorrow after service to prepare! She gave a little laugh, hoping that he mistook it for joy rather than nerves. "Imagine my obtaining an interview so quickly. I'll be by Monday at eleven o'clock on the dot," Winnifred promised, tucking the card in her reticule.

Jude stood in the shadows, gripping the glass of water. The man was entirely too close to Miss Wylde. He clenched his jaw as he watched the man bow to her, his hand edging for his gun when he saw the man extend his hand to her. *Don't go with him. Don't. You're not prepared.* In all their time searching, Jude never thought they'd actually run into the suspect, and he'd secretly hoped Miss Wylde would give up this ridiculous scheme of hers and set her mind on something else, anything else. His shoulders sagged with relief when she turned away unscathed, but his scowl returned as the man's gaze never left her retreating figure, studying her petite, hourglass form. Jude had to fight the urge to confront the man for his impudence. Despite his feelings on the matter, he would have to trust that Miss Wylde knew what she was doing.

Not seeing him behind the children's exhibit, she began to pass him. "Miss Wylde," Jude hissed. To her credit, she appeared as if her interest was being drawn to the Horticulture Building. She turned the corner and away from the man's line of sight before clutching her lavender skirts and running to him, allowing him to draw her into the shadows of the Children's Building.

"Oh my goodness. My heart is pounding out of my very chest. I didn't know if I could pull it off. I was so worried you wouldn't be back in time if he decided to take me then and there." She brushed back a golden lock from her perspiring forehead, her cheeks bright.

Seeing the trembling in her shoulders, Jude grasped her by the elbows, steadying her. "You are shaking. Come, let's find you a place to sit."

She nodded, closing her eyes for a long breath. "I'm only thankful to know that you were watching me. I never could have done this on my own. Thank you."

"Of course. Guarding you is my job at the moment, after all." He handed her the glass of water, which she gulped, some splashing down her chin in her haste. He handed her his handkerchief. "Tell me what happened. What did he say?"

"His name is Doctor Henry Howard Holmes, and he wants to interview me for the position of secretary." She pulled a card out of her reticule and handed it to him. "Here's his address."

Jude thumped his finger against the card. "He doesn't live that far from here." His brow furrowed at the excited gleam in her eye. "Even though I think this Mr. Holmes is, at the most, a suspect of an *attempted* theft, we need to tell your father. But you should know that an interview alone won't be enough proof for us to hold Mr. Holmes."

"Attempted theft? I knew you didn't believe that I witnessed a kidnapping. Well, if I can get in for this interview, I'm sure I will be able to procure the position and find the proof we need to confirm that this is our man."

Jude inwardly cringed at the idea of her going undercover in a potentially dangerous situation. "If Holmes is indeed the man behind the recent disappearances, what makes you think he will allow you to leave the interview?" he asked.

"I'll pack my pistol. Besides, I know that if he tries to take me, you will be there to protect me." She turned those wide eyes to him, full of trust.

He shook his head to break the spell and took the glass from her to return it as promised to the waiter of the teahouse. "You put far too much stock in my abilities."

"Well, weren't you the best in New York?" She gave him a coy grin and fastened her hat into place.

"I can't risk your safety. I promised your father that I'd report to him anything dangerous. I'm sorry, Miss Wylde, but I have to tell him of your findings."

She sighed. "Then I'll tell him tonight. Better for him to hear it from me. Now that Aunt Lillian is away, there is no reason to delay."

Winnifred piled baked ham onto a china plate along with two sweet potato rolls, each with a pat of butter atop, and a side of steaming green beans. She set the plate at her father's place and checked that his coffee was filled to the brim.

Finding her fluttering over his plate, her father's brows rose. "What's all this? What are you buttering me up for this time? I told you, Winnifred, that ten dollars a month is more than a fair budget for books. If you have already spent your allotment—"

"Have a seat, Father." She held the back of the Queen Anne chair for him.

"If it's not books, it's something far costlier. The last time you fixed my plate, you wanted a trip to Europe." He eyed her suspiciously.

That was the problem with having an inspector for a father. She could never get away with anything. "It's nothing like that, and it won't cost you a penny."

"Oh, well then, I'm all ears after we pray," he said, taking his seat and reaching for his dinner napkin before bowing his head.

She took her seat beside him and folded her hands over her own plate, waiting for the blessing to end before leaning toward him. "I wanted to discuss the case I've been working on."

He laughed and took a sip of his coffee. "I knew you wouldn't let it go so easily. What have you found, Daughter?"

Winnifred slid the business card across the pristine white tablecloth to her father. "The man in question is Doctor Henry Howard Holmes, and he has asked me to apply for the position of his secretary. If you give me permission, I will take the interview on Monday morning. With Aunt Lillian away visiting her friends for the summer, my calendar is completely free, allowing me to accept the position and find the information we need without any cost to the department."

He set his cup down and rubbed his hand over his chin. "Your aunt is gone for not even a week and you are already asking me if you can take a job with a man whom you believe is the devil behind the mysterious White City's disappearances? You are being ridiculous."

Her mouth twisted at his mocking tone. "If you really think my theory is as ridiculous as you claim, why would you object? If Mr. Holmes is indeed innocent, then no harm would be done, and I will have extra spending money for my books. But if not, you will have another feather in your cap with the arrest of a kidnapper." Her words came out all in a rush. "Besides, you will want me to keep busy with Aunt Lillian away or you'll say I'm underfoot."

Father sighed and lifted a finger to her. "Very well. However, you are only allowed to take the job if you carry your muff pistol at all times and have an undercover detective posted outside the house and this Englewood building, acting as your bodyguard. You may not have realized it, but my men have been watching out for you since you brought this to my attention."

Oh, I realized it. Her heart lifted at the thought of spending more time with the enigmatic Jude Thorpe, but to her father she merely raised her brows. "Have they? Well, hopefully this will lead to naught and you can return them to their normal duties, but if I'm right, we could be saving lives."

"But if you do not uncover anything in six weeks, by which time your aunt will return, you must give up this nonsense you've picked up from those Valentine books and begin to seriously consider a suitor. A girl your age shouldn't be consumed with ransom notes and finding kidnappers and filling her head with all sorts of unrealistic romantic adventures." He narrowed his gaze to her, impressing the seriousness of his words. "I mean it, Winnie. This is my offer. Take it or leave it."

Confident in what she had witnessed, Winnifred extended her hand. "And if *I* am right, you and Aunt Lillian are to stop this endless parade of suitors and give me the freedom to find my own suitor."

Father clasped her hand. "Agreed. I'll send Detective Thorpe over tomorrow morning and he can coach you on creating an alias."

Chapter Five

"Through the mirror blue, the knights come riding two and two."
~Lord Alfred Tennyson, *The Lady of Shalott*

J ude stepped into the front parlor, hat in hand, and took in the
cozy room. While the cottage had a Lakeshore Drive address,
it was certainly one of the most modest homes on the shore. His
fingers traced the carved mantel above the dormant fireplace that
was decorated with a basket of dried lavender, lending a sweet
aroma to the room. On an end table next to the settee, he spied
a pile of books, the one atop with a coral ribbon marking a spot.
Picking up the book, he read the title—*His Secret Wife* by Percival
Valentine. He opened the book and read a few lines, chuckling over
the flowery language before setting it back on the table.

Near the window was an easel holding a half-completed painting of a cherry tree bearing ripe fruit, or at least he thought it was
a tree. He tilted his head, trying to make sense of the blurry image.
It was difficult to say. He brushed his hair from his forehead and
glanced about the room, noticing at least another half-dozen rather
odd, poorly executed paintings and smiled, thinking of Miss Wylde
attempting to sit still long enough to paint them, no doubt at her
aunt's insistence.

In the corner of the room, there stood a piano with a lace over-
lay and a framed picture of Miss Wylde from when she was a young
girl. Even though she had become quite the lady, she still had that
same spark of mischief in her eyes. He filtered through a stack of
music beside the picture and found many of the popular songs his
sister played on the piano Victor had bought her when they were
first married nearly a decade ago. Jude looked over his shoulder and,
as no one was near as far as he could tell, he returned the stack of

sheet music, leaned over the piano stool, and played a few notes. The piano's rich tone put Mary's piano to shame.

"Detective Thorpe, I'm sorry I kept you waiting. We had a guest speaker at church today and the service ran a bit long." Miss Wylde entered the room in a cloud of powder-blue skirts. "I didn't know you could play."

He turned away from the piano, grinning. "Oh, I don't. The violin is my instrument."

"The violin!" Her eyes grew wide. "How unique. None of my friends play the violin. You will have to play for me sometime."

The thought of performing for her, sharing his music, excited him, but the inspector had assigned him to teach her how to go undercover, not entertain her. "Maybe someday, but I do believe we will be quite busy without any music."

"I'm so glad you could make it on a Sunday." She reclined on a wingback chair and motioned for him to take a seat on the settee. "I do hope my father's request didn't ruin any plans you may have had with your family."

He blinked against the light falling on her golden hair. She was entirely too pretty for him to concentrate on much of anything. "I'll miss the family luncheon after church, but my mother and sister will be fine without me for a few hours."

"No lunch?" She frowned, crossed the room, and called out into the hallway. "Clara?"

"Yes, Miss Wylde?" A short, rotund woman with mousy-brown hair appeared at the threshold in a serviceable gray gown and stained white apron.

"Would you be a dear and fetch a tray of sandwiches to the parlor?"

"Tilda has already prepared them, miss." Clara gave her a smile and a pat on the arm. "I'll fetch them right away and bring a couple of glasses of fresh lemonade to help with this heat."

Thanking the maid, Miss Wylde took a seat next to Jude on the settee, her nearness unsettling him. "Thank you, though I hate to be a bother," he said, clearing his throat and shifting in his seat.

"Nonsense. You heard Clara, and besides, who can work on an empty stomach?" She tucked a golden strand behind her ear, her eyes sparking with excitement. "So, where shall we start?"

"Start?" He gave a short laugh. "I honestly still can't believe your father agreed to allow you into the home of a suspect. Didn't you read the article in the *Chicago Tribune* about Holmes's secret rooms? Didn't your father read the copy I left on his desk? Holmes is a swindler at the very least with all the supposed 'hotel' supplies hidden between floors in the secret compartments that the creditors found."

She pressed her lips into a firm line. "Yes. I suppose most readers think that it is only an interesting design to his house for hiding objects, but I'm happy we agree that there is more to it than having a place to hide creditors' furniture. He is up to something, and we will find out what."

The scent of Miss Wylde's delicate, alluring gardenia perfume distracted him. Jude rose and, clearing his throat, strode to the mantel and leaned his elbow against the wood, looking back at her. "I was thinking that we should start by composing your background. What name did you give Mr. Holmes?"

"Cordelia Swan."

His brows rose at the name. "Miss Swan? As in the heroine from *His Secret Wife?*"

Her jaw dropped. "You are familiar with Mr. Valentine's work? What did you think of it? Miss Montgomery only just returned it, and I finished it last night. I could hardly sleep after the climax. I had no idea his secret wife was—" She pressed her hand to her chest and laughed. "But I won't ruin the ending for you if you haven't finished it. Quite the suspenseful novel."

He gave her a smile to soften his response and tilted his head toward the end table. "I saw the title in that stack of books and flipped through the novel before you came."

"Oh." Her mouth twisted in disappointment as her cheeks tinged with a bit of pink. "Well, Cordelia Swan was all I could think of off the top of my head. Anyway, I figured that if I could pick any name I wanted, I might as well pick something elegant."

"Very well, *Miss Swan*. Let's talk about your childhood, your parents, your siblings, and then move on to your professional background."

She grinned and pulled a writing pad out from behind the cushion. "I thought of a few things already." She arched her brow at him, an impish smile playing at the corner of her lips as if she enjoyed surprising him by being two steps ahead.

He chuckled. "I guess I keep forgetting that I'm working with the daughter of an inspector, don't I?"

"You'll remember, given time." She gave a small laugh as she rose and, taking the pencil from between the pages, flipped through her notes before clearing her throat. "Ah, here they are. Are you ready to hear my ideas?"

"Ready."

"As you know, my name is Cordelia Swan. My father died when I was only a tender child and my mother this past year. Alas, I have no siblings or relatives to call my own." She pressed her hand to her heart, lifting her gaze to the small chandelier.

"All alone in the world?" He nodded with approval. "Basically, you are making yourself the perfect potential victim."

She pointed her pencil at him. "Exactly. If Mr. Holmes is indeed our kidnapper, he won't be able to resist me." She tapped her pencil against her full bottom lip. "Now, as for my past position, I figured it might be best if I had some kind of experience as a secretary since I am interviewing for that position? Say three years?"

He drummed his fingers on the mantel. "That would be too coincidental. I think it might be more realistic if you had, say, a teacher's position in Michigan and came to the Windy City for an opportunity as a tutor to a high society family, which inevitably fell through."

"Oh, I like that." She wrote, murmuring to herself. "Tutor. Fell through. Dire need."

"And what about your personal life? While you do not have family, surely you have friends or a beau?" Jude clasped his hands behind his back and began pacing the width of the small parlor.

The color in her cheeks heightened. "Friends, yes, but no beau, which is why Aunt Lillian keeps pushing suitors on me." She dropped her gaze to her blue skirts. "But I haven't found one worth keeping around yet."

"I was asking on behalf of Cordelia," Jude clarified, finding himself relieved that she didn't have a beau. The realization stopped him in his tracks. *Why would I care whether she has a beau or not?*

Her cheeks brightened to the hue of the ripening cherries in her painting. "Oh, of course. I suppose my character should have a beau in Michigan? That might keep me a bit safer than if I had no connections whatsoever." She paused. "And by safer, I mean that Holmes won't think I'm available and try anything beyond kidnapping me."

The thought of the man touching her made his fists curl, but before she could notice his reaction to her musings, Jude replied, "He won't hurt you, Miss Wylde. You have your pistol, and should he try to take you out of that building against your will, I'll be there to stop him." He gritted his teeth. "I would like to be on the inside, protecting you, but your father insists that you know how to use your weapon should the need arise, which the inspector thinks is as likely as you giving up reading."

"Thank you." She rewarded his promise with a wavering smile, flickering between her bravery and visible nerves. "And please, won't you call me Winnifred? Or even Winnie, if you prefer. It seems rather silly to remain so formal when we will be working together for the foreseeable future."

"If that would please you." Jude cleared his throat, feeling as if he were doing something wrong by allowing himself the familiarity of calling her by her Christian name. He extended his hand to her. "Pleasure to meet you, Winnifred. I'm Jude."

She accepted his hand in a surprisingly firm grip. "Jude."

He loved the way his name sounded on her lips, endearing her further. At the squeak of wheels in the hall, he released her hand. The maid brought in the teacart with sandwiches, chocolate-covered fruit, and lemonade, causing his mouth to water at the thought of the tart treat.

"Thank you, Clara," Winnifred called after the retreating maid. She held up a plate for Jude to take and fill for himself with whatever he liked from the veritable feast for two.

He accepted the plate, his fingers brushing hers before he turned his attention to the fare. He placed a turkey sandwich on the pink floral china. "So, how well do you wield your pistol?"

She selected two cucumber sandwiches and a chocolate-dipped strawberry, forgoing the tongs and using her fingers before licking away a bit of the chocolate stuck to her thumb. Her eyes widened as if realizing what she had done in front of him. "Oh, uh, quite well. My father insists that I go every year with him out to the country to practice. He says there's no sense in my owning a pistol if I don't know how to use it properly. It would be more of a danger to myself and other civilians if that were the case."

"Your father is exactly right. After a few lessons focusing solely on developing your alias, we will take an afternoon to refresh your skills with a firearm." *What can't this woman do? Well, besides painting, what can't she do?* Fighting his urge to grin, he bit into his sandwich.

Winnifred was enjoying her time with Jude far too much. She was here to learn from him and nothing more. Standing in front of the mantel, she couldn't help but glance into the looking glass to ensure that her curls were still tucked neatly away in her coiffure. She spied a stray hair sticking wildly out of place and her hands twitched to adjust it, but instead, she fought the urge and folded her hands, waiting for the moment when his beautiful gaze moved from her own and she could pounce on it.

She took her seat and concentrated on his directions on what to say, do, and wear while working as a potential secretary to H. H. Holmes, all the while taking notes. She couldn't help but admire him for his extensive knowledge of going undercover, and it gave her a little thrill knowing that the next morning, she, Winnifred Wylde, would no longer be only reading or hearing about being a detective, but would be the one going undercover, preventing crimes.

"Excuse me, Miss Wylde?" Clara appeared at the door. "There is a Mr. Percival Covington at the front door asking to see you. Do you know a Mr. Covington?"

Percival Covington. . . ? "I don't know—blast," Winnifred murmured under her breath. She had forgotten that before Aunt Lillian left, she had informed Winnifred to expect one last caller, who was returning from an extended business trip in London. At the time, she had tried to get out of it, but Aunt Lillian insisted, and if she insisted, there was little Winnifred could do but humor her. Rising, she shook her head. "I'm so sorry, Detective Thorpe, but I have to receive him. It shouldn't take long. Show him in, Clara."

The maid curtsied and hurried off to do Winnifred's bidding.

"But weren't you just seeing Mr. Saunders?" Jude asked. He seemed amused, but she sensed an undertone of censure that made her want to crawl under the settee.

She shrugged, hoping to negate any perception of being fickle. "I suppose that since I'm about to turn twenty, Aunt Lillian sees me as an old maid who should be desperate to marry. It's her goal to see me engaged or married by the time the next season starts."

"My, that's a quick turnaround." He tucked away his notepad. "Shall I leave you and return in the morning?"

"We haven't much time to waste, as my interview is tomorrow." She smoothed down her dress, pinched her cheeks, pulled her curl over her shoulder, and patted back that flyaway hair, giving him a smile. "I'm going to practice my undercover skills as Miss Wylde, the potential bride, who is exuberant to receive a suitor yet will find a way of dismissing him within fifteen minutes."

Mr. Covington stepped into the parlor, his tall form and brilliant smile capturing her attention at once. She studied him discreetly under her lashes, finding him a great deal more muscular than she would have imagined a rich gentleman could be, and in spite of the massive, furry blond caterpillar under his nose, she had to admit to herself that he was far handsomer than any of the other prospects she had been forced to see. If she looked beyond his mustache, she could tell that Mr. Covington possessed a charming, boyish face while his tanned complexion and white-blond hair bespoke a love of the outdoors. *First a handsome detective and now a suitor that looks like he has been chiseled by Michelangelo. If I didn't know any better, I'd say I'd fallen asleep in the middle of a Valentine novel.*

"Mr. Covington." She dipped into a curtsy as he bowed to her, his eye roving to Jude, who rose from the settee with a clenched jaw. "Allow me to introduce Detective Jude Thorpe."

"Ah yes, your aunt mentioned that someone was acting as your bodyguard during this tumultuous time." He extended his hand toward Jude, who grasped it, and they nodded to each other. "Pleased to meet you, sir."

Realizing that she was staring at them both, Winnifred cleared her throat and attempted to calm herself as the maid rolled in the teacart again, but this time laden with hot tea and pastries. She pressed a hand to her straining corset, still full from their luncheon. She didn't know how she'd manage to eat one more bite. "Please, have a seat, gentlemen."

Mr. Covington looked to Jude as if expecting him to leave, but she ignored any hint of a desired dismissal. She glanced at Jude from the corner of her eye and found him watching her as if try-ing to gauge her reaction. Well, she wouldn't give him any clues. She rustled to the cart and poured each of them a cup of tea. She straightened her shoulders and arranged her features into those of a china doll, frozen in a smile that was neither cold nor overeager. "Detective Thorpe has been so kind to see me on his day off," she began, dispersing the refreshments.

"Well, it is a relief to hear that you are being so well guarded. I read in the *Chicago Tribune* that the world's fair was going to be a beacon to every thief far and wide, so I understand why your father insists that Detective Thorpe stay by your side, even on a Sunday. . . inside your parlor." He lifted his teacup to Jude. "Thank you for your service."

Jude shifted in his seat and bit into a dainty puffed pastry. "It's my job."

Winnifred kept the flinch in her heart from spreading to her face. *Of course he thinks of you as an assignment. Why did you ever think he was interested in anything more than his task? Because he is kind? Friendly?* She dipped her head and gathered herself before turning her smile to her caller. "So, I heard you were in London. Have you had a chance yet to visit our world's fair?"

"I have. I went the day before yesterday, not even twenty-four hours after my return. I have to admit that I was so enchanted that I purchased a season pass, which Inspector Wylde tells me you too have acquired as you quite enjoy the fair as well." Mr. Covington grinned conspiratorially as if he were sharing some daring secret with her. "I am quite enthralled with the Fine Arts building. What is your favorite exhibit?"

"I adored my time on the Ferris wheel," she said, thinking that it may have had more to do with Jude's arms protecting her than the actual ride. She turned to Jude, half expecting him to join in the conversation, but instead of adding to the exchange, he popped the rest of his pastry into his mouth and stood, brushing his hands free from invisible crumbs.

"If you'll excuse me, Miss Wylde, I must return to my post. Thank you for the refreshments." Grabbing his hat from atop the piano, he bowed to them and made for the door.

"Oh? Must you?" she asked boldly, rising and snatching her napkin before it fell to the rug. While she did wish to spend time with him, the thought of entering her interview tomorrow with only three hours of training almost made her want to give up the whole scheme. . .if not for those missing women. She ran her fingers over the length of the napkin, her eyes wide. *Lord, give me the strength to go through with this and not create a complete disaster in the first ten minutes of the interview.*

Jude's gaze flicked toward Mr. Covington and back to her. "It is for the best. I will be here first thing in the morning." He turned on the heel of his black boot, not waiting for her to show him out.

With a sigh, she returned her attention to Mr. Covington, praying that he would start speaking on the gloriousness of the orange towers and set her world to rights, for no man could be this attractive and rich and remain unattached as long as Mr. Covington had for no reason.

Chapter Six

"No man, for any considerable period, can wear one face to himself and another to the multitude, without finally getting bewildered as to which may be the true."
~Nathaniel Hawthorne, *The Scarlet Letter*

Winnifred's hands shook as the grip car halted in Englewood. *Dear Lord, help me.* She looked over at her companion, hoping for an encouraging word, but he was staring off into space with a deep scowl pressing his brows together. "Jude?" she ventured, waving her hand in front of his face. "We are two blocks from South Wallace Street. Are you ready?"

"Oh, sorry." He hopped off the car first, lifting his hand to help her down.

At the sight of the street sign, she paused and gripped about for a scripture to steady herself, but she was so nervous only jumbled pieces of verses came to her. *Dear Lord, please protect me and calm my soul,* she prayed to keep her panic at bay. Then the scripture from Isaiah she had long held onto since those dark days after her mother's death, when her father had been so consumed with grief he had nearly forgotten her, flooded her being. Her grandmother had embroidered it on a sampler for her as a reminder that she was never alone, never unprotected. Those verses gave her the courage she lacked. *Fear not: for I have redeemed thee, I have called thee by thy name; thou art mine. When thou passest through the waters, I will be with thee; and through the rivers, they shall not overflow thee: when thou walkest through the fire, thou shalt not be burned.*

She paused on the sidewalk and drew a deep breath. *I am Yours, Lord. I am Yours. I am never alone.* She straightened her shoulders and focused on the plan, finding further comfort that Jude would be within earshot of a scream. Even though she knew she wasn't alone, she couldn't help the tremors that began to overtake her. Clearing her throat, she clutched her plainest reticule, comforted by the scripture in her heart and the hard thump of her pistol against her unassuming navy skirt. "I guess this is it."

Jude grabbed her by the shoulders. "Winnifred, you don't have to do this."

"I must." She squeezed his hand and whispered, "Pray for me?"

"I won't stop praying until you leave that building," he returned, a grim color washing over him that did nothing to calm her frazzled nerves as she turned away from him, the distance chilling her even in the warm morning.

Taking a deep breath, she drew back her shoulders and, with confident strides, entered what appeared to be the main door of Holmes's building, sending the copper bell overhead to ringing. Spying shelves of glass bottles, gauze, and medical paraphernalia, she paused yet again, surprised to find herself in a pharmacy. She smiled at the woman behind the counter. "Excuse me? Do you know where I might find Doctor Henry Howard Holmes? I have an appointment with him, and this is the address he gave me." She withdrew the card from her reticule and handed it to the pharmacist.

The woman's bun was drawn so taut that it lifted her wrinkles to an unnatural height, and the rouge smeared onto her pale cheeks did nothing to aid in the youthful glow she was attempting. "You've come in the wrong entrance. I'll show you to the second-floor landing, but only this once. You need to take the side entrance to reach his apartments and staff on the second floor. Mr. Holmes's office and hotel are located on the third floor. His housekeeper will have to fetch him for you." She motioned for Winnifred to follow her behind the counter and up the back stairs, mumbling to herself, "I keep telling him to add a note to his business card so I don't have to keep doing this nonsense."

Gathering her skirts in one hand, Winnifred followed the

pharmacist, pausing at the second-floor landing while the woman fetched the housekeeper.

"You Miss Swan?" a middle-aged woman with an ebony complexion asked, wiping her hands on her apron as the pharmacist brushed past Winnifred with nary a glance.

Winnifred nodded, her throat parched. She would have to do better if she wanted to fake her way into this position. *Give me courage, Lord.* "Yes, ma'am. I have an interview with Dr. Holmes."

"I'll show you to the parlor and find *Mr.* Holmes. He likes to go by Mr. Holmes around here. Thinks the title of doctor makes him stand out too much. Come along." She led Winnifred down the hall. By the creaking of the floorboards and a baby's piercing cry coming from down the hall, she could tell the second floor was poorly built, with paper-thin walls. The dingy parlor was decorated simply with an old Persian rug that had seen far better days; an overstuffed, faded velvet settee; and a wingback chair, all directed toward a fireplace with dried bits of branches left in the ash-filled corners.

Knowing that she needed to appear collected, Winnifred perched primly on the edge of the settee and attempted to loosen her grip on her purse strings. She reminded herself yet again that she had her muff pistol tucked inside if she had need of it, but her heart still raced. She attempted to calm herself with the thought that Mr. Holmes would not be brazen enough to try anything with the housekeeper right there and the drugstore below. Hearing someone enter from behind, she rose, dropping her reticule in her haste.

"There you are, Miss Swan. I am so glad that you were able to come today for your interview." He extended his hand to her, palm up.

She placed her hand in his and gave him a slight curtsy. "I wouldn't miss our appointment for the world, sir."

"Please, have a seat and tell me a little more about yourself." He waved her to the settee and bent to retrieve her bag.

Her heart stopped. *If he feels the barrel. . .this is over before it begins.* With a smile, he handed her the bag and joined her on the settee, sitting entirely too close. "Thank you," she whispered, and refrained from scooting into the corner of the couch. He was not a particularly handsome man with his strabismic left eye, thick mustache, and lean form, but he smiled at her as if expecting her to be charmed. *What makes women trust you, Mr. Holmes?* Winnifred summoned a blush as she dropped her gaze demurely to her lap. "I appreciate the opportunity to interview with you, Mr. Holmes. It's been a few weeks since my tutoring position was terminated, and I'm greatly in need of funds."

His brows rose. "Terminated? Were you fired?"

"Oh no. You see, the young lady I was teaching decided to attend tutoring sessions with her best friend on Lakeshore Drive, and I couldn't compete with a French tutor." She dipped her head again. "Unfortunately, her father decided to release me even though I'd traveled across the state to come here."

He shook his head, his gaze never breaking away from her own. "Such a shame. Did you leave your family behind?"

Her blood pulsed at his leading question. "My family is originally from Michigan. My mother passed away last year, and my father has been gone since I was a child. I have no siblings." She smoothed her skirt. "My beau is not happy that I left, but I wanted to see a bit of the world, starting with the world's fair. However, if I don't get this position, I'm afraid I won't be able to afford to do so on my own and I'll have to return to Michigan to marry him after all." She blinked at Holmes through her long lashes in what she hoped was an alluring manner and not like she had dust caught in her eye. "What else is there for a girl to do if she doesn't have a position that enables her to provide for herself?"

"I see." He stroked his fingers over his thick mustache before folding his hands over his crossed knee. "I'd like to do whatever I can to help you. I have almost exclusively employed young women as my secretaries. I am attempting to open the third floor as a hotel, but the fates are working against me. I have had to fire contractor after contractor, and I have lost two good secretaries back to back. Once the hotel is up and running, I'd like you to keep track of our visitors. But until it is at full capacity, I'd like you to take dictation, type up any notes, and generally keep me better organized. I think from your manner of speech and obvious education, that you'll be a good fit for us." He rose, extending his hand to her. "Would you like to work for the Campbell-Yates Company? I can only offer you half days for now. When the hotel is up and running, we can talk about you coming in full-time."

"Thank you. I won't let you down, sir," she gushed, placing her gloved hand in his as she too rose. "When would you like me to start?"

He cupped his other hand over hers, giving her a benevolent smile. "I'm going to be in Wilmette for the rest of the week, so let's plan on you coming in first thing on Monday morning next week. And in the meantime, you can fill out the necessary paperwork to set up your insurance policy."

"An insurance policy?" Her brows rose along with her voice.

"Oh yes, I always set up an insurance policy for each of my new employees. Now, if you'll follow me to the third floor, I can show you to my office, where you will be working. Are you staying nearby? A long commute will not be easy or financially responsible." Without waiting for her to reply, he climbed the stairs, adding, "If you are interested, I rent out rooms here in the building. I have a few houseguests already, a Mr. Beardsley and his wife, but they have only been staying with me for about a week. I think they will be staying with me for at least a month longer. Then there is Dr. Lawrence and his wife and child. And you met Auntie Ann. She's my housekeeper and cook." He opened the door to his third-floor office and crossed the room to where a briefcase was tucked beside a worn leather chair. Riffling through it, he withdrew some papers, handing them to her. "I always keep extra insurance papers for new employees and friends. It's sort of a side business of mine."

"I see," she said, cracking her knuckles in her anxiety before she could catch herself.

"Of course you can look over the papers before signing if you wish, but it's a standard document. Take your time filling them out and then bring them back for my lawyer to verify and file through the insurance company."

He spoke so fast her head spun, but she nodded and accepted the small stack of papers as she took in the large room with two desks. *The larger one must be Mr. Holmes's desk,* she assumed, judging by the papers scattered about it. The smaller one stood under the lone window and bore only a typewriter sitting neatly on top, devoid of paperwork.

"I can give you a good rate on a room," he said, going back to the matter of her housing, causing her heart to lurch.

It was one of the few points that she and Jude had not discussed. Winnifred acted as though she were studying the papers and nodded absentmindedly, all the while scrambling for an answer. "Oh?"

"One of my last secretaries, Miss Emeline Cigrand, roomed nearby with a pastor and his wife for a dollar and a half a week. I can give you a room for a dollar and a quarter a week, which I must say is a more than generous rate with the world's fair so close by."

"Why, thank you. That is most generous of you, but, uh. . ." Unsure of what to say, she floundered. Her father would certainly forbid her from staying here, and she wouldn't dare risk it. "I will have to check with my landlady and let you know as soon as possible," she answered noncommittally, and prayed he would leave the matter be.

With every tick of his pocket watch, Jude's gaze followed the length of the building, searching for Winnifred and thinking about the file on his kitchen table. Victor's research was inconclusive. He had found something, and it was that something that got him murdered.

He shoved his pocket watch in his waistcoat pocket and returned to not reading his newspaper, his eyes on the third-floor window. Even though he believed Holmes was only a two-bit swindler taking advantage of tourists, Jude couldn't shake the feeling that Winnifred might find out something that would put her in danger just like Victor.

His mind raced with possibilities as to why it was taking her so long to reappear. *Lord, protect her,* Jude prayed. An hour was far too long for a simple interview. *Unless Holmes hired her on the spot.* But there was no way to confirm that Holmes had indeed hired her, without entering the drugstore. Jude attempted to spot her through the windows of the second and third stories, but as they were rather sooty and unkempt, he couldn't see any movement. He had to get closer. Tossing his paper into the bin next to the bench he had been occupying, he crossed the street and stepped into the store, his gaze drifting to the stairwell in the back of the room.

The woman behind the counter looked up from her work of counting pills, lips pursed in concentration. "Can I help you, sir?"

He removed his hat and wiped his sleeve over his eyes, adopting a hazy expression. "Yes, ma'am. I'm looking for something to help me with my headache."

"We've several options." She lifted a binder from under the counter, opened it, and began rattling off which medicines were the best for headaches.

He nodded and replied as needed, but listened for the voices from upstairs. When she'd finished, Jude scratched the tip of his nose and pretended to be reading the binder upside down, stalling.

The woman slammed the book shut. "This is for a qualified pharmacist's eyes only. You want something or not?"

Jude ran his hand over the back of his neck and gave her the smoldering look that he had found useful in the past to melt even the most suspicious of women. "Would you mind terribly reading it to me one more time, please?"

A tinge appeared beneath the layers of makeup as she sent him a pretty smile, revealing her yellowed, crooked teeth overlapping in multiple places, and obliged.

Just as he was beginning to think he needed to charge upstairs with his firearm drawn, he heard a soft footfall above and the tap, tap of heels that sounded like Winnifred's. Snapping his fingers, he nodded. "That powder you mentioned is the stuff for me. May I have a packet?" He gave her a smile for her effort and dug out some change. With the medicine in hand, he slipped outside and waited on the street corner, wanting to catch a closer glimpse of Holmes if he escorted Winnifred outside. When he heard her light voice behind him, he dropped his packet to the sidewalk and bending to retrieve it, caught sight of Holmes bowing to Winnifred, his hands lingering too long on her own.

"Until next week, Miss Swan," he said, pressing a kiss atop her gloved hand and churning Jude's stomach in the process.

He didn't even try to curb his unkind thoughts of the man as Winnifred looked over her shoulder at Holmes with a parting smile that would capture any man's heart. She waved as she walked away from them both.

Jude crossed the street again and followed her a couple blocks behind, noting that she looked well enough, but her pace was brisker than normal. She was excited, nervous. Winnifred appeared not to notice him, but Jude knew she was aware of his presence as he trailed behind her to the next grip stop.

He kept an eye trained behind him for Holmes and stayed at the back of the line for the grip car. When he was certain she had not been followed, he joined her in line as the car pulled up to the station. "How did it go?" he whispered, his hand on her elbow, helping her up the steps and onto the wooden bench.

"Oh Jude. It was positively thrilling and terrifying, but I've got the position!" She dove into her tale, giving him an animated version filled with descriptions of Holmes's Englewood estate that would rival an experienced detective. "And then he offered me a room," she ended, breathless, as they hopped off the car.

"No. Absolutely not. I have no control in that situation, and I need to be able to get to you if there is trouble. Besides, your father would never allow it." He shoved his hands into his pockets, half expecting her to protest in her excitement.

"Believe me, I would never willingly stay there. I was only telling you what he said. We will need to find an address for me to put down on these insurance papers, lest he track me down to my real home."

"Good." He nearly laughed with relief until he saw a carriage parked in front of her cottage. *No doubt it's that darn Percival Covington again.* Jude scowled. He had seen the way her eyes lit with interest when she first met the man. He knew he should be happy Winnifred was distracted by Mr. Covington's impressive presence. Covington could well be what would cause her to walk away from the case and stop putting herself in danger. But he didn't like the fact that she would be staying safe with some man who wasn't him. "Finding a new address is easy enough. I'll get to work on it now. If you decide to go anywhere else today, call the office, and I'll come by for you." With a tip of his hat, he forced himself to disappear.

Chapter Seven

"She preferred imaginary heroes to real ones, because when tired of them, the former could be shut up in the tin kitchen till called for, and the latter were less manageable."
~Louisa May Alcott, *Little Women*

Recognizing the carriage, Winnifred hurried into the front parlor to find Danielle sprawled out on the settee with her feet up as she read. "Danielle! How on earth did you manage to slip away?"

Danielle's gaze slowly rose from a Valentine book, and she blinked in the afternoon light. "I don't know how this story could possibly end well."

"I wouldn't know either. I'm almost done with it, and you already commandeered my other book, so hand it over." She flipped her palm open and wiggled her fingers.

"I brought it back ages ago. I'm not some monster who goes around borrowing limited-edition books and never returns them." She rolled her eyes.

"It wouldn't be the first time you've tried to take my books." Winnifred tossed her hat onto the piano stool and joined her friend on the lumpy settee that they kept in the corner of the room near the side garden window. Her aunt had attempted to replace it on multiple occasions, but as it was her favorite place to read on the first floor, Winnifred refused her aunt time after time. "Fine. You can borrow it, but only because you are my best friend."

"Borrow? I'm going to be a bride on Saturday, and I should be *given* a book for a gift, at the very least. The bookshop said they won't have any in stock for at least another two weeks, and I will be on my honeymoon for ever so much longer than that."

Winnifred rubbed her hand over her eyes. "Very well. It is my gift to the future Mrs. Edward Fairfield, but this is the last time you can use that excuse."

"Thank you!" Danielle squealed and tucked the novel inside her reticule as if to hide it away before Winnifred could change her mind.

"Now, tell me what brings you to my parlor when it is your wedding week."

"My mother heard through the grapevine that you had a gentleman caller, none other than my brother's university chum, Percival Covington!" She grasped Winnifred's hands. "You have to tell me all about it." She settled back into the settee, drawing her knees up to her chin as if they were girls again without a care in the world. "What did you think of him?"

Winnifred bit her lip against her smile. "I have to admit that he is the most eligible of all my suitors."

"Eligible? Winnie, the man is a dream." She giggled. "How did it go? Did he ask to see you again?"

Winnifred felt her insides turn. She had far more important matters at hand and here she was twittering over a gentleman. "He concluded our teatime by asking if he could escort me to the fair Sunday after church."

"And?" She leaned forward, her eyes wide. "Don't be so infuriating, Winnie, and tell me."

"And I said yes." She dipped her head, surprised to feel herself blushing. "I didn't want to like him, but he was so kind and attentive."

"And handsome," Danielle added, lifting her gaze heavenward. "But what of Detective Thorpe? I thought I saw a spark of interest between you two?"

"We are working together, nothing more." Winnifred shrugged. "Besides, you know Father's rule as well as I."

"No lawmen," she quoted with a dramatic sigh. "Such a pity.

Surely your father would reconsider if he knew you really were interested. . . ." At Winnifred's crossed arms and raised brows, she nodded. "I know, I know. He will never alter his stance." The clock on the mantel chimed four times, and Danielle hung her head with a grunt. "Unfortunately, my time is up. I promised Mother that I'd only stay for an hour, and you were gone for so long."

Standing, Winnifred embraced her friend. "I'm sorry. I'll be sure to come over tomorrow and help you with whatever I can."

Danielle leaned her head on Winnifred's shoulder. "If only I didn't have so many sisters, I could have had you as my bridesmaid and then you could have come over for every hour of every day and helped me through this wedding planning nonsense. I wish the ceremony and the reception to be over with and be married. Shouldn't our marriage be the focus? And not society's opinion on how much my father spent on the occasion?"

Winnifred squeezed her hand. "When you return from your honeymoon journey, you will be free to come to the bookshop with me whenever you please." Winnifred followed her friend to the front door as Father returned, nearly bumping into them both.

"I didn't know you had a visitor today." Father hugged Danielle. "Congratulations on your upcoming nuptials. I wish I could be here to celebrate, but I couldn't get out of a business trip and won't be home until late Saturday evening."

"As long as you send me a gift as an apology, I'll attempt to understand and forgive you." Danielle gave him a teasing smile along with a peck on the cheek.

Father chuckled. "I will send you ten novels of your choice along with something crystal for your new home. How does that sound?"

"Simply marvelous." With a farewell wave, Danielle slipped away.

Winnifred helped her father out of his coat and hung it over the banister, her heart pounding with the weight of her request. "Did you and Detective Thorpe have a moment to discuss my meeting with Mr. Holmes?"

Father nodded and took a seat on the bottom step and set to untying his boots. "Thorpe caught me before I left the office. I agree with him that we should be wary of this fellow. However, as far as we can prove, Henry Howard Holmes is only a swindler who has narrowly evaded any consequences as of yet. None of the articles or information available has led me to believe that he is anything more."

"But—"

He held up a hand, halting her. "To the best of our knowledge, Holmes hasn't proven to be a danger, so, as long as you keep your pistol and Thorpe nearby, I am comfortable with you working for him if you wish to continue this plan of yours. If you catch him in any illegal dealings while working as his secretary, I can arrest him, but you are not to say anything to my men at the precinct until you are certain a crime has been committed, understand?"

She nodded, relieved to have his permission though it still stung that he didn't believe her. "I will. I hope that I am wrong about him, but I know what I saw that day at the fair, Father."

"I know what you *think* you saw, my dear." Father sighed as he grabbed the rail and lifted himself up, shuffling in his socks toward the kitchen, no doubt looking for a snack. He swung open the kitchen door, scuttling around the busy Tilda who was quite used to his before-dinner munching. "Did you have the chance to do any baking today?"

"No, sir, I'm sorry, but perhaps Miss Winnifred can go fetch some goods from the bakery? Whatever she finds to her liking. It's Clara's evening off. Otherwise, I would have sent her." The cook looked to Winnifred, lifting her hands covered in an egg mixture. "I'm trying to get this meat pie ready in time for dinner."

"I'd be happy to fetch something for you, Father. I need the walk to clear my head." She rose on her tiptoes and pressed a kiss onto his bristly cheek. "I'll be back soon."

He scowled, rubbing his neck. "Since I came home a bit earlier today, I sent Thorpe home for the day, and his replacement won't arrive for an hour, so there won't be anyone to escort—"

"I can take care of myself," she reassured Father.

Gathering her things, she left the house. Winnifred strolled toward the park, humming to herself as she took the longest route to her family's favorite bakery. Walking through the wooded park, she spied Mr. Covington down the lane on a bench bending over a portfolio with a stilled pencil, working so intently that he didn't even hear her approaching him. "Mr. Covington?"

He jolted, dropping his pencil, but managed to use his portfolio to catch it before it fell on the ground. "Miss Wylde! What a pleasant surprise to see you so soon. It must be fate drawing us together."

She laughed. "Fate, or the fact that my father has a sweet tooth and needs dessert after work every day." She nodded to his notes. "For work?"

"Mmhm." He closed his notebook with a snap and rose. "Are you out alone?"

"Of course. I'm not one of those ladies who needs to be rescued at the drop of her handkerchief." She smiled to soften her rebuke. She knew that most ladies in his class were escorted at all times, but she was thankful that her father didn't require it of her. . . except when there was an abductor on the loose.

"No, of course not," he grinned, a dimple appearing in his right cheek. "Well, even though you are not in need of your handkerchief being rescued, would you mind if I joined you? I am rather stuck in my, uh, notes, and a walk sounds like just the thing. Nothing like fresh air to stir the mind."

Winnifred laughed and lifted her arms, gesturing to their surroundings. "Fresh air? Have you forgotten where you are sitting?"

"Well, the air by the bench is not quite as refreshing as the air beside you. You smell like a meadow," he teased, tucking his notes under his arm.

Winnifred shook her head at his logic, smiling to herself. "You, sir, have more lines than the heroes from my novels."

"Why thank you, Miss Wylde." With a flourished bow, he extended his arm to her. "Shall we?"

He was far too attractive to be calling on her when she had merely six weeks to ensnare Mr. Holmes. Aunt Lillian and Father's plan to distract her with handsome men must not succeed. Straightening her shoulders, Winnifred resolved once more that she needed to minimize distractions. She couldn't have Mr. Covington sidetracking her from her work, no matter how intriguing she found him. She thought of the times when Miss Swan, the heroine from *His Secret Wife*, was forced to make a similar choice. If Miss Swan could give up the beau of her dreams for the sake of her beloved sister, Winnifred could relinquish her dashing suitor for the sake of the women of Chicago.

"What do you think, Miss Wylde? I can get reservations tomorrow if that will work with your schedule?" He gave her a fetching grin, a blond curl escaping his pompadour and falling onto his forehead, lending him a charming, boyish look.

She blinked, trying to find her voice in the face of such uncanny beauty. *No man should be this attractive.* "Uh, I'm not sure tomorrow will be best. I have a prior engagement with my friend, Miss Montgomery. She is to be married this week, so I doubt I will have much time to spare." Winnifred lifted her lady's watch that was pinned beneath her shoulder.

"Ah, that is where the stars have aligned. I know Miss Montgomery's older brother quite well and was invited to the wedding. Your aunt sent me a note this morning asking if I'd act as your escort as your father will be out of town and will not be able to accompany you to the wedding."

Before she could even think to be embarrassed that her aunt had yet again orchestrated a call, Winnifred made the mistake of looking directly into his expectant blue eyes. "Lovely. I mean, that sounds lovely, but I'm afraid I really must be on my way now. I need to reach the bakery before they close or Father will be in a foul mood for the rest of the evening and our cook will be forced to bake something to soothe his temper."

"Then I shall allow you to be on your way and I will count the days to Saturday." He tipped his hat to her and released her arm as a mangy dog leapt out of the bushes, charging headlong into their path, tripping her into Mr. Covington's shoulder and knocking the portfolio out of his hands. "No!" He dove to retrieve his work as the dog disappeared around the bend and the wind picked up, scattering his pages about the park. He scrambled on his hands and knees, gathering each piece of paper to his chest as if they were gold, not minding the dirt soiling his perfectly tailored suit.

Spying more sheets tumbling toward the pond, Winnifred ran down the hill after them, saving all but one from the terrible fate of drowning. She sank onto the grass and painstakingly stacked the papers. Shaking out bits of debris caught between the papers, her gaze fell to the top page and she began to read.

Lady Seraphine knelt beside the grave of her mother. Her tears fell freely as she rocked back and forth, clinging to the only remnant of her mother's that had survived the fire, a golden diadem. She prayed that God would at long last grant her heart a moment of happiness, a moment of love. How could she wed another when Lord Winston was the only one she could ever—

Winnifred gasped as she recognized the tone and flipped through the pages, scanning for a title, her pulse already hammering with the truth as she found a chapter heading. *The Mysterious Death of Lady Ashton by Percival Valentine.* Her hands shook at the realization that Mr. Percival Covington was the author, her favorite author, Percival Valentine. She pressed the papers to her heart and looked up to see Mr. Covington, having finished collecting papers from above, trotting down to her.

The suitor that Aunt Lillian selected for her began to make sense. She had chosen him not only because of his wealth and standing with society's elite set, but because he was a writer. Aunt Lillian knew that out of all the women in Chicago, Winnifred would appreciate him the most. She swayed a bit at the thought that this was the man who created the heroes of her dreams.

He reached for the papers in her hand, pausing at the sight of her open mouth. "What? Did I get dirt on my face from crawling under that park bench?" He laughed, rubbing his handkerchief over his face before extending his hand to help her up.

"You are Percival Valentine? The famous mystery writer?"

If his cheeks hadn't been so colored from the exertion of collecting his papers, she was certain he would have blushed even more. "You've read my work?"

"Only everything you've ever written, three times over. My friends and I have your books set aside for us the morning they are released, but even then, the bookshop has a waiting list." She handed him the stack, her hands fairly shaking as he took them. "I can't believe I finally know who the author is. Why don't you write under your real name? Is it because people would treat you like this?" She giggled nervously, dropping her hands to her sides and pushing herself to standing.

He grasped her by the elbow to assist her. "Not at all. I never intended to be an author, and the name came about quite by chance."

Not a writer? If anyone was destined to write it was him. Having a difficult time speaking in the presence of her hero, she simply lifted her brows.

"My father had grand plans for me to become a lawyer and sent me off to the university, but how I studied criminal justice was by molding those true crime stories into works of fiction, and before I knew it, I had written a novel, which I left in a drawer at my parents' home after the Christmas holidays. Well, Mother discovered my scribblings and sent it off to a publisher under a pseudonym. The publisher loved it, and I have been writing novels ever since."

"Goodness." She pressed a hand to her ruffled jabot. "I never would have thought that Percival Valentine was so young. You sound so experienced, and you've written, what, fifteen novels? How old were you when you were first published?" She paused, taking a deep breath. "I'm sorry if I'm asking a lot of questions, but, well, I have a lot of questions."

Mr. Covington dipped his head and smiled. "Thank you for flattering me with your interest. It's not every day a beautiful woman compliments my work." With his portfolio under his arm, he tucked his hands into his pockets, kicking a small rock down the path. "I've been writing since I was twenty, so about six years now, much to my father's dismay. I know he hoped my infatuation with the pen would wear off, as he would rather I make a living doing something more glorious than writing romantic mystery novels, but my mother enjoys them, and it makes for a good laugh over the holidays when the relatives talk of my books without knowing they are mine." He tilted his head. "My being an author doesn't cause a problem, does it?"

If anything, being an author makes you far more attractive. "Not in the least. What do you tell people you do for a living, since you write in secret?"

"Being from the upper set has its benefits." He winked at her. "I pretend I'm nothing more than a lazy dandy. You would be surprised how many people believe it without a word."

"I can hardly believe that you are the writer I love." She blushed and added, "To read. But, no one would ever accuse you of being lazy." *Not with those muscles,* she finished silently, averting her gaze as she kicked the rock forward, earning another grin from Mr. Covington.

"I'm glad to hear that you aren't disappointed in my works. I was rather nervous when your aunt told me you were such an avid reader."

"Quite. I must admit I am already longing to read your next work."

He sucked in his breath through his teeth. "My next book is due in three months, and I have no idea what I'm going to write about." He lifted up his portfolio. "Well, I've had a few thoughts, but they're so jumbled that I'm having a hard time sorting through them. Having written so many books all at once, I may have used up everything I have to offer." He rubbed his forehead.

"Nonsense. You are a brilliant author, Mr. Covington. You only need a little push, and I might be just the one to help." She fell into step beside him. "After all, I am the daughter of an inspector, so I'm sure I can help you work through some of the plot points that are pinning you down."

He stopped, turning to her. "You would do that for me?"

"I feel it is my duty to society, nay, to women everywhere, to help you with your writing." She threaded her hand through his arm. "We cannot live without your work."

His ears reddened at her praise. "Then tell me, Miss Wylde, what should I write about next?"

"Well, I am privy to a rather plot-worthy scenario at the moment," she confided in a whisper as she pulled him along in the direction of the bakery and told him of the scene at the fair, her interview with the suspect, and of Detective Thorpe's training her to go undercover. "And, since I have the job, I'm sure our next step will be to visit the countryside for some target practice."

Mr. Covington openly stared at her, a single brow lifting. "Miss Wylde, you have shocked me to my very core. Imagine a gentle-woman going into danger for the sake of justice." He took a seat on a park bench and opened his portfolio. Licking the tip of his pencil, he nodded to her. "Please, continue with your tale. I need to jot this down. It sounds too fantastical to be true. Tell me about your alias."

"I took the surname of the latest heroine I was reading about in your book and applied it to my favorite name to form Cordelia

Swan. It was all I could think of on the spot."

"Miss Swan? Now *that's* a heroine's name." He winked at her. "I must say I am impressed that you managed to get this far, Miss Wylde." He tapped his pencil against his paper. "This is excellent. I can already feel the story pulsing once again. Do you think that one day next week I can tag along? And as for target practice, we could take a drive down to my family's country estate. We have quite the course set up."

"We'll have to ask Detective Thorpe, but I don't see why not." Winnifred nodded toward the park exit. "Now, what do you say we pick up a chocolate cake for Father and you come over for dinner tonight and we can see about getting your story outline written?"

Taking her elbow, he grinned. "I say, is that even a question? You had me at chocolate cake."

Jude stepped into the first-floor office of a building that had seen far better days. The storefront window's upper corner had been smashed with a rock, and from the looks of the mildew surrounding the fissure, it had been that way for months. He gritted his teeth. A loan office that didn't even care to spend the funds to repair their own window did not sound promising.

"Can I help you?" a raspy voice called to him.

He turned his attention to a stout man sitting behind a large desk. Jude opened his coat to display his badge. "I was hoping to speak with someone about a loan that was filed here not too long ago."

The man's eye lingered on the badge before he slowly nodded. "Name on the loan?"

"H. A. Williams."

"Mr. Williams. . ." the man repeated, pressing his hand atop his desk and hefting himself up. He shuffled over to one of many filing cabinets, muttering to himself as he riffled through papers. With a harrumph, he slapped a file on the desk, sliding it toward Jude.

Flipping through the paperwork, Jude found another name. "Who is Miss M. Williams? His wife?"

The man crossed his arms and leaned against the window frame. "Not a very talkative fellow. Said he was taking out a loan for his sister for a real estate transaction. My guess is that if you can't find Mr. Williams, start with Miss M. Williams."

At long last, a lead. Jude lifted a prayer of thanks as he gathered the paperwork. "I'll be taking this. Once I have made my notes, I may return the file, unless it is needed for evidence."

The man grunted, jotted a note down on a yellowed piece of paper that had a coffee stain on the corner, and then turned the paper to Jude along with the pen, nodding to the inkwell. "Sign your name and leave your station's address for the release. Can't have papers going about without knowing where they are heading."

Nodding, Jude scrawled out the information, tucked the file under his arm, and headed to his favorite pub to order a pot of coffee. He would not be sleeping tonight, not until he had searched every inch of the file for any clue left behind.

Chapter Eight

"Love is very sweet, when it is simple and sincere."
~Louisa May Alcott, *Jo's Boys*

Dressed in her new gown of a pale pink trimmed with ivory lace and puffed sleeves, Winnifred descended the stairs to await Mr. Covington in the front parlor, ready for a morning of celebration after a harried week. In the midst of preparing for the wedding with Danielle every day, perfecting her alias with Jude every evening, and practicing her typing, she had little time to dwell on the danger in which she was about to place herself. But, if she were honest, Jude was a wonderful distraction from her fear, as she thoroughly enjoyed her time with him.

During their hour before dinner and before Father returned, Jude would coach her on what to say and do and what topics to avoid. To keep her from being trailed to her true address, he had rented a room for Winnifred two miles from Holmes's Englewood building. Jude even spoke with the landlady on Winnifred's behalf, flashing his badge to impress the seriousness of the situation on the woman so she wouldn't divulge the fact, if asked, that Winnifred didn't actually stay there.

His thoughtfulness touched Winnifred again and again, but she had to remind herself that it was his job to look after her. After that first morning on the Ferris wheel, he had maintained a respectful distance, only touching her arm if something appeared out of the ordinary. She sighed as she sank onto the settee, tracing the spines of her Valentine novels stacked on the side table. Percival's books did nothing for keeping her imagination in hand with all his tales of forbidden, star-crossed love. Father had always said that she was not meant to be a lawman's wife. So why was she daydreaming about it in that moment on the Ferris wheel?

She dropped her hand from the books and gathered herself. Jude was not an option, unlike Percival. She couldn't think of Jude as anything more than her protector, her instructor. At the knock on the front door, Winnifred straightened her shoulders and let her thoughts fall aside. She rose to answer the door herself to find Percival standing with a bouquet of two dozen tulips. The blooms took her breath away. *Surely, he knows that, in the language of flowers, to give a woman tulips is a declaration of. . .love?*

Percival started at the sight of her standing in the doorway and bowed, a smile overtaking his features as he presented her with the tulips. "Miss Wylde, may I say that with the morning light casting its radiant glow on your golden locks, you look like an angel among mortals."

She felt heat creep into her cheeks at his praise and dipped her head as she accepted the flowers. She was unused to such blatant flattery.

"Miss Wylde, you should have allowed me to answer." Clara's cheeks puffed from the effort of rushing to the door. She reached out for the flowers. "I'll put these in some water. You two best be on your way to the church."

Percival extended his arm to Winnifred and escorted her out to an impressive carriage with two white horses hitched to it. *Of course Percival would have white horses. All the heroes in his books do, so why would he be any different?* Forcing herself to swallow her laughter, she pressed her hand over her smile.

Pausing with her foot atop the carriage step, she looked over her shoulder and spied Jude down the sidewalk, leaning against a streetlamp with his *Tribune*, keeping an eye on her. She chided herself for not thinking of sending him breakfast or some kind of refreshment, but as she didn't wish to be late for Danielle's wedding ceremony, she merely sent him a smile and a small wave.

Winnifred stared out the window as the carriage rolled toward the church, watching the people and vendors meandering down the sidewalk, a significant portion traveling in the direction of the world's fair. Her city, along with her life, had forever changed when the fair opened.

She turned her gaze to Percival, finding him quite handsome if not a bit silent, as he stared out the window, mouth pressed in a firm line. It wasn't like the quiet moments between her and Jude. This felt awkward and a bit ridiculous after their time in the park, but the excitement she had felt of discovering his secret had faded into nervousness when she thought on their dinner afterward where she had boldly expounded on a possible new plot for her favorite author. *Is he upset with me? Is that why he is silent?* But, remembering the tulips, she dismissed the notion and cleared her throat, breaking the silence. "So, can you tell me what you've decided to do with your next book?"

He blinked as if in a faraway land and slowly turned to her, smile bright. "I'm sorry for my absentmindedness. I have a tendency to get lost in my thoughts. I was actually thinking about my new plot involving a swindler turned murderer."

"Oh?" Elation sparked within her. She hadn't truly believed Percival when he said he was interested in her suggestions. Danielle would melt if she discovered the truth.

"Since you've told me of your adventure, I've put my other story on hold, feeling that it should be finished later. This story is more important to tell at the moment." He rubbed his hands together, unable to keep his enthusiasm from showing. "I am thrilled that Detective Thorpe agreed to let me shadow him. I want to write this from the perspective of the detective, and what better way to learn than from one of New York City's finest?"

"And now one of Chicago's finest." She nodded with approval. "Detective Thorpe is the perfect hero." *His eyes, build, smile, and kind spirit combined with his fierce manliness and drive to protect.* She held in a sigh as the carriage rolled to a stop. The world would swoon at his feet as she wanted to, if only her father would relent.

The church was alive with the hushed flurry of wedding guests finding their seats before the ceremony began. Taking her place in the pew beside Mr. Covington, Winnifred felt a twinge of sadness that she had not been able to join the wedding party. However, she understood that Danielle had little to no power in whom she had chosen to stand with her. Besides, when one had four single sisters, there was no room for another bridesmaid.

The music began along with the procession, and when the bride appeared in the doorway, the crowd rose, murmuring with admiration as she glided down the aisle on the arm of her father, who placed her hand in Edward's without so much as a tear. Danielle looked ethereal in her cloud of white, and the expression on Edward's face told Winnifred everything she needed to know about him. Even though Danielle may not be in love with him at the moment, Edward adored her, and Winnifred was certain that his adoration would, in time, woo Danielle.

After the short ceremony and drive to the Montgomerys' mansion for the reception, Winnifred grasped her friend's hands in her own, offering her congratulations. With a quick hello to Edward, she focused her full attention on Danielle. "You did it! I cannot believe that you, the last of my single friends, are married. Mrs. Edward Fairfield. It has such a nice ring to it."

"Oh good. I felt positively ill," Danielle confided. "I was terrified that I would lose the single piece of toast that I managed to eat this morning."

"You look stunning. I'm certain that if *I* did not notice your queasy stomach, no one else did." She gave Danielle a peck on the cheek, whispering, "Are you feeling better though?"

"Now that the ceremony is over and I am seeing the presents flow into the front parlor, I am wondering why I was so worried in the first place." Danielle laughed as Edward slipped his hand under her elbow, gently reminding her of the others in the line that was beginning to grow. Danielle sighed and embraced Winnifred again.

"I don't know if we will get any more time together today, but I wanted to wish you the happiest of honeymoons." Winnifred slowly pulled away to join Percival in the dining room, sighing. If only she could find the love, the sense of belonging she had been reading about for years. She knew her father loved her. But sometimes, it seemed as if he loved his work more, and it kept him away so often that she felt quite alone in the world.

At the sound of Percival's laughter, she spotted him across the room, her heart skipping as his gaze met her own and lit with unencumbered delight.

Jostling in the rear of the grip car, Jude felt a twinge of something akin to jealousy as the memory of Percival Covington in his black coattails escorting Winnifred to the wedding flashed to the forefront of his thoughts. He was reluctant to allow her out of his sight, but he had been instructed to watch her only until Percival's arrival. Apparently, the inspector trusted that dandy to watch out for his daughter, but Jude did not believe that the pen was mightier than a pistol when it came to confronting danger, and he was disinclined to leave her. But, as he had to obey orders, he had made his way to the grip car line to meet his sister and nephew for a much-needed day of fun at the fair.

It felt odd taking the entire day to himself. In New York, he only took a half day on Sunday to attend church. He enjoyed his work and, as he had no family in New York City and all of his friends worked at the precinct, he felt lonely if he was not working on a project or near his desk with a cup of coffee in hand and his friends at his elbow. While he missed his old precinct, he was finding that he enjoyed having some time to himself and spending it with his family despite the melancholy cloud that constantly hovered over them.

Hopping off the grip car, he strolled to the corner intersection on 60th Street where he'd agreed to meet Mary and Georgie and found they were already waiting on him. Jude chuckled as his sister struggled to keep Georgie at her side in his eagerness to enter the fairgrounds. Georgie, catching sight of his uncle, jumped up and down, waving his hat over his head to ensure that Jude had seen him. With a wave, Jude ran up and scooped his nephew into his arms, tossing him in the air, much to his sister's unease.

"Uncle Jude, I'm getting too old for you to toss me." Georgie giggled, which betrayed that he was anything but too old for such antics.

Five years of age was far too young for a boy to lose his father, and Jude meant to be there for Georgie to guide and help him in any way he could. Extending his arm to Mary and grasping the boy's hand in his own, he stepped up to the ticket counter and purchased day passes. At the sight of a vendor selling molasses taffy out of a cart, Georgie tugged on Jude's arm, pulling him toward the sweets.

Mary smiled, shaking her head. "Georgie, honey, we have been here for all of three minutes and you already want your one treat of the day?" She lifted her brows, placing a hand on her hip, reminding her son of their prior agreement.

His crystal-blue eyes widened as he vigorously nodded with his little tongue licking the side of his mouth. He pointed to the candy. "Please?"

At his sister's smile of consent, Jude dug a coin from his pocket and handed it to the man, purchasing two small sacks of the sweet. Giving one to Georgie, he reached into the other and winked at his sister. "Never too old for candy."

"So, tell me. What sights did you and Miss Wylde see at the fair this past week?" Mary's dark eyes sparkled with mischief. "I've never heard you talk about one of your cases quite so much, and that is saying something. Everything is 'Miss Wylde' this and 'Miss Wylde' that."

Jude had to catch his jaw from dropping. It had been months since Mary had shown interest in anything but Georgie's well-being. For him and him alone did she smile or feign a light heart. "Uh, well, since we found our suspect last week, we haven't been back to the fair. I have been preparing Miss Wylde for the week ahead of her. However, I did find a few places that I think Georgie might like," he replied, pulling them toward the Midway. "There is even a place where I heard that a tiger actually rides a velocipede," he added, looking toward Georgie.

Georgie's mouth dropped open at the mention of the tiger. "Can we go? Mama, can we go?"

They laughed at his fervor enhanced by the copious amounts of sugar he had consumed. Mary bent down to kiss his cherub cheeks. "Of course. We need to see what time the next show starts though. It may not be for a while, so don't be too disappointed if we have to wait."

Jude paused in front of the crowded Hagenbeck Arena building and read the billing. "Georgie, we are in luck. The next show starts in ten minutes. Hopefully, we can still find a seat," he called over the din, guiding them inside the overly crowded arena.

Children swarmed with their parents clutching their little hands for fear of losing them. Keeping to the edge of the crowd, Jude skimmed the seats but didn't see a vacancy. Then he saw a child, two rows up on his left, clutch his tummy and beg his father to leave. Without hesitation, Jude helped his sister to the now empty seats and placed Georgie on his lap, thankful for the moment's respite from the blazing sun as the show began.

They had only reached the second act when Jude spied fingers stretching toward his sister's purse that was dangling from her wrist. His gazed locked with the dark glare of the pickpocket and he shifted to grab the man, startling his sister into realizing what was happening. But the thief was faster, vanishing with the purse.

"Stop!" Mary cried out, but in the pandemonium of the cheering crowd, no one heard her, not even Georgie. "Jude, my locket with Victor's picture. It's in my purse." Mary seized his arm, panic edging her every word. "I was going to have the clasp repaired. I didn't think—"

"I'll catch him. Don't tell Georgie." Jude transferred Georgie to his mother's lap and scrambled through the crowds. Exiting the building, he spied the pickpocket sprinting away. Jude took chase, vaulting over and around anything in his path. The thief led him on for nearly a half mile, only stopping when he reached a dark alley outside the fair, joining a tall, scruffy-looking man who came out of the shadows.

The thief spread his arms out with the beaded reticule dangling in his fist. "What? Are you really going to fight me for this? It's two against one. Me and my pal here will kill you if you try to mess with us." His brows narrowed as his breath came in short gasps.

Jude lifted his coat, flashing his badge. "Don't make this harder than it needs to be. Hand over the purse."

The men laughed, elbowing one another. "He thinks his badge is going to make a difference?"

Jude stepped forward, his fists at the ready. "This is your last warning."

The man lunged at him, but Jude easily dodged him and his friend's jab. It had been a while since he had last taken a boxing class in New York, but the lessons of old were seared into his muscles. With a single blow, he knocked the tall one out, but the pickpocket landed a solid right hook, knocking Jude to his back. Jude rolled to his feet with a grunt, moving in a circle, and was calculating his next move when yet another form appeared in the alley, a black bandana covering his face, his bowler hat pulled too low for Jude to make out his features. He could fight two at once, but three? Jude's hands twitched for his revolver, but the man lifted his hand, brandishing his own firearm at the ready.

The man took a seat on one of the crates, bracing his heel on the base of the crate. "I heard you were looking for me."

His stomach twisted at the man's words. "H. Williams?" *How could I be so stupid? I ran straight into this thug's trap.* Jude faltered in his defense and his opponent landed a punch to his gut. Jude doubled over as the other henchman rose from the dirt with a groan, shaking his head as if to wake himself from a deep slumber. He clenched his hands, stepping toward Jude. Jude attempted to straighten and lift his fists, but the man's iron fist found its mark on Jude's jaw, sending him reeling backward and falling to his side. Too weakened by the blow, Jude barely had time to raise his arm to attempt to block the men's kicks to his torso. Together, the two pummeled Jude until the masked man grunted.

"Enough boys." Williams squatted in the shadows, a foot from Jude's throbbing face. "I don't like to kill lawmen, as it raises too many questions, but I do so enjoy creating little accidents."

Jude lifted his gaze, the cut above his eye fissuring even more. *I wonder if he gave Victor the courtesy of a warning too, before he killed him?* He thought of the pain this man had caused his family and pulled himself up onto his elbows with a guttural yell. "I won't stop until you are marching to your judgment—" At the kick to his ribs, he curled inward, the pain nearly blinding him.

"Hold off." Williams flicked his wrist at the two men and turned back to Jude, his masked face growing hazy. "Tell anyone about this and I'll make sure your sister attends her son's funeral shortly before her own."

Jude lunged at the man, his hands reaching for his throat before the two henchmen grabbed him by the arms and hauled him back. "If you dare hurt my family, I'll kill you myself. You hear? Stay away from them."

Williams laughed, turning his back to Jude. "They live across the street from that little Italian bakery, don't they?"

Jude's head spun at the murderer's words, and his arms went limp. Knowing Jude was defeated, the two henchmen shoved him backward into a stack of crates before joining their leader.

"Drop your search for me and maybe your family won't end up like Victor." He stepped into the shadows and disappeared with his men, Mary's purse forgotten in the dirt.

Shaken, Jude dusted his coat as best he could and ran his hands through his hair, grunting at the pain in his ribs. Testing his injuries, he pressed his hand over his ribcage. His ribs felt tender, but he didn't have the searing pain his friends told him that broken ribs caused. Using his handkerchief and a bit of spit, he patted away the blood from his eye before stepping out of the alley. He paused in front of a storefront window and examined his swollen lip, his bruised cheek, and the cut above his eye. Other than those injuries, he appeared well enough. He was thankful that most of his bruising would be hidden from Mary and Georgie.

Stiff and sore, he returned to the animal show to find Mary and Georgie waiting outside, the threat cutting him anew. He would report this incident to the inspector, but withhold any information about why the threat had been made. Until he had that man behind bars, he would have someone watching each member of his family, even if he had to hire private bodyguards to do it.

At the sight of him, Mary pressed her hands to her mouth, halting any outburst, her gaze darting to Georgie. But he was so busy finishing off his candy and watching two men on stilts walking by, he didn't seem to notice anything amiss.

"Oh Jude, what happened? Mother will be worried sick when she sees you."

With a kiss on her cheek, Jude pulled the reticule from his pocket and pressed it into her hands. "Don't fret over me. It was only a small scuffle. They escaped, but I managed to retrieve your bag. Victor's picture is still there."

"Thank you," she whispered, her voice wavering as she clutched her bag to her heart.

He grasped his nephew's hand and sent Mary a wink, hoping to lighten the mood and ignore the throbbing pain rippling through his body. As soon as the inspector returned, he would request protection for his family. In the meantime, he would find an excuse to stay with them. "Well, I suppose I'm never really off duty, am I? Come on, let's go see the rest of what the fair has to offer."

Chapter Nine

"Not knowing when the dawn will come I open every door."
~Emily Dickinson

Winnifred paused at the corner of South Wallace Street and 63rd and drew a ragged breath as she smoothed down the front of her flawless navy skirt, trying to summon her nerve and ignore her misgivings. Jude's swollen face and bruises had awakened her from her fanciful musings of the romance of detective work. She was leaving the shelter of her home and placing herself at risk, and she needed to be aware. One sobering glance at Jude was enough to remind her of the danger.

As her will began to crumble, she remembered Jude's advice to embrace her character. Cordelia Swan wasn't afraid of anything, let alone a position as a secretary. The thought gave her only a false sense of bravery, but it would have to bolster her enough until she found courage of her own. Straightening her shoulders, she pressed a hand to her plain jabot, feeling for the hard lump underneath her gown where she was secretly wearing her mother's pearl ring on a ribbon about her neck.

Help me, Lord, she prayed, and used the apartment entrance as instructed to find Mr. Holmes waiting for her on the bottom stair. "Oh, good morning, sir."

Glancing up from his pocket watch, Mr. Holmes snapped it shut with a smile, tucked it into his striped waistcoat pocket, and extended his hand to her in greeting. "Right on time. I am so glad you are punctual, Miss Swan."

She accepted his hand. "I am rarely ever late, Mr. Holmes, and I did not intend to start off on the wrong foot today of all days."

He motioned her up the stairs. "I appreciate that in my workers.

As an employee of the Campbell-Yates Company, your position will require a lot of typing, clerical work for the business, and, of course, the signing of your name as my representative on transactions regarding the apartments and the new hotel. Many, many documents and bills cross my desk, and I don't have the time to sign them all."

At the third floor, he opened the first door to the office, which had been transformed since last week. There was now only one desk, with a faded Persian rug, two overstuffed chairs, a small side table with a hurricane lamp atop, and red curtains covering the windows. Her desk remained facing the window, the typewriter securely in the middle of the desk, but the larger desk had been moved to where she could barely spot it through the adjoining room's open door.

"I moved my desk into the turret space to afford us both some privacy for when I have contractors and potential investors over."

She swallowed, uncomfortable with having him so near and not within her line of sight, but she couldn't think of a way to suggest rearranging her desk without causing suspicion. *Dear Lord, protect me in this position.* She tugged off each finger of her gloves before slipping her hat pin from its place and setting her chapeau on the rack by the door. "How lovely."

"I'm pleased that it is to your liking. I had the furniture brought up from Mrs. Conner's old room, or the green room I call it now, as I thought that you might be more comfortable if it didn't look quite so vacant." He stepped to the window, looking out onto the street below. "If you'd like a settee or anything else, have a look in the green room. It acts as my storage space for furniture, so feel free to decorate from the pickings there. But hopefully the view is to your liking?"

She joined him by the window and looked out to the neighborhood already bustling with people. She purposefully did not look in the direction where Jude was watching the building from his park bench. She calculated her response. "It is quite nice, but if it proves too distracting from my work, I may turn my desk from the window to face the room." Not wanting to miss her chance to explore, she gave him an enthusiastic smile. "I love what you've done with the place, but I may check out the storage room. What kind of woman would I be if I didn't jump at the chance to do a little shopping?" She winked at him.

She was awarded with a barking laugh. "I knew you would enjoy it. See Auntie Ann, and she will be happy to let you in the room."

"Thank you for your kindness, Mr. Holmes. You have already proven yourself to be quite the ideal employer." She clutched her hands in front of her skirt and gave an eager bounce on her toes. "Would you like me to start with the stack of papers on your desk?"

"Those?" He gave a nervous laugh. "Oh no. I'll have Mr. Owens go over those. Anything I need you to work on, I'll have Mr. Owens bring it to you or I'll give it to you myself."

"Mr. Owens, sir?"

"I forgot to mention that you will share your clerical duties with Mr. Joe Owens. I hired him a couple of weeks ago. He understands the workings of the business a little bit more at this point, so I would prefer that he deal with those particular papers until you are up to speed."

Winnifred's instincts pulsed. If there were papers that he did not want her to touch, it was obvious to her that they were in Mr. Holmes's office.

He shifted through one of the stacks on her desk, thumping the top with his finger. "Sort through and file these. All have been opened by Owens, but he only scanned them. If something needs my attention, make a note and set it aside, but if a letter simply requires a signature, I would prefer not to be bothered. I am often away attending to business, and when I am in my office, I will be focusing on getting my hotel up and running, which is the main reason why you have been hired. You are to get me to a place in my paperwork where I can concentrate solely on the hotel. I have a lot of funds tied up in this building and there are many people I do not want to disappoint."

She tucked her hands behind her skirt and nodded. "I will do my best, sir, to have your office organized as soon as possible."

"Thank you. Now, did you have a chance to fill out those insurance papers? I know it sounds rather eccentric, but as a precaution, I require each and every one of my employees to carry an insurance policy in case the worst should happen."

She retrieved the folded papers from her black reticule and handed them to him. "I don't have any next of kin, so whom should I sign the money to should something happen? My beau and I had a disagreement and aren't speaking at the moment. I'm not sure if we will recover from it."

He rubbed a hand over his mustache and shrugged as he spread the papers on her desk. "I suppose you could put my name down for now and amend it when you can think of someone suitable."

She inwardly cringed as she bent to fill out the last line, but if she signed it as Cordelia Swan, she supposed it wouldn't be illegal, since she had the sanction of her father. Signing her alias with a flourish, she handed the documents back to him, feeling as if she had signed her life away. *Well, if I was trying to give him an incentive to kill me, I just did.*

"I will notarize it and have it sent to the insurance office to be filed by this afternoon." He crossed the room to the adjoining door. "I'll be here this morning if you have any questions, but most of the time, Mr. Owens will be on hand to answer on my behalf."

Winnifred filtered through the first stack, sorting them into piles of bills and contracts and receipts, humming to herself as she imagined Cordelia would be likely to do as she searched for any clue of nefarious activity.

After nearly three hours of categorizing, she was beginning to feel uncomfortable with the amount of water she had been sipping, but Holmes had yet to leave, giving her a moment to quietly seek the necessary. Feeling a blush creeping into her cheeks, she murmured an excuse about visiting the kitchen for more water and rose from her chair, stepping out of the office. Following the hallway, she tentatively opened doors to empty rooms and rooms with sparse furnishings. Finding a space without windows, she heard a throat clear behind her.

Auntie Ann adjusted her grip on the tray filled with dirty dishware, a scowl furrowing her forehead. "Miss Swan, what on earth are you about?"

Winnifred blushed, not wanting to mention her state, but seeing no way out of it, she cleared her throat. "I seem to have forgotten where the necessary is located. There are so many doors up here. Could you point it out to me?"

Auntie Ann motioned back down the hall toward the landing. "We use the facilities on the second floor. The upstairs is still under construction. Follow me."

The steps creaked beneath their feet, proclaiming their route to the whole floor. She waved her down the hall. "Second door on your left."

"And the green room?" At Auntie Ann's pointed look, Winnifred added, "Mr. Holmes said I might check and see what furniture I could use for the office."

Auntie Ann patted the chatelaine at her waist, keys rattling from the chain. "It's the first door on the left, but come and see me when you are ready and I'll open it for you."

Alone at last, Winnifred rested her head in her hands and sighed, her shoulders sagging from the pressure of appearing composed all morning while keeping up her alias. She poured the pitcher of water into the porcelain basin and rinsed off her face, enjoying the coolness against her flushed cheeks. The hair caressing her face curled from the dampness as she dried her face with the less than clean white towel.

Smoothing her modest lace collar, she tugged on her ivory cuffs and peeked into the kitchen where Auntie Ann was already wrist deep in dough, pounding it into a mound of flour on the table, shaking the floor with her strength and making Winnifred take note of the instability of the second floor.

"Would you mind opening the green room for me now, Miss Ann?"

She grunted, dusting off her hands as they headed to the locked door. "Everyone calls me Auntie Ann, so don't be giving off airs by adding a 'miss' in front of my name." She harrumphed as she found the key that unlocked the door. "I don't know why he decided to switch the name of this room. To me, it will always be Mrs. Julia Conner's room."

"Where is Mrs. Conner now?"

"Gone. Mind yourself. Lots of boxes in here that could easily topple over and crush a little thing like you," she warned.

Winnifred massaged the palms of her hands. "So, um, how long have you been working for Mr. Holmes?"

"Long enough to know that you best not flirt with your employer. The last two little girls who worked for him were all kinds of in love with Mr. Holmes, and both even went on to say that they were going to get married." She pushed the door open. The room was piled high with crates and Queen Anne chairs stacked on one another along with white cloths covering massive pieces of furniture.

"Oh? And what happened?" Winnifred asked, feeling slightly admonished for her alluring smiles to Holmes, but then instantly remembering that she was there to do a job and flirting with Holmes was part of it.

"Do you see them about?" She waved her hand around the room. "I have a hearty suspicion that Mrs. Conner had her eye on Holmes as well. Think that is why her husband left, but I'm surprised he left his daughter behind too. A pretty little thing she was." Auntie Ann surveyed the room, picking through a crate of blue-and-white dishes before curling her lip at a chipped edge and returning it to its nest of straw.

"Was?" Winnifred lifted one of the white sheets to find a worn leather wingback chair. "What do you mean *was?*"

"They seemed to disappear overnight. Holmes said that Mrs. Julia Conner left in quite a state with little Pearl in tow, but the strange thing is that she left behind most all of her things." She shook her head. "Doesn't seem like a lady would leave behind her toiletries."

Winnifred's skin prickled at this, but before she could ask another question, Auntie Ann dusted off her hands and moved for the door, calling over her shoulder, "I'll be in the kitchen. Let me know when I can lock up."

A cloud of dust billowed beneath her skirts, creating the illusion of fog as Winnifred ambled about the room, searching. She opened the closet door and paused at the sight of a china-headed stuffed doll, tucked haphazardly in a small wooden box. Kneeling down, she scooped the doll into her hand, remembering the doll her own mother had given her. If she had lost it as a child, she would have been devastated. She never would have parted from it, even if the house was on fire. Her gaze fell to the left of the box onto something rusty in color. *Is that paint?* She ran her finger over it and a tiny bit rubbed onto her skin. She had read enough novels to know what it was. Winnifred's stomach roiled as she pressed her hand to her mouth. *Blood.*

Chapter Ten

"Anxiety is good for nothing if we can't turn it into a defense."
~George Eliot, *Daniel Deronda*

Jude eyed the targets on the manicured meadow of the Covington's vast country estate. After Winnifred's discovery yesterday, he'd cleared his afternoon schedule for shooting practice with Percival Covington. If he hadn't truly believed she was in danger, he would have excused himself from attending the practice and avoided the awkwardness of being a third to a courting couple's outing, but as it was his job to ensure that Winnifred had the proper skills for defending herself, he set aside his feelings and focused on the task at hand.

Percy rested his hand on the puffed sleeve of Winifred's red blazer, pointing to one of the targets in the field. "Normally, I would use this target for long-range practice, but since we are working on defense, I figured it would be best if we stepped closer."

Jude inwardly cringed at the obvious conclusion, but was thankful that at least Percy provided a distraction for the reason *why* Winnifred would need time to practice. If she had indeed found blood in the room of the mother and child who had disappeared, Holmes may be far more dangerous than the inspector or anyone had believed.

As he watched her laugh with Percy over something, his thoughts began to drift, but instead of traveling to Victor's case, he found them wandering to Winnifred and how the sun caught her golden locks and her laughter rippled in the air and the way her fine eyes sparkled at him when he said something she found humorous. And how she always buried her nose in a book every chance she got. He was confident that if she took only a moment to look up from her pages, she would find herself inundated with suitors.

"What do you say, Detective?" Percy called to him, breaking Jude's reverie. "Shall we make this a bit more challenging? Have a competition of sorts?"

Winnifred clapped her hands. "Oh, I like the sound of that. Detective Thorpe, are you up for a bit of shooting?"

"Are you sure you want me to join in? It would hardly be fair with all the practice I've had over the years," Jude replied, not wishing to quash the fun of a competition between the couple.

Winnifred's mouth twisted in what looked to be suppressed mirth. "That's very benevolent of you, but I think it will be more than fair. What do you say, shall we go shot for shot? The first time someone misses, they are eliminated. The last one standing wins."

Jude stuffed his hands into his pockets, seeing no polite way out of the competition without insulting her. He held back a sigh and slowly nodded, thinking he would go easy on Winnifred to bolster her confidence.

"Perfect. Shall we make it even more interesting with a prize?" Percy selected a revolver from the small table that held their weapons.

Curiosity piqued, Jude asked, "What kind of prize?"

Percy turned his weapon over in his hands, examining it. "If you or Miss Wylde wins, you will have the honor of naming the hero in my next novel."

Jude grinned, stepping up to the table. "I think that sounds like a fine idea." *This is going to be quite entertaining after all.*

Winnifred shot him a sly smile. "Sounds like you won't be throwing the match now?"

"I'll say." Jude hooted with glee. "I think Sir Marion Shirley would do quite nicely for a hero's name."

"You wouldn't!" Winnifred smothered her laughter with her hand.

Percy rubbed his hand over his face with an exaggerated groan.

"That, my friend, might be the worst name I have heard to date for one of my male leads. And judging by Miss Wylde's reaction, I'm not sure it will go over so well with the ladies."

"Well, one of you will just have to win is all." Jude chuckled at this turn of events. "And Mr. Covington, what would your prize be should you win?" He asked out of politeness.

"Why, the glory of besting an inspector's daughter and one of New York's and now Chicago's finest detectives." Brandishing his weapon in a circle above his head, Percy shouted, "Lady and gentleman, take your places for the first annual game of glory!" Percy gave Winnifred a flourished bow. "Shall the lady go first?"

For her answer, Winnifred planted her feet in a wide stance. Turning her shoulders, she gripped the pearl handle of one of Percy's smaller revolvers in one hand and wrapped the other on top with her finger resting right outside the trigger as she aimed. Even if she didn't make her first shot, Jude was already impressed with her stance. Closing one eye, she moved her finger to the trigger and a crack filled the air as a puff of smoke drifted from the barrel. She had hit the target dead center.

Setting the gun on the table, she gave a happy twirl and looked up at him. "One of these days, you will stop underestimating me, Detective Thorpe."

Jude returned her grin, but before he could reply, Mr. Covington stepped up beside her to take his place.

"Well, I must say I am quite impressed, Miss Wylde, and I hope I never cease being surprised by your talents," he said before taking aim and making his shot.

Blast. Winnifred lowered her firearm, her cheeks burning from missing such an easy shot on the fifth round of the game. She couldn't blame Jude's presence for distracting her. She had not taken the proper time to aim, and she was dismayed to think that she would have even less time in the moment should Holmes attack her. If she missed this shot, how could she defend herself if it came down to it? She shook her head. Her father would have been shocked by her mistake.

One of the few outings she and her father had taken after her mother died were trips to the country solely for target practice. For two days out of the year, they would spend hours together practicing. Before one such outing, Winnifred had set up discarded glass bottles on the rear fence line of her aunt's mansion for targets to impress her father with her improvement. However, before she had time to follow through with her disastrous plan, Aunt Lillian had stepped in and stopped her, saying that a twelve-year-old girl should know better than to discharge a firearm in the middle of civilization. Winnifred supposed that some part of her thought that if she impressed her father, he would remember he had a daughter more often than once a year.

"No need to look so downcast." Mr. Covington took her hand in his, misinterpreting her silence. "I will win for you, so you can still name my next lead character if you wish."

Giving him a bright smile to dispel her clouded thoughts, she pulled her lace-trimmed handkerchief from her sleeve and looped it through his buttonhole. "If you are to be my champion, you will need to sport my colors, Percy."

"This shot is for you, Winnie." Percy bent and kissed her cheek with a tenderness that stole her breath. She blushed at his bold action, but was surprised to find it was not disagreeable. She glanced out of the corner of her eye to her guardian, but Jude had already averted his gaze to the targets.

"Are we going to shoot or talk all day?" Jude motioned for Percy to take his place.

She stepped back from Percy as he took his shot and watched the two men closely. Jude shot with a practiced hand, but Percy seemed as equally at ease with a gun in his hand as a pen, and she couldn't help but admire his skill. The men took a pace back with every shot, and Winnifred grew more and more impressed over how well Percy was doing against a seasoned detective, until finally someone missed.

She gasped, twisting to look up at the unexpected winner.

Percy gave them a wry laugh as he set aside his weapon. "I quite enjoyed target practice as a boy, short and long range, archery, and hunting and the like, and I still shoot clays every chance I can get. Thank goodness too, else I might be at the mercy of Detective Thorpe's choosing my character's name." He turned to Winnifred and kissed her hand, sending her heart into confusing flutters. "Hopefully my fair lady will be a bit more generous in naming the hero."

Chapter Eleven

"There is love in me the likes of which you've never seen.
There is rage in me the likes of which should never escape.
If I am not satisfied in the one, I will indulge the other."
~Mary Shelley, *Frankenstein*

Miss Swan?" Holmes called from the adjoining room door, bowler hat in hand. "From the looks of your desk, I'd say you have done six hours of work in half the time and deserve a cup of coffee from the café."

Joe Owens, whom she had met before leaving on her first day, sent her a smirk as if Winnifred was already falling in love with her employer. Owens had even gone as far as to say that he and one of the other male boarders were betting to see how long it would take for her to step out with Holmes.

She looked from him to Owens, who was making himself look busy with a file she had just finished. "This is only my third day here, Mr. Holmes, and there is still so much to be done. I don't want to postpone your hotel opening—"

"Nonsense. One should always have the time for a cup of something hot." Mr. Holmes twirled his bowler hat before flipping it on in a single motion.

Push yourself. You are here to engage the suspect and find clues! "Yes, I'd like that very much," she replied, thankful that she had managed to keep her voice steady. Snatching up her hat and reticule, she followed him down to the ground level and stepped outside, blinking in the afternoon light as Holmes offered her his arm.

"Since I invited you out for coffee, there will be no talk of you paying for your libations."

"But, sir, I hardly think it proper for you to pay for me, as I am an employee." She protested as she imagined Cordelia might, weakly, and with a hint of flirtation, as if she were only objecting because that was what a lady should do.

"Nonsense. What kind of gentleman would I be if I allowed that? Don't look so worried." He chuckled as she glanced over her shoulder looking for her guardian, mistaking her motive. "We are only going down one block to the coffeehouse."

She observed a vendor pushing a cart, children with their nurse, and a couple arm-in-arm strolling by, but no Jude. Her stomach dropped, and she gripped her reticule a little tighter as she stepped inside the dark coffeehouse. It was nothing like the light, airy café near her home on Lakeshore Drive, but she acted as if she had been in many such coffeehouses. Inhaling the heavy scent of freshly ground beans, she slid into a seat near a smudged window, allowing Holmes to order for them both.

"So, how were your first few days?" he asked, turning his attention back to her as the girl placed his order of two black coffees and two pastries of the day.

She forced her fidgeting hands to still, folding them on the table as she looked up at him through her lashes. "Excellent, sir. I am grateful for the work, and I look forward to learning more about the business."

"Good. Good. And did you get along with Auntie Ann? She seemed a bit put out with you." He chuckled, shaking his head.

Did he overhear the housekeeper's warning? She searched for the right words. "She certainly is, um, to the point."

"I half asked you to coffee as an apology for her insinuations on your very first day. I hope she did not frighten you away, because I need a pretty worker like you to brighten my day." He gave her a conspiratorial grin. "Did she give you her little speech, warning you to remain in a professional relationship with me?"

She got the feeling that Holmes was testing her attraction to him, and she knew that if she failed to return his flattery, she would not get much out of him. Holmes seemed like a man who enjoyed being made much of. Why else would he have so much ambition to set up a hotel when he obviously had no money to pay back creditors? He was desperate for wealth and approval, and she would use that weakness against him. If Auntie Ann was worried that she might charm Holmes into her confidence, maybe Cordelia really could.

She smiled at him, blinking her lashes like the heroines she had read about in Percy's novels, stepped into her character, returned his smile, and leaned forward. "I'm sure you must be aware of the effect that you have on your female staff? She meant to protect you, but... you know what they say about forbidden fruit."

He threw his head back and laughed as the coffee and eclairs were placed on the table, and Winnifred could see his pleasure in his features. "I don't know about all of that, but there have been a few incidents that may have led her to believe that assessment." He lifted his palms helplessly. "Who am I to turn away a maiden in distress? It's not my fault if they mistake a comforting shoulder for that of a lover's."

She traced the rim of her coffee cup with her forefinger. "I heard that one girl thought she would marry you."

His smile seemed strained before he allowed a confident light back into his eyes. "A few did, but I am a hard man to pin down."

"Only a few?" She giggled as if he told a great joke and gently laid her hand on his arm, allowing a blush to reach her cheeks and her eyes to widen at her boldness.

A grin spread under his thick mustache as he leaned toward her, his breath on her ear. "We are going to work quite well together. Did you find accommodations elsewhere, or should I have the housekeeper prepare a room for you?"

A room? Too far! I took it much too far. She slowly withdrew her hand, hoping to assure him that she did so, not because of what he'd said, but rather her remembering to act like a lady. "Alas, the owner of the boardinghouse would not release me from our agreement. Fortunately, it is only a short grip car ride away and is a fair price."

"If money is the issue, I can lower the price. I would hate to have you take the extra commute because of money." His gaze lingered on her fingers curled around her coffee cup handle.

She absentmindedly twirled a curl at the base of her neck. "Oh Mr. Holmes, I couldn't. A room like yours should go for a much higher price. I heard from one of the boarders that you charged far more than what you're asking from me. I appreciate your generosity, but I cannot allow myself to accept such a steep discount even from the kindest and, might I add, handsomest of gentlemen."

"Can we get closer?" Covington asked for the third time in twenty minutes. "Surely I can purchase a cup of coffee without him suspecting anything."

Jude crossed his arms, anger bubbling in his chest. "No. As I told you before, you might destroy her cover and put her and the mission in danger."

"You said he's a known swindler. Maybe I can bump into him and try to invest in his so-called hotel business?" He gave the ends of his blond mustache a little curl with the waxing kit from his pocket.

Despite their time shooting, the respect Jude had gained for Percival Covington was slowly deteriorating with each obstinate suggestion that he knew better than a man who had been professionally trained as an undercover detective. "Do you really wish to risk Miss Wylde's safety for the sake of your own curiosity?" *And for your next novel?*

"I think it would be perfectly natural if I went in there and threw some money around to catch his attention. Imagine the information I could glean from speaking with him as a potential investor." He scribbled down a thought on his wretched notepad before slapping it shut and tucking it into his pocket. "Well, I guess that's about it for me. I think I have enough to get started with my new story, but will you fill me in if something interesting comes up?"

"You got it." *Anything to keep you from scratching your pencil across the page for a minute longer.*

"Thank you. I have complete confidence in your ability to protect Miss Wylde in my absence. I have to say, your job is quite exciting. If I hadn't decided to write stories, I know I would have loved to be *in* the stories like you are. Who wouldn't jump at the chance to protect a beautiful young maiden from the hands of a notorious villain? And look at you. It takes quite the man to look even better with a black eye."

Jude couldn't help but laugh at Covington's simple summation of his job. "It isn't always as glamorous as this, and it's not just a story. It's real life with real dangers. Oftentimes, I am watching out for trouble in the worst of places. Places that you have only written about."

Covington clapped him on the shoulder. "And that is why there are photographers, my friend. So I do not have to dance in the squalor to depict the dirt one might find there. I must simply look at a picture and paint it in my words." He shrugged and added, "Sometimes my paint is laid on a little bit thicker than needed, but it makes for a good story, and the ladies seem to love it. They are my best customers, after all. Have a good day, Detective." He grinned and tipped his bowler hat, swinging his walking cane as he practically pranced down the sidewalk.

Breathing a sigh in the blessed silence following Covington's wake, Jude returned his gaze to the window where he could see Winnifred sipping on her coffee. To maintain his cover, he pulled out his newspaper and leaned against a lamppost across from the coffeehouse and pretended to read, all the while keeping one eye on the couple.

He hadn't been able to do any more digging into Victor's murder since the threat on his family's lives, but the threat had only caused him to renew his vow to find the killer. Last night, after he had returned Winnifred safely home from target practice, he had sought out the inspector and told him of the incident. The inspector was reluctant to accept Jude's lack of explanation behind the threat, but he approved the need for security. Jude's family, though now guarded by the precinct's men, would not truly be safe until Victor's murderer was behind bars.

Jude brought his thoughts back to the case in front of him. Even if this Holmes fellow turned out to be nothing more than a swindler, the man would certainly try to steal a kiss at some point. Winnifred was far too beautiful to be flirting with him and not expect repercussions, and Jude couldn't protect her from the outside.

His stomach turned as she laid a hand on Holmes's arm, but to his relief, they stood and exited the building. Jude followed them with his gaze as Holmes walked her toward the grip line, where he paused and bowed to kiss her hand and, with a winning smile, Winnifred waved to Holmes as the car pulled away.

Chapter Twelve

"Let us be elegant or die!"
~Louisa May Alcott, *Little Women*

As a thank-you for allowing him to tag along on her investigation for the past week, Percy surprised Winnifred with two
box tickets to the Chicago Orchestra playing in the Auditorium
Theatre. Since she would be seated in the most coveted box in the
house, she dressed in her finest sapphire damask evening gown, the
garland of pearls woven into the tulle at the bust casting a luminous
glow in the candlelight. With Aunt Lillian's burgundy opera cloak
hanging from her shoulders, she twirled before the long looking
glass. *I could be a heroine from one of Percy's books.* She grinned at her
reflection before shaking her head at her silliness, dismissing it as
overexcitement for the evening. It was a luxury for her to sit anywhere but in the general admission, where one could hardly see the
face of the soloist.

The front doorbell rang, and she snatched the two tickets from
atop her vanity and hurried down, unable to hide her anticipation
for the night. But instead of finding Percy at the door, she was
greeted by a messenger boy in a navy uniform with his cap in hand
as he drew a message from his brown leather satchel.

"Miss Wylde? I have a note from Mr. Covington." He extended
the note to her and stepped down to the sidewalk to give her a
moment of privacy and to await her reply.

She tore open the note, a hint of fear in her spine.

My Dear Miss Wylde,
Inspiration has struck me at long last. Please forgive me for
the unfortunate timing, but I must listen to the beckoning of

my muse. I am all anguish for ruining our night out at the orchestra.

Regards, Percival Valentine

She sighed, her heart aching with disappointment more from missing the symphony than from missing her suitor. "Please inform Mr. Covington that it's quite all right," she said to the boy, dismissing him with a wave of the wretched letter before sinking onto the step in a sapphire cloud of skirts, not caring that she might soil her ensemble.

"Winnie?" Jude called to her, awakening her out of her trance as he trotted into view and up the path toward her. "Did you have bad news? Are you unwell?" He sank onto the step beside her.

She lifted the tickets and the note. "Apparently my escort will not be able to come tonight, and my evening is spoiled."

Jude pressed his lips into a thin line, slapped his hands on his knees and, pushing off them, rose and extended his hand to her. "No sense in letting those tickets go to waste, or your efforts of dressing up. Shall we go?"

Blinking at his hand, she looked up at him. "But you aren't dressed for the symphony."

"I'll stop at my apartment on the way there. It will take me all of five minutes to change into my black coattails."

Her heart sparked with excitement at the thought of attending the symphony with him. "Are you sure? I'd hate to put you out," she said, before remembering his love of the violin. Surely it wouldn't be *that* much of an affliction for him to escort her.

"I was going to be posted outside of the theatre all night to keep an eye on the perimeter, so it would be an unexpected pleasure to be the one enjoying it from the inside." He wiggled his fingers, inviting her to stand with him. "Come on, it will be fun."

He would enjoy it as much as I, and why should we let those seats go unoccupied? Winnifred's heart tried to convince her head that it was a good idea in spite of the risk of being seen by the high society ladies who might report back to her aunt. But after the dangers she had recently experienced, caring about society's fair-weather opinion seemed a bit foolish. Grinning, she placed her hand in his and allowed him to pull her up. She threaded her arm through his offered arm, a thrill traveling through her at the feel of him being so close once again. "Let's do it."

With a cheer, he led her to the street and lifted his arm to hail a passing carriage. "No time for a grip car tonight, Miss Wylde. I have a symphony to dress for and a lady to escort. Only the best for you, my lady," he exclaimed with a wink and a deep bow.

She laughed and enjoyed the freedom of being able to do so without feeling awkward. In a quarter of an hour that had passed far too quickly for her taste, they were parked in front of his apartment building, and while he was a bit apprehensive to leave her alone in the carriage to wait for him to change, Winnifred patted her heavy reticule, silently reassuring him that she would be quite safe. She watched his retreating figure and was once again struck with how kind he was to her. Not every young detective would willingly go to the symphony with his charge. *Is it really only kindness, or is there something more behind his thoughtful gesture?* She bit her lip as he disappeared.

She studied the outside of his building and found herself longing to see what his home looked like, aching to know him beyond his work persona. Did he have a small library? What songs did he play on his violin? Was his place well kept? Did he cook? She shook her head, trying to keep the questions at bay when he came trotting down the steps with a slightly faded top hat in hand.

Jude tapped the roof, signaling the driver to move on, and settled into the seat next to her, breathless. "So, you should know that I've never actually attended the symphony before, but I shall endeavor not to embarrass you."

"Have no fear. I'll take care of you," she reassured him, admiring his clean jawline and full lips, devoid of that horrid mustache that almost every man in Chicago deemed a necessary part of their attire. Why they tried to hide their faces under a furry caterpillar, she'd never know, but of course, not all men could be as handsome as her escort. *Stop it. He is paid to protect you. Nothing more. You best remember that before you allow your heart to be broken.*

"What? Is my tie crooked?" Jude tucked his chin down in an attempt to check for himself.

Winnifred laughed and tugged off her gloves before reaching out to straighten it. The carriage wheel struck a rut in the road, jostling her into him, her hands inadvertently wrapping about his collar. She gazed up into his eyes and forgot to remove her hands for a few fleeting moments as the carriage rolled to a stop.

"Can't get any closer, sir," the cabby called, wrenching them both out of the moment. "The place is packed. I could try to wade through, but you would be late for the opening. My suggestion is shank's pony."

She jerked back, and Jude opened the door for them, assisting her out onto the sidewalk two blocks from the theatre. They walked in silence, her heart racing over what had just occurred. *Dear Lord, let me not have frightened him off by my imprudence. Why did I linger? Why did I not pull away instantly?*

Jude handed their tickets to an usher, who bowed and motioned them to follow him as he expertly wove through the crowd to their seats. Any inhibitions she harbored melted away at the sight of the opulent theatre. The room hummed with excitement as the instruments performed their scales, warming up for the performance.

"I have to admit that I feel almost guilty for enjoying this when I know that every minute I spend not studying Holmes's case is another minute a criminal is going free and possibly plotting something dire," she confessed. A man jostled her shoulder and Jude drew his arm about her waist, tucking her to him until the press of people lessened.

His hand found the small of her back as he gently guided her through the curtain to their seats beyond. Thanking the usher, Jude handed him a folded bill and held the back of her chair. "I know how you feel, but I learned long ago that in order to survive this job and to continue helping people, you need to learn how to take a break from the hardness of life and savor the sweet moments."

Savor the sweet moments? Like this one? Her breath caught as she met his steady gaze, thankful he could not read her thoughts as she sank into the red velvet cushion.

Jude released his hold on the back of her chair and, leaning forward, whispered into her ear. "Let's forget Holmes for tonight."

She bowed her head, trying to cool her cheeks with her silk fan as the orchestra finished warming up, their sweet trills and low notes that had been filling the air only seconds before silencing as the famous maestro, Theodore Thomas, tapped his baton against his music stand. The arched ceilings magnified the melody, the music pulsating through her body and clearing her mind of all but the music.

Feeling someone watching her, she looked across the theatre to see acquaintances of Percy's in the other boxes, staring at her. She smiled and nodded to them, but instead of a warm return, they awarded her with barely veiled disdain as they turned away. She gripped her fan in her fist. *What snobs.* While attending the symphony in Percy's box with another man may look odd to them, she was too excited about being so close to the stage to give up the chance to experience it. She lifted her head and turned her attention back to the music.

That notebook and scribbling pencil had finally become his friend. Percy was a fool for missing out on an evening with Miss Wylde. Sitting slightly behind her left side, Jude was free to observe her without fear of her noticing as the music carried her into another land. She always seemed so strong and confident, but he loved seeing the gentleness unfold in her countenance tonight. Again and again he'd heard from older officers how she was exactly like her mother in looks and spirit, but more often than not, he saw her father in her actions. Tonight, he saw what the others were talking about.

Officer Baxter had recounted the tragic story of how Mrs. Wylde passed away, and he couldn't imagine, after being in the presence of such a winsome, playful spirit full of joy, how Inspector Wylde bore such a loss. It was little wonder to him that the inspector wished for his daughter to always be protected.

At intermission, Winnifred turned to him with shining eyes. "Wasn't that marvelous? I felt like I was on stage myself, we were so close."

"I doubt I'll ever be able to watch the symphony in general admissions now." He gave her a smile, refraining from winking at her should others catch him.

She rolled her eyes. "I know you are teasing, but I have to admit I also had the thought that the symphony will never quite be the same again." She extended her hand to him. "I'm a bit parched. Shall we adjourn to the refreshment hall?"

He rose and slipped her hand into the crook of his arm before guiding her out into the crowded hall, keeping her as near as he could to avoid her being jostled by a passerby again.

"I may need to stop by the powder room to freshen up," she whispered to him.

"Of course," he said, moving toward the requested room. "I'll fetch the drinks, or shall I wait for you?"

She gave him a smile. "I doubt that I will be accosted by any women in the powder room, Detective Thorpe, but if I am, I'll be sure to use the maneuvers Father taught me as a young girl to defend myself against marauders."

He laughed, but he had to concur that the lady's powder room should be no cause for alarm, when he spied Mr. Saunders with a woman.

Winnifred, having seen her old suitor as well, paused in their promenade and offered the couple a bright smile. The woman looked at Winnifred with her right brow angled before she turned up her nose and, without a word to Winnifred, turned her attention back to Mr. Saunders and whispered loud enough for them to hear as they approached, "*That* is the woman you recently courted? It's only Winnifred Wylde, and I'd say she's hardly pretty enough for all the trouble she caused you."

His gaze on Winnifred, Saunders moved toward them, causing the lady to fairly hiss. Saunders nodded to Jude before addressing Winnifred. "Detective Thorpe is still by your side, I see."

"Yes, Father wishes for me to be protected." She smiled at the woman. "And how are you this fine—"

"I'm sorry, we don't have much time before intermission concludes. If you'll excuse us, I have some important people to introduce my fiancée to," Mr. Saunders interrupted, his mustache dipping below his chin.

"You're engaged? Congrat—" She stopped talking, as he was already moving away. Winnifred's face reddened, and she flicked open her fan and disappeared into the powder room.

Jude bristled, finding it odd that they would be so rude to her. Was it because of him? Or was it because of the woman's jealousy over Winnifred's beauty? Concealing his concern for Winnifred, he secured two glasses of punch and waited a discreet distance from the powder room. When she finally appeared, he searched her face for any sign of distress, but as her gaze found his in the crowd, he read nothing but pleasure.

She took the cup and, with a whispered thanks, downed it. "I've come to expect that treatment from others, but I never would have thought that she, of all people, would turn on me like this."

"You *know* the woman? Then why would she—?"

"Slight me? With a marriage to Mr. Saunders, Nellie will rise quite a bit above her current station. In fact, one could technically say I was above Nellie on society's ladder, but now that she is engaged to a Saunders, she has eclipsed me and finds herself far too good for me or anyone else who is below her now."

"What a lonely way to live." Jude set aside their empty glasses and took her arm, longing to embrace her.

She shrugged as if it mattered little to her. "It's one of the reasons why Aunt Lillian wishes me to marry well and quickly. She is afraid that if I wait too long, my friends—no, my acquaintances—will move on with their lives and leave me behind. And then, by the time I do marry, they will have forgotten about me and I will never receive an invitation to anywhere else in my life, unless I marry *very* well at that point. But what Aunt Lillian fails to see is that I do not wish for such fair-weather friends." She leaned her head on his arm for a half second before catching herself. "Come, intermission is almost over. We had better find our—" She gasped and yanked him into the shadows of a potted plant, pressing his shoulder down with her palm and keeping her arm over his shoulder as if afraid to move.

Jude, his senses instantly awakened, twisted in the direction of her wide-eyed gaze. Holmes was at the refreshment bar merely yards away with a woman draped on his arm.

"He can't see me here. Not dressed like this." She whispered up to him, her chin nearly in his chest in the close quarters behind the foliage.

He lifted a finger to his lips and crouched even farther down beside her, watching through the leaves. The woman, though well-dressed, did not have the attire of one from the box seats, but that of general admission, the seating for which was in the opposite direction. He and Winnifred would be safe if they waited until the couple was out of sight.

"You hardly have time for us anymore. I'd wager that Lucy would not even recognize you." The woman's voice choked.

"Darling, I'm sure you are exaggerating. You know that business keeps me quite busy." Holmes drew his arm over her shoulders, producing a handkerchief from his breast pocket and pressing it into her hand as he kissed her cheek.

"Too busy even for us?"

He rested a hand on her elbow. "Let's not argue on our anniversary, my sweet. Come, the orchestra is about to begin again, and I know how you love the next piece." Giving her a gentle smile, he escorted her away.

Winnifred turned to Jude, their faces an inch apart. "Holmes is seeing someone? No one has mentioned his calling on anyone. And an anniversary? They've obviously been seeing one another for quite some time then."

"Maybe no one knows." He shook his head against the scent of her delicate perfume filling his senses, trying to grasp what this meant. Hearing the music, he held out his hand. "Do you want to go back in?"

She grasped his hand, and he could feel her tremble. "I would be much too afraid that he would spot me in my box. I pray that he did not already."

"But would he even recognize you?" He gazed at her embroidered gown with its yards of lace and pearls accentuating the delicate neckline, dipping gracefully to expose her creamy skin. "You are dressed far differently than your stern navy suit and with your hair arranged so, you look like a socialite tonight, not a secretary."

She exhaled and gripped his arm. "I pray you are right."

Chapter Thirteen

"If I had a flower for every time I thought of you. . .
I could walk through my garden forever."
~Lord Alfred Tennyson

Winnifred stretched under her feather-filled duvet, smiling softly to herself as memories of the sweetness of last night flooded over her. After Jude had returned her safely home, she'd dreamt of him professing his love to her and of her kissing him with a consuming longing. The thought of their kiss, fictional though it may have been, brought a blush to her cheeks. It was at times like these that she ached for Danielle to hurry home from her honeymoon, but she knew Danielle's husband still had a business trip following and it would be months before they returned and Winnifred could share her heart's yearnings.

The clock over the carved mantel chimed, reminding her to begin her preparations for the day. Rolling out of bed, she reached for her toothpowder, thinking of Jude's smile. She brushed her hair, all the while remembering his kindness toward her last night. Selecting her gray suit with the cream lace trim, she recalled how Jude's eyes sparked when he saw her in her sapphire damask last night.

At the chime of the clock yet again, Winnifred realized she was far too late for breakfast. She would have to go to work on an empty stomach and, as if on cue, her stomach rumbled in protest. She patted her corset. She never liked to be hungry. Snapping her fingers, she rummaged through her drawers and found one last piece of chocolate left over from the box Saunders had brought her. Popping the formerly rejected orange-flavored sweet into her mouth, she hurried down the stairs, taking the steps two at a time, eager to see Jude.

Since she had begun working at the Englewood house, her father had increased Jude's days of watching her to six, taking away all his other duties so he could focus on her. She couldn't help her smile as she pinned on her plain navy hat, knowing that he would be waiting for her. She stepped out into the warm summer morning and looked about expectantly for him, but instead found Officer Baxter at the bottom of her steps, hat in hand as he leaned his hip against the gate, waiting.

"Officer Baxter! What are you doing here? What happened to Jude? I mean, Detective Thorpe?" Her body tensed. Nothing could keep him away. . .nothing except a tragedy or her father.

"He came down with a cold this morning and was unable to make his shift." He grinned. "I was at the station when he sent word through one of the officers who lives in the same building, and your father assigned me to your case in Thorpe's stead. Winnifred Wylde, I cannot believe you got your father to agree to this." He chuckled, slapping his hat against his thigh. "Here the boys and I've been thinking that Thorpe was being assigned to a highly classified case, and now I come to find out that instead of thwarting criminals, he's been gallivanting around the fair with the prettiest girl in Chicago, the lucky rascal."

Her stomach knotted. No ordinary cold would keep Jude from his post. "Did he say how he was feeling?"

"It had to have been bad enough to keep him from you. Must be a weakling under all that muscle after all." He rolled his shoulders back and sniffed. "It would take more than a cold to keep me from a post like this."

Winnifred was too worried to reply to his ridiculous statement. *Dear Lord, let Jude not be too ill,* she prayed as memories of her mother's sudden death flooded her being. She gripped the iron gate to steady herself.

"Now, don't you go getting upset and ruining your morning,"

Baxter said, taking her by the elbow, concern shining in his eyes. "I'm sure it really is only a cold. Even the most robust of us have to get a little sick sometime. It's only fair."

She gave him a half smile and gathered her wits.

He extended his arm to her. "Does Thorpe get to escort you on his arm?"

She sighed, shying away from him, knowing he was a hopeless flirt. "Only on rare occasions. Most of the time he trails behind, keeping an eye on me."

He sighed, feigning colossal disappointment. "Can't this be one of those occasions?"

She smothered her laughter and kept her hands folded demurely around her dangling reticule. "I'm afraid not, Officer Baxter."

He shrugged and fell into step beside her. "I can't wait to tell the others that while we've been working, he's been out of the office day after perfect day like this one and in the company of an angel."

Winnifred attempted to make coherent replies to his constant chatter, but all the way to work, her thoughts were with Jude, and all through work she thought of him, imagining him home alone and writhing in pain from a fever. *Most likely his mother and sister are looking after him,* Winnifred told herself, trying to reassure herself that he wasn't in any danger. Fear flickered through her at the thought that Holmes had poisoned him. She shook her head. "That is ridiculous," she muttered under her breath.

Joe Owens looked up from Holmes's rolltop desk in the adjoining room. "Did you say something?"

"Sorry. Talking to myself," she called. She pressed her lips together and set to work typing up her notes from her uneventful meeting with Holmes and a supplier the other morning. The typewriter was harder to master than she'd anticipated, and her page was constantly getting marred with little mistakes that caused her to have to stop and retype the whole sheet.

The only thing she'd found strange about her job so far was that

Holmes had ordered more supplies but had used her name on the form. When she had asked him about it, he'd said that should she need to sign for the delivery on Friday when he was out of town, it would be easier to have the name matching that on the order.

Hovering over the ledger, studying the items coming in and the very few payments going out, Winnifred laced her hands and tapped her thumbs together, counting the minutes until her half day would come to a close and she could discover how Jude was doing for herself.

"Something on your mind today, miss?" Joe asked as he came with a fresh pile of papers for her to sort.

She tapped the ledger. "I'm seeing a lot of building materials coming in, but few payments being made to the suppliers. Am I missing some documentation?"

"Mr. Holmes likes to keep that private and won't even allow me to see, but I'll ask him for you," Joe replied as the grandfather clock chimed downstairs, its bell sounding through the floorboards. "Well, I guess that's it for you today, Miss Swan. See you tomorrow." He nodded to her and returned to his own stack of papers.

"I can go over those tomorrow if you'd like, Mr. Owens," she offered casually as she slipped her hatpin into place.

"I would take you up on it, but Mr. Holmes was extremely clear that you were only to manage the mail that was already sifted through by him or on occasion by me. And as slow as you type"— he chuckled—"you have your hands full. Better get faster before Mr. Holmes finds out how long it's been taking you."

"Hilarious." She waved to him, bidding him farewell. Stepping outside, she determined to call on Jude to set her mind at ease. He had seemed perfectly well the night before. No cold could possibly set in that quickly and take him away from his post. She tugged on her gloves and formulated her plan to take the grip car, stop at the café near his house, and pick up some soup and pie and bring it to him as a valid excuse to see him.

The car thumped and swayed as someone hopped onto the back of the already moving car, and she twisted around to see Baxter doubled over in the back. She blinked. She had forgotten about him.

He slipped into the vacant seat beside her, panting. "I barely knew you had left before you hopped on the car! You could've left me. Where are you off to in such an all-fired hurry?"

She bit back a laugh at his labored breaths, thinking it would not be charitable. "We're off to do a good deed."

At the knock on the door, Jude groaned and heaved himself out of bed, praying it was only his mother and sister coming for a visit and they had forgotten their keys. He held his stomach and slowly shuffled to the door. Once he was well, he would find the barkeeper who gave him that rotten meat sandwich and throw him in jail for obstruction of a lawman doing his job. He shook his head, regret trailing his every step toward the door, wishing he'd never stopped for a late-night snack at that germ-infested pub on the way home from dropping off Winnifred.

Opening the door, he felt the blood drain from his face at the sight of Winnifred, standing in his door, looking radiant in his drab hallway with an armful of food, and Officer Baxter standing behind her. *Of all the officers in the station, she had to bring him. I will never live this down. He'll spread it all over that a sandwich laid waste to me.* "Miss Wylde!" He ran his hands through his tousled hair, thankful that he had at least managed to put on a clean shirt this morning. His hands fumbled to fasten the top three buttons.

Her cheeks turned a rosy hue as her lips parted, and she averted her gaze from his open shirt front to his face. "Detective Thorpe, I'm sorry to intrude, but I couldn't help but feel that you needed some soup." She extended the small jar to him with the tips of her gloved fingers. "Careful, it's hot."

"How kind," he managed to say before the scent of the hot food wafted to his nose, sending his stomach tumbling as he accepted it, gripping the jar from the lid. *Dear Lord, please don't let me get sick in front of her.* He ran his hand over his scruffy chin and tried to give her a lighthearted grin. "I would ask you in, but. . ." But he couldn't think of an excuse as his body gripped in pain.

She nodded, taking a step back, obviously repulsed by his appearance. "Maybe another day when you are feeling better."

"Thank you for stopping by," he said all in a rush, snatching the pie from her hand and quickly closing the door to the sound of Baxter's snorting laughter. Jude leaned his head against the door and wished she could have been left with the image of him in his fine coattails the night before, not the pale, sweating—The aroma of the soup was too powerful and sent him lurching for the necessary.

While her visit wasn't nearly as romantic as it had played out in her head, Winnifred was glad she was able to put her mind at ease that Jude wasn't fever ridden. Leaving Officer Baxter at her front door, she spotted Aunt Lillian's favorite wrap hanging on the coatrack. *Oh no. What on earth is she doing here a month early?*

"There you are. What took you so long? Clara said you should have been home two hours ago."

"Aunt Lillian," she said, embracing her aunt. "I'm sorry. I was dropping off some soup to a sick friend."

Aunt Lillian plunked her fists on her still girlishly slender hips. "I know who your sick friend is, Winnifred Rose Wylde. I've just returned from the police station where your father mentioned that your bodyguard has been in this very parlor every day for the past two weeks while I was away." Aunt Lillian pinched the bridge of her nose, not waiting for a response. "I thought you would like Percival. His mother and I are great friends from finishing school, and when I told her that you loved this certain author's writing, she told me in confidence about her son's true occupation." She sank onto the settee, motioning for Winnifred to join her.

"So, you did know." Winnifred perched on the edge of her seat, wishing she had stopped by the bookshop instead of coming home to accusations without Father to defend her.

"Of course. Now, please tell me, what is the problem with this one?" She counted off her fingers. "He's handsome. He's young. He's wealthy. He loves books. What more can I do for you? Why would you put that all in jeopardy by attending the symphony with a lowly detective?"

Ignoring Aunt Lillian's barb at Jude, Winnifred scowled. "How could you have possibly found out about that?"

Aunt Lillian threw her hands over her head. "I was stopping by here before I left for Newport for the rest of the summer when I ran into Percival's mother. Do you know what she told me?"

It must've been something, to cause you to purposefully miss your train and delay your trip. She grimaced. "No."

Aunt Lillian crossed her arms. "She told me that Percy is very attracted to you and has even gone so far as to call you his muse."

Well, that doesn't sound like terrible news.

As if she could read her thoughts, Aunt Lillian nodded. "Which I *thought* was wonderful news, but then, she continued to say that she didn't think you were enthusiastic about the match after all, because Percy's friends saw you at the symphony with another man last night. And not just any man, but a man obviously from the lower classes, judging from his worn coattails."

Winnifred heard the rattle of keys and nearly sagged with relief that her father was home, but he must have heard Aunt Lillian's high-pitched voice and seen her wrap, because Winnifred could make out the delicate tap of retreating footsteps. Aunt Lillian must have heard too. She rustled to the parlor door and called into the hallway after him, pointing her finger. "Randolph Wylde. Don't think you can escape. You tell your daughter what you told me," she said, pulling him into the room.

Winnifred would have laughed at the discomfort on her father's face if not for the topic of conversation. She gave her father wide eyes, silently begging him to end Aunt Lillian's rant.

"Your father said that the man escorting you was none other than that detective of his, Jude Thorpe."

Winnifred suddenly became fascinated with the lace at her cuff. "Why would that be a problem? Jude is my bodyguard whom *Father* personally selected for me."

"The problem is that you can't be seen gallivanting around with a detective. I have worked tirelessly to set you up to return your family to high society where you belong. Where your mother belonged. And you will drastically hurt your chances of continuing your climb if you start associating with the middle class."

Winnifred's mouth gaped. She had taken the lessons, obeyed her aunt, and remained respectful even when she didn't feel like it was warranted, but this was too far, to insult her father's roots along with Jude's. "How can you allow her to say things like this? She is insulting your trade!" She twirled away from her father to Aunt Lillian. "Detective Thorpe was a perfect gentleman. Percy cancelled on me at the final hour and Detective Thorpe kindly stepped in and escorted me to the Chicago Orchestra. It took me hours to dress to perfection, and there was no reason for me to miss a perfectly good symphony because Percy's inspiration struck at a most inconvenient time."

Aunt Lillian frowned, crossing her arms as she paced in front of the fireplace. "Be that as it may, if you are being seen by Percival Covington, you are not to associate with that detective outside of him escorting you about town while he is acting as your guardian for the duration of the world's fair. I understand the need for him to be with you when you take your walks and such, but I don't see why he has to be with you all day every day if you're attending tea parties like you should be—"

Winnifred lifted her hand. "Aunt Lillian, I'm sorry to interrupt, but you were supposed to be gone until the end of August, and

Father and I have a plan for how we wish to spend our time. Father, please explain."

"Lillian, you were never supposed to find out," her father said in a tone that revealed he was rather afraid of his wife's sister.

"Oh Randolph." Lillian paused in her pacing, gaze locked on him. "What did you tell Winnifred she could do?"

Father rubbed his hand over his sideburns, crossing over his chin and back.

"Randolph?"

"I told her she could go undercover as a secretary for six weeks to investigate a suspect that she brought to me."

Aunt Lillian threw her hands in the air. "Really, Randolph. I do my best for this family. I have given up years of my life." She reached out, stroked Winnifred's cheek, and softly added, "Albeit gladly. But if my opinion is not going to be considered, I feel it might be best if I be on my way and return to my role as Winnie's aunt and not her stand-in mother, guiding her."

"Lillian, you know we couldn't manage without you."

Winnifred sighed. Even though she didn't quite see eye to eye with her aunt, she did love her. When her mother died, Grandmother and Aunt Lillian had been her anchor when her father was too consumed with grief to see beyond his own pain. And when her grandmother passed away when Winnifred was fifteen, her relationship with her aunt had shifted from one of comfort to one of preparation for marriage. *If only I can get her to understand.*

"Very well then, I shall cancel my Newport plans. I will stay and help repair the damage Winnifred has done to her reputation by neglecting to pay morning calls in my absence. Winnifred, you are going to have to come with me first thing in the morning to call on Mrs. Covington."

"I'm sorry, but I have already committed my mornings, and I will not give them up. This assignment is far too important. I can make calls in the late afternoon, but that is all. I'm sorry, but that's final." She rose, feeling like it was not her place to battle any further with her aunt, and slipped away to her room.

Sinking onto her window seat, she took a deep breath and exhaled her anger, still hearing her aunt's agitated voice trailing up the stairs to her room. She reached for her book and attempted to lose herself in Lady Rowena's love story, but every line reminded her of Percy being her only viable option in her father and aunt's opinion, and every reference to those fiery amber eyes made her think of the man she could never have.

Chapter Fourteen

"The pain of parting is nothing to the joy of meeting again."
~Charles Dickens, *Nicholas Nickleby*

Officer Baxter was no Jude, and Winnifred found herself missing her detective more and more as each day passed, thinking that she might have taken his company for granted along with the sense of security Jude gave her. Baxter was always ready to flirt, yet he never really engaged Winnifred in much talk outside of complimenting her, which was kind of him, but she ached for a conversation.

On the third day, after a long morning of looking over papers, she had a pounding headache from her constant retyping of documents and from her search for facts and details, trying to capture Holmes in a mistake, but she had discovered that he was a careful man. Her desk was always piled with rabbit-trail receipts that led to little more than nothing, and as Owens never left his desk unattended while she was working, she was beginning to think Holmes had instructed him to always be near.

Closing her eyes and rubbing her temples, she sighed. She only had an hour and a half left to work today, but the pain had finally become too much for her to bear without medication. "Mr. Owens, I might pick up some headache powder from downstairs and take a walk. Hopefully between the medicine and the fresh air, I will feel better soon, but if I don't, I'll make up my time tomorrow."

Having no authority over her schedule, Owens shrugged. "Better be back before Mr. Holmes returns from his errands."

"He won't mind if I move my hours to Saturday if necessary." She jotted down a note, explaining that she would only be gone for a couple of hours, but quite possibly the rest of the day if her headache did not get better, and that she would make up the hours on Saturday morning. She handed Owens the note and, with her hat in hand, hurried down to the drugstore and ordered a packet of headache powder and water.

She stirred the powder into her glass of water and downed it, smacking her mouth against the bitter taste. Picking up a small box of her favorite chocolates, she retrieved a bill from her reticule and purchased it as well, hoping the sugar would soothe her throbbing head into a peaceful state again. She popped a candy into her mouth as she stepped out onto the street, discreetly licking the tips of her fingers clean and casually glancing about for Baxter, but he was nowhere to be found. Her heart thudded. *Where is he?* She looked over her shoulder as stealthily as she could, growing agitated at the thought that she had been inside without someone listening if she cried for help.

She gritted her teeth against the pain of the midday sun and threaded her decorative pin through her hat to keep it in place. Not daring to go back inside Holmes's building without someone on the outside to protect her, she ambled into a nearby park, seeking comfort in the soothing green glow of the trees as she nibbled on the chocolates. It was difficult not to think of Holmes following her, but Winnifred doubted that anyone would dare accost her in the middle of the day with people milling about.

Since she hadn't explored this park yet, she chose a path that looked well-traveled, hoping it would take her in the direction of the fair or to a grip car. But, turning the corner, she found that the path led deeper into the park, not toward the fairgrounds. Trying to decide which way to turn, her neck bristled with the distinct feeling that someone was watching her.

Remembering Jude's advice, she casually dropped one of the candy wrappers on the ground and bent to retrieve it. She glanced for Baxter and in the secret corner of her heart, hoped to find Jude, but Winnifred didn't see him, or anyone for that matter. She shrugged off the sensation, thinking it must be her nerves getting to her or possibly the headache powder was dulling her senses. Instead of continuing down the path, she collected a small bouquet from the wildflowers growing alongside the gravel path, humming to herself and feeling comforted by every passerby and every piece of chocolate that passed her lips.

She saw a girl beneath a cherry tree reading one of Percival's novels and remembered that he was coming to dinner this evening. In her concern for Jude and her work, she had nearly forgotten. *Come to think of it, Percival hasn't come to see me lately on the job either.* He'd been more than excited to stand guard outside the building while Jude was there, but maybe Baxter wasn't his cup of tea either. The thought made her duck her head and laugh into her bouquet.

She'd paused to retrieve a stunning burgundy wildflower when she heard footsteps behind her. Someone was following her, and it wasn't one of her father's detectives. Plucking the bloom, she sank onto a bench and pretended to be absorbed with the beauty surrounding her, praying she did not look like someone who was aware someone was hiding in the bushes. Nearby, a nanny pushed a pram and three children skipped about. Two men in business attire strode briskly past her. She looked beyond the obvious and found him standing at a vendor's cart, ordering a cup of lemonade.

Her heart raced at the sight of the lean man's thick mustache beneath a familiar bowler hat. *Why is Holmes following me, and why hasn't he come up to talk with me? If he had only happened upon me in the park, he would speak with me, wouldn't he?* Her stomach dropped as her body tensed. *It's about to happen. Baxter is nowhere to be found, and Holmes is going to take me like he took the woman in green. No one is going to know where I went!* She slipped her hand into her reticule, the cool metal giving her the confidence that at the very least, she could defend herself.

Rising, she strode down the path with purpose in her step even though she had no idea where to go beyond getting to the grip car line. She couldn't return home. Her family's safety would be compromised. And she certainly couldn't go to the police station. Maybe she could lose him if she took the car to the fake apartment that Jude had rented for her. *It's only two miles from here. But if I am cornered. . .* She shivered. She would be in trouble.

She reached into her purse to retrieve enough coins for the grip car ticket. But she felt nothing. Her knees weakened as she realized that she had inadvertently left her change on the drugstore counter. She couldn't go back. If she did, she would be there on her own at Holmes's mercy, so she kept walking, the shadow following her every step. Thinking quickly, she read the street sign, thanking the Lord when she realized that Jude's apartment was about a mile away. She could walk there if she just kept far enough ahead of Holmes.

Her heels clicking on the sidewalk, she fairly trotted, praying for the Lord to protect her and that Jude would be home. She breathed a prayer of relief when she saw Jude's apartment building, and took the stairs two steps at a time, nearly gasping for air as she pounded on his third-floor door. "Jude!" she whispered, nearly in tears, "Jude." *Oh Lord, please let him be home. Let me not have cornered myself.*

Her frantic whisper clawed at him as he wrenched open the door, revolver at the ready. Winnifred slipped inside and slammed the door shut behind her, eyes wild as she sank with her back against the door to the floor, a withered bouquet and a box of chocolates tumbling from her arms.

"Winnifred! Are you hurt?" He knelt on the floor beside her

and holstered his firearm in the back waist of his pants, not wanting to move her until he was certain she was well enough.

She sobbed into her hands, her shoulders shaking. "Baxter wasn't there. I couldn't find him, and Holmes was after me. He's behind me now. I'm *sure* of it."

"He's in the building?" He scowled at the door as if he could burn a hole into it and see who was lying in wait beyond in the hall. He moved to rise, but her hand reached out, clasping his in her clammy grip.

"Don't. Please don't leave me again."

He took a seat next to her, allowing his arm to drape around her shoulders, and pulled her close in an attempt to calm her. Winnifred rested her head against his chest, her hair brushing his chin. Waiting until her breathing slowed, he said, "Baxter wasn't watching you?"

"No. He escorted me to work this morning, but then disappeared. I came outside on account of a headache, and I couldn't find him. I thought I'd be safer in the park than in the building without reinforcements." Her voice dithered. "I haven't felt safe since you've been sick." She rubbed her hand over her eyes, wiping away her tears. "I apologize for barging in on you at home, but I didn't know where else to go."

"You did the right thing." He reached into his pocket and retrieved a fresh handkerchief. "I'm so sorry. I felt well enough to come today, but then there was a plumbing emergency, and I figured since I had the day off already, I'd fix it first, but one thing led to another and my sister and mother came over—" He raked his hand through his hair, berating himself for leaving her unattended.

She blinked as if aware for the first time of her surroundings, her hands fluttering to life over her hair and gown. "Your mother and sister are *here*? Oh my goodness. You best help me to my feet or else they will think me a mess to find me sprawled against your front door."

"They came by to drop off some more soup before they picked up Georgie from school. But don't worry. I told them to stay put in the kitchen." He stood and offered her his hand. She placed her small hand in his and he fairly hoisted her to her feet, unprepared for how light she was. "Will you join us at the kitchen table for a moment while you catch your breath?"

She nodded, grabbing onto his shirtsleeve and swaying slightly. He moved to pick her up, but she whispered, "No, you can't carry me, not with your mother in the next room."

"You'll have to at least allow me to assist you. I can't have you passing out." He wrapped his arm about her waist and, with slow strides, assisted her into the kitchen. "Mother, Mary, and Detective Holt, this is Miss Wylde."

His sister and mother rose along with the detective, their chairs grating against the hardwood floor. "Is she quite all right?" his mother asked as Mary moved to help Winnifred into a chair.

"She's had a fright, but is physically unharmed." He set her down, reluctant to remove his hand for fear she would faint.

"Poor dear. Shall we talk of something to take your mind off your ordeal while Jude fetches you something hot to drink and a bite of something?" his mother asked, patting her hand.

Winnifred offered them a feeble smile. "Thank you."

"I'll put on the kettle for tea," Jude murmured, his heart pounding out of his chest as he attempted to maintain a calm façade. He kept an ear out for anything happening in the hallway as he filled the kettle. His mind hummed with scenarios of how bad it could have been, all the while the terror in her eyes haunting him. He was going to tear into Baxter for leaving his post. He slammed the kettle onto the stove with unnecessary force.

The women jumped, his mother shooting him a scowl. "Really, Jude." She pressed her hand against her chest.

He gave them an apologetic grin. "Sorry. Don't know my own strength sometimes." With the women returning to their discussion of Georgie's first trip to the fair and Holt sitting silently with his newspaper, Jude's mind wandered to the street below. *If Holmes is still outside, we will need to lose him before I take her home.* He leaned against the countertop, crossing his arms as he racked his mind for the best course of action.

"Are you going to keep scowling at the kettle or are you going to take it off the stove?" his mother called.

Jude blinked as he registered the piercing whistle of the steaming kettle. Grabbing a kitchen towel and removing it from the stove, he reached for the tin of tea leaves and carefully measured out three tablespoons, sprinkling them into the pot along with a dash of cool water before adding the boiling water.

"Did you add the cool water first to the leaves so they wouldn't singe?" His mother lifted her gaze to his tea making.

"Of course. I'm not a complete novice." He carried the pot to the table before retrieving five mismatched cups that he had collected over the years from wives of friends who took pity on his lack of dishware.

"Jude, I'm surprised you are so domestic," Winnifred said with a teasing lilt in her voice as he set the tea strainer over a yellow cup with a slightly chipped base.

"I lived on my own for a long time in New York after these two abandoned me for Chicago," he replied, pouring the tea from a daring height to make the ladies laugh and distill the tension he still detected in Winnifred's shoulders. With a flourish, he presented each guest with their cup. "I have also prepared for you a plate of the finest oatmeal cookies in the land." Jude whipped the checkered napkin off the single china plate he owned.

"Did you really bake these?" Winnifred asked, her eyes widening at the taste.

Detective Holt clamped his lips together to no doubt keep a snort contained and lifted his cookie. "Tea is about the extent of our detective's domestic talents. These are from the bakery down the street. And if his mother and sister didn't bring him a casserole twice a week, I am sure he would starve."

"Being someone who has never touched a stove, I appreciate the existence of bakeries when in a pinch," Winnifred replied, a reassuring smile on her lips for Jude before turning to Detective Holt. "Are you visiting Detective Thorpe as well? Or does business bring you here?"

Holt looked to Jude, and at his nod, Holt replied, "I'm on duty, Miss Wylde. There's been a threat, and I'm here to protect Detective Thorpe's family."

Winnifred blanched, looking to the women. "I'm so sorry. After all you have been through this year, this is the last thing your family needs."

Mary dipped her head, and Jude's mother again patted Winnifred on the arm before sipping her tea as the clock on the mantel chimed one o'clock.

Jude was grateful to his mother and sister for distracting Winnifred for a quarter of an hour, but if he were to lose Holmes and get Winnifred home at a reasonable hour, they would need to leave now. "Winnifred, I'm afraid we don't have time for you to finish your tea."

"Finish? She's taken maybe three sips," Mother interjected.

Jude shrugged. "I'm sorry, but we need time to lose Holmes. If she's not home well before dinner to change, I'm sure her father will begin to worry."

Winnifred smoothed her skirts and rose. "Good point. Aunt Lillian would sound the alarm if I'm not back in time for dinner with Mr. Covington." She curtsied to his guests, who rose and returned her farewell. She gave them a wobbly smile. "Good day, Detective Holt and ladies, it was lovely meeting you all, and I hope we shall see one another soon."

Ignoring the part about dinner being with Covington, Jude shrugged on his coat and retrieved his hat. "Your Aunt Lillian is back? I thought you said she'd be gone all summer."

"She was supposed to be." Winnifred sighed, twisting the pearl ring on her finger and betraying her nerves.

He would have to remind her not to wear jewelry while working undercover, but he couldn't scold her now, not when she was so worked up. "Well then, we shall be sure to get you home as soon as possible." Jude held his arm out to her and, with a trembling hand, she slipped her arm through his as they stepped into the shared hallway.

"Shall I drop my glove so you can look for Holmes?" she whispered, turning her wide blue-green eyes up to him.

He nodded, pleased with her cleverness. He bent and retrieved her soft cream glove, scanning the area, but thankfully, he did not see anyone lurking.

"I tried to use the techniques that you taught me, but they didn't seem to work for me this time. I think I might have been a little too rattled to execute them properly." She slipped her gloves on, blushing. "I'm sorry for my dramatic entrance earlier," she whispered as she fitted her hat.

He reached for her hand, ashamed of himself for allowing this to happen. If he had been there, she wouldn't be so frightened "We will lose him together this time." He stroked her palm with his thumb before tugging on his hat and leading them to the stairs. He could tell from her breathing that her panic from earlier was returning, and he could hardly keep his anger in check at Baxter's actions that led to her being in such a state.

Jude paused at the second-floor landing, took Winnifred by the shoulders, and turned her to him. "Holmes will most likely be waiting just outside the building. I think that you and I should act as if we are courting and are off to enjoy an afternoon at the fair. The crowds will provide the perfect place to lose him."

She swallowed and nodded, her eyes wide. "Whatever you think best."

He squeezed her hand once again as they descended the steps. It would not be difficult for him to pretend that she was his girl. Once this was over, maybe he could summon the courage to speak with her father even though he knew what the inspector would say. It was well known about the office that the inspector did not wish for his daughter to marry an officer of the law.

Jude poked his head through the front door before holding it open for her to pass beneath his arm. On the sidewalk, he tucked a stray golden curl behind her ear, his eyes searching behind her for a form waiting in the shadows. There he was, waiting for Winnifred. Jude slipped her arm through his and whispered, "He's here. Don't worry. I won't leave you, not for one second."

She clutched his upper arm, her voice low and trembling. "What do we do?"

He reached across his chest to her hand and squeezed it. "We will stick to our plan." Then, he added a bit louder for Holmes's benefit, "Miss Swan, I'm sorry you had such a bad headache, but I'm glad the medicine is working now. Hopefully the fresh air will complete your healing." To her credit, she let nothing in her countenance betray her fear as he hailed a carriage and helped her inside, quietly giving the cabby instructions to drop them at the Stoney Island Avenue entrance to the fair before settling in the seat beside Winnifred, his arm around her shoulders.

With a sigh, she leaned into his side, closing her eyes as she rested her head on his shoulder. "I don't know if I can keep doing this, Jude."

"No one is forcing you to, Winnie." He grasped her hand in his to bring her some small measure of comfort. "After we lose him at the fair today, you don't have to interact with him ever again. However, as much as I want to tell you not to return, I think it is only right to admit to you that I feel as if you're very close to uncovering something. Holmes has been careful, but he's beginning to show more interest in you, and I think that his attraction will cause him to make a mistake."

She tilted her gaze up to him and nodded. "I'll have to agree with you there. Owens is growing more comfortable too. He usually keeps Holmes's papers under lock and key, but one of these days, he is going to leave them unattended in plain view or forget to lock the desk. I'm certain I will find enough in one of those papers to bring Holmes in for an investigation and enough for us to get a search warrant." She pressed her handkerchief to her temple and laughed. "At least my headache really is going away. But if I'm honest, I think that might have more to do with you being here with me and Baxter, not."

He clenched his fists on top of his thighs. "When I get my hands on that officer, he will regret the day he ever—"

She held her hand up. "Please don't tell Father. I'm sure Baxter didn't mean any harm. And I really don't wish for him to get fired. However, he does need to be reprimanded, so if you could get on to him rather than having Father find out and fire him, I'm sure it would benefit everyone."

He nodded as the carriage stopped at the fair entrance. "If your father found out, I have no doubt he would fire him, so I will reluctantly keep it from the inspector." He hopped out and held the door for her. "I'm famished. The other day when I was here with Mary viewing the various state buildings, I discovered that the Louisiana building has a café with Creole cuisine. I tried some of their étouffée and found it positively delectable. If we perchance have not lost Holmes on the drive, then maybe we could show him that we are on a regular outing and that nothing underhanded is going on by sitting down for a late lunch?"

"That sounds lovely, but I don't have my season pass with me." She lifted her hands up, helpless. "I don't have enough to pay for a ticket, much less dinner."

He laughed, taking a place in line. "What kind of gentleman caller would I be if I did not treat you?" He checked his pocket watch, casually glancing down the street for Holmes possibly following in a hired carriage. While Jude didn't see Holmes, his gut told him not to underestimate the man. "But, after we eat, I think we may need to weave through the crowds a bit more. Any suggestions for somewhere we could lose him?"

She tapped her lip in her father's fashion before snapping her fingers. "I think I have just the place. In the horticultural building, under the central dome, there is an exhibit called the Mammoth Crystal Cave that we can explore for an extra fee. I don't know if Holmes is aware of it. He might be. . .but he might not, and it would be a good place to hide away."

Paying for their tickets, he took her arm in his, loving how perfectly natural it felt. "Perfect," he murmured.

Chapter Fifteen

"You don't need scores of suitors.
You need only one. . .if he's the right one."
~Louisa May Alcott, *Little Women*

Jude held the door of the Louisiana plantation-style building as Winnifred stepped inside to discover various artifacts from the state along with notable agricultural products. But all she could focus on was the mouthwatering aroma wafting out of the Creole café that Jude had been praising on the walk over. She pressed a hand against her corset stays to quiet her rumbling stomach. It had been far too long since her lunch, which she only nibbled on because of her splitting headache. She dabbed her handkerchief to her perspiring temples, praying that the sweltering afternoon sun would not cause the throbbing to return.

Jude led her to one of the vacant tables in the corner of the restaurant, concern etched between his brows. He waved one of the waiters over and ordered them each a glass of iced tea, french bread, and some oysters on ice to begin.

"Oysters?" she questioned, having never tried the delicacy. "Shall we get something a little less ambitious?"

"I was thinking of something cool to get for you, but perhaps we could try gumbo? It's a sort of soup." He called to the waiter's retreating back. "Please change that to two bowls of gumbo."

The front door slammed shut, causing her to jump and turn toward the entrance before catching herself and whipping back to face Jude. "Sorry. So, um, when are you going to tell me why someone is guarding your family? Does it have anything to do with those men accosting you that day?"

Jude pressed his lips into a firm line and nodded, whispering,

"If I tell you, you cannot breathe a word to anyone, not even your father."

Her eyes widened, and she leaned forward to pick up his words. "Of course."

"The beating was a warning." Jude bowed his head. "I've told you about my brother-in-law's passing, but Victor's death was not an accident. I picked up the case that he had been working on before the fair began and asked one too many questions to the wrong person. The man threatened my family if I didn't stop my investigation."

Winnifred gasped, pressing her hand to her chest. "Oh Jude. And you couldn't tell anyone, because Victor's case was originally ruled as an accident." She leaned back in the chair, scowling. "I am so sorry. Here I've been so consumed with my own problems, I never once thought to ask if you were dealing with something other than our case."

He reached across the table and took her hand. "It's all right. I hadn't confided in a single soul until today. And just the telling makes my burden lighter for being shared."

At the strength his hands lent her, she gained the courage to whisper, "You know that I'll always be here for you should you ever have need." And for a moment, she thought she could see her longing mirrored in his gaze before it flickered away. Clearing her throat, she asked, "Do you see Holmes?"

"No, but that doesn't mean he's not here. If he is lurking about where we can't see him, we best keep playacting that we're on an outing."

"I almost wish we could confront him, now that you are here," she admitted, all the while knowing it to be a foolish notion.

He gave her a sympathetic smile. "If we acknowledge him now, it would destroy your cover. It's not about the immediate danger at this point." He leaned toward her as if he were about to whisper into her ear, but the waiter reappeared with their iced sweet tea, his presence pulling them apart. When he left, Jude whispered, "You are safe with me, Winnifred. Please don't be frightened. I won't allow anything to happen to you."

At his words, her tumultuous spirit calmed a bit, and she met his gaze, feeling as if he could peer into her very soul, and confusion washed over her anew. *I must control my feelings. My heart cannot rule.*

The waiter placed a bowl of brown goop in front of her and, once he left, she leaned in and whispered, "It smells delicious, but truly, it looks like we were served a puddle of mud with bits of dried leaves and. . .are those *legs* in my bowl?"

He threw back his head and laughed. "Now, I know it doesn't look like much, but I've heard it's amazing. And yes, those are crab legs."

She swirled her spoon around in the bowl, discovering rice hidden under the gumbo. "This is bizarre." She tasted it and gave a disbelieving laugh. "And surprisingly delicious." Settling back in her chair, Winnifred found she really was relaxing under Jude's watch.

"So, I've been meaning to ask how things are going with Mr. Covington." He scooped up a bite, the steam curling above his spoon.

She stiffened, not liking the sound of her suitor's name on his lips. She didn't wish to talk about Percy at the moment, much less with the one person she wished were courting her instead. "He is working away on his book. I haven't seen him since before the symphony."

His brows raised as he dipped his french bread into the bowl, sopping up the last bit of his gumbo. "But you are still seeing him?"

"As you know, my aunt came home," she replied as if he should know what that meant, and hoped he would catch the hint.

"Meaning *she* still wishes for you to continue the relationship," he deduced.

"Exactly." She took a few more bites of her gumbo, savoring the flavor before her stomach pressed against her corset, staying her spoon as it always did before she was entirely full, which her aunt said was the point of the corset. "Well, good sir, shall we continue on our way to the next exhibit?"

Tucking a couple of bills under the lip of his clean bowl, Jude extended his arm to her. It felt wonderful to be back with him and to have her arm securely through his as they made their way to the horticultural building. Strolling by one of the largest displays of roses that she had ever beheld, she paused to drink in their fragrance, overtaken by their beauty. "Stunning."

"Yes," he replied, his eyes meeting hers.

She blushed, uncertain if he was speaking of the roses or of her, and a shyness stole over her before she pulled him into the large horticulture building and toward the central dome where there was an artificial mountain surrounded by a mound of flora and fauna. Near the cave entrance that was roped off, there were signs promoting the grand sights they could experience for an extra fee.

Jude dug into his pockets and fished out twenty cents, paying the gatekeeper before they took the small cave entrance down into the makeshift mountain. At the sight of the giant white crystal clusters glistening in the glow of some kind of disguised electric lighting, Winnifred's breath caught in her throat. She threaded her hand through Jude's, and, to her shock, his fingers wrapped protectively around hers.

For a moment, she almost forgot they were only pretending to be lovers in the beauty surrounding them. She surveyed Jude's strong jawline in the glimmer of the crystals, wondering why she felt so safe with him. *Well, it might be because he is an excellent marksman or that he has more muscles than any one man should have.* At the thought, she turned her heated cheeks away from him, absorbed in examining the white crystals before once again forgetting herself as she leaned her head against his shoulder. She felt him tense, and she was thankful that the darkness masked her blush. "I'm so sorry," she whispered, and pulled away. "But we're supposed to be pretending, are we not? Is this too much?"

"No, it's not too much." His voice sounded hoarse as he wove his hand in hers, pulling her close again and pressing a kiss to her forehead.

Her heart stilled as she lifted her gaze to him, her fingers pressing to her parted lips.

"Too much?"

Winnifred knew she should say yes, but she couldn't find it in her to whisper the lie. Instead, she gave him a gentle smile and returned her attention to the exhibit, wondering how the designer of the cave had managed to capture the beauty of the real Mammoth Crystal Cave. Jude's arm tightened about her waist, alerting her, and before she could even look to see what had been the cause, she found herself with her back to the wall as he put himself between her and danger.

While Jude felt a pinch of self-reproach for pretending to spot Holmes in the crowd, he knew it was the only way he could get her between his arms once again as he had that first day on the Ferris wheel. It felt so right to have her close to him even if the means were not quite innocent. The delicate floral scent of her golden tresses nearly blinded him with the desire to kiss her again, propelling him forward. *Did I really kiss her on the forehead?* He wished that he could repeat the act, but he would not take advantage of her for Holmes's benefit. That is, not any more than he already was by putting his arms around her.

She looked up to him with trust in her gaze. "Is he still watching?"

Feeling the nudge of the Holy Spirit to end the charade, he begrudgingly dropped his arms. "False alarm." He offered Winnifred his arm and became the picture of propriety even though his heart was riotous. "We best be getting you home. I'm sure your aunt will begin to worry if you aren't back in time to dress for dinner."

"Dinner? Is it that late?" She checked her watch pin. "Goodness. Aunt Lillian is going to be livid." She tucked a curl behind her ear and gave him that charming smile of hers. "Thank you for rescuing me once again. As much as I enjoy being my own heroine, plunging headlong into danger, I admit that being on my own when danger is near is not a feeling I wish to repeat."

"Are you going to feel safe enough to return to work for that man?" He gauged her reaction.

"No, but as you said, we cannot detain him on the grounds of him following me. It's a free country. If I give in to my fear and don't find something soon to prove his guilt, he is going to capture another girl. I know if I tell Father I am growing uncomfortable and about what happened today, he would put someone else on the case immediately. However, the problem with that is we would have to get another female to go undercover, and it could take days or weeks for Holmes to hire her as a secretary, when I am already in the very room with the evidence."

"But I don't want to make you feel like you must go back. You have options."

"None of which are unselfish. I had a moment of weakness today brought on by fear." She pressed her hand to her chest. "I know the Lord will protect me. I had the feeling that since I was alone, something could happen."

"And who is to say that feeling wasn't Him protecting you? You always want to have reinforcements when you are undercover. It is never safe to be completely alone. Even if it turns out he's only a swindler, Holmes did follow you today, and strange men don't go around following an unaccompanied lady without less-than-honorable intentions." He guided her to the street outside the fairgrounds and hailed a cab, assisting her into the carriage. He glanced over his shoulder once more to ensure they were completely and totally alone before he gave the man her home address and climbed inside.

"Holmes will question me about why I left. What should I tell him?" Winnifred asked, a nervous tremor in her voice.

"Mostly the truth, that you had a headache and found yourself at a friend's house for a cup of strong tea to take the edge off while you waited for the medicine to take effect."

"And while there," she added, averting her gaze, "I met my friend's brother who offered to take me to dinner at the fair. I think he would believe that."

"What if he gets jealous? Because I assure you, he will."

She shrugged. "Then I will tell him that once I learned of your occupation, I wanted nothing to do with you and will flirt with him until he is convinced that my affections are not with you."

"And if he spots me outside?"

"I'll say you're stalking me."

He didn't quite care for the idea of her flirting with Holmes, but agreed it was the best course of action. Jude observed Winnifred as she kept her eyes on the window, searching the waning light for any sign of danger. He longed to comfort her, to sweep her into his arms and take her away from Holmes and out of danger, but he knew that she wouldn't respond well to him whisking her away completely. She felt called to do this job, and he must honor her calling and help her, even if it meant keeping his feelings at bay and placing the woman he cared about in harm's way.

They pulled up to Winnifred's cottage and, much to Jude's annoyance, he recognized Covington's carriage already parked outside. Jude tapped his fingers together, not happy with the situation, wishing he himself could be one of her suitors—better still, her only suitor. He had been fighting this long enough. He would speak with Inspector Wylde tomorrow, but first he would find Baxter and give him a tongue lashing he would not soon forget.

Winnifred ran her fingers over her ruffled jabot, giving it a little tug before passing her hands over her hair in an attempt to smooth back any wild wisps. "Thank you, Jude. I don't know what I would have done without you today."

"I'll always be here if you need me." Jude repeated her promise from earlier and moved to open the carriage door for her before assisting her up the stairs, lingering on the bottom step, reluctant to part with her. "I hope you get some rest, Miss Wylde."

"Miss Wylde?" She looked up at him even though she was a step higher than him. "After what we've been through today, I think anyone would agree that to return to such formality is unwarranted and rather silly." She placed her petite gloved hand in his and opened her mouth to say something when the sound of running footsteps came from behind. Jude whirled around, throwing one arm out in front of Winnifred before spying Baxter.

"Oh Miss Wylde. Thank the good Lord in heaven. I was about to ask your father if he had seen you." He panted, pressing his hand into his side as he bent over double.

Winnifred's scowl turned her into a fierce feminine version of the inspector. "Officer Baxter. I don't intend to tell my father about your lapse in your duty today, but I think Detective Thorpe would like a word with you." She turned back to Jude and rested her hand on his shoulder for one second then two before she slid her hand down his arm to his hand and clasped it. "Thank you. Until tomorrow," she whispered, and slipped inside.

Winnifred rested her head on the front door, a smile on her lips. Despite her harried afternoon, she was unfathomably happy. Jude had kissed her! She could hardly wait to write Danielle and tell her that she had been given her first kiss. *Well, first kiss on my forehead.* She sighed with delight and looked heavenward. *Lord, thank You for sending me Jude Thorpe.*

"Winnifred Rose Wylde! Where have you been?" Aunt Lillian grasped her by the shoulders, took in her plain navy gown, and scowled. She raked her fingers down her cheeks, in a rare show of her absolute annoyance with Winnifred. "You don't have time to change."

Winnifred scowled in return as she removed her hat. "I know we spoke about my working until one o'clock, but I've returned in plenty of time to freshen up—"

Aunt Lillian waved her hand. "We can't discuss that now. Percival and his *mother* are here for dinner. They arrived unfathomably early because Percy wanted to ask you about a new scene he has written, which was terribly rude of them, especially when I wasn't expecting Mrs. Covington, but it is what it is and they have been here for nearly an hour waiting for your appearance. It makes me look like an abysmal aunt to not even know where you are." She tugged on Winnifred's collar, straightening the white lace, before pulling a curl loose from the tight low coiffure. "Your hairstyle is so prudish, and yet you are entirely too flushed," she murmured and ran her hands over the back of Winnifred's skirt, whacking the dust clinging to her hem. "But there's nothing we can do about that at this point." She pulled back her shoulders and cleared her throat. "Come now. Don't put me to shame."

Before Winnifred could even respond, she was pulled into the front parlor where she found herself very underdressed compared to the formal attire of Percy and his mother. Mrs. Covington's copper silk made their parlor, which Winnifred's mother had been so proud of, look drab. However, Aunt Lillian's burgundy gown brought the surroundings up a notch. Father was also dressed in his formal dinner coattails, but his absentminded tugging at his cuffs betrayed his discomfort.

Winnifred took after her father in that way. Extreme formality made her uncomfortable. Unfortunately, she rarely had a choice about what she could dress herself in as her aunt believed that in order to capture the right man, Winnifred must make sacrifices and maintain a corseted hourglass figure. If that meant sacrificing the luxury of breathing, so be it. Folding her hands, she held herself as regally as possible to keep from shaming her aunt as Percy crossed the room to greet her with a flourished bow.

He pressed a kiss atop her hand before securing it in his and guiding her to Mrs. Covington. "Mother, I'd like you to meet someone very special to me. This is Miss Winnifred Wylde. She is the one who has finally reawakened my muse."

To Mrs. Covington's credit, she bestowed a gracious smile on Winnifred and extended her hand, overlooking her informal attire. "My son speaks highly of you. I look forward to getting to know you better over dinner."

Taking the hint, Aunt Lillian quickly ushered them into the dining room where Winnifred was surprised to see that Aunt Lillian had used the delicate china Mother had kept for only the most auspicious occasions. The beautiful gold-trimmed plates did wonders to transform the small dining room into a place of elegance.

Percy held the back of her chair and, as she slipped into her seat, he whispered, "Did something go wrong today? You seem a bit out of sorts and rather quiet."

She gave him a small nod, and glancing toward her father, she saw his concerned gaze on her as well. She couldn't have him thinking something was amiss and remove her from her case. "It was nothing," she whispered back. "Jude sorted it out."

The conversation hummed about her as she traced her finger around the gold rim of her plate. The last time she'd used these plates, she was a little girl. The day's frightening events dulled to the background as the china pulled her to a simpler time. She remembered the soft tone of her mother's voice when she spoke to her father paired with an adoration in her eyes as she embraced him. Her father had been so young and carefree then. Was that what love was supposed to do to a person? She smiled as she thought about Jude. He had looked at her that way today, and if she were honest with herself, she had felt a stirring in her soul that she had only read about in Percy's novels. Even in the midst of danger, Jude's presence calmed her. Maybe her father would relent in his decree against her wedding a lawman if she was adamant in expressing her feelings for him. After all, hadn't Mother done the same so many years ago?

"Miss Wylde?"

She blinked, and at Aunt Lillian's pointed stare, she realized she had done it again. She had lost track of the conversation. Her cheeks tinted with the secret burning inside. "I am so sorry, Mrs. Covington. Please excuse me. I had a rather long day. What was the question, please?"

"I asked what you did with your day," Mrs. Covington repeated, her spoon poised above her bowl of tomato basil soup.

Winnifred, being too tired to conjure a suitable excuse, settled on the truth. "I spent the afternoon at the fair with an associate of Father's, Detective Jude Thorpe."

Percy stiffened next to her. Under his breath, he whispered, "Mother doesn't know about you-know-what."

"Ah yes, Detective Thorpe. Randolph has assigned a detail to watch after Winnifred while the world's fair is taking place," Aunt Lillian hastened to explain. She rested her hand on Winnifred's and gave a bright smile to cover her annoyance. "Wherever she goes, a chaperone is there to protect her and her reputation. Nothing is more important to us than Winnifred's safety."

The blunder avoided, dinner passed slowly, and it took everything in her to focus on the topics at hand. When the Covingtons had finally departed, Winnifred stifled her yawns and climbed the stairs, anxious for her feather bed and novel.

"Winnie," her father called from the bottom of the steps.

She covered her yawn and turned to him. "Yes, Father? I'm sorry. I must have forgotten to say good night in my exhaustion." She returned to the first step and lightly kissed his cheek. "Sleep well."

He took her hand in his and placed his other hand atop. "I'm afraid that you might be getting too attached to Detective Thorpe. I noticed you mentioned him quite often at dinner."

"Did I?" She felt the now familiar heat rising in her cheeks.

"You didn't notice Percy bristling at his name? The first time, he took it in stride, but by the third or fourth, I think he realized he has a rival in Thorpe."

Her ears were stinging now too, but she didn't deny it. She couldn't.

"That's what I thought. I'm afraid I may have to assign someone else to you." He dug his hands into his pockets.

"No!" She gripped his sleeve. "Please. I need to have him guarding me. I don't feel safe without him. There is no one, besides you, that I trust more. Please."

He shook his head. "But you see, that's what I worry about. Jude is not an option for you, Daughter."

She did not cry easily, but she felt the tears rising, threatening to spill over onto her cheeks. She ducked her face and attempted to gather herself for fear her father would recognize the fact that she was already in love with his detective. "Please," she whispered. "Don't take him away too."

He took her chin between his fingers, lifting her gaze. "If you continue to allow Mr. Covington to call, I won't dismiss Thorpe from your case, but you have to promise to give Percival Covington a chance."

Chapter Sixteen

"I delay so long, because I fear; because my whole life hangs in balance
on a single word; because what I have near me now may never
be more near me after, though more than all the
world, or than a thousand worlds, to me."
~R. D. Blackmore, *Lorna Doone*

Winnifred could not believe her luck. Holmes had left last night for business and Owens was preoccupied cleaning up the basement that had, based on Auntie Ann's account, a putrid smell that would not go away. With Owens out of the way, she neglected her stack of paperwork and went straight for Holmes's rolltop desk. It was, of course, locked.

Winnifred slipped a hairpin from her coiffure and set to work on the desk lock as she had so often in the past to get into her mother's old desk in the cottage attic. Her father kept Mother's letters and diaries there, saying that they were best left untouched. However, by the age of ten, she had mastered the art of popping the lock to read the sweet letters her mother had written to her father while they were courting. She held her breath as she turned it to the left, adjusted the pin, and. . . . At the click, she exhaled and lifted the rolltop, grimacing at each thunk of wood hitting wood as it slid back into place.

She filtered the papers as quietly as possible, fearing that even the slightest crinkle would somehow sound the alarm. Winnifred read over the names on several deeds to properties and countless insurance policies, pausing at the names of Emeline Cigrand, Minnie Williams, and Myrta Belknap. She recognized the first two as the names of the former secretaries of Holmes but the third. . . Who was Myrta Belknap? She was not surprised to find the insurance policies, but she was puzzled as to why he would have deeds in their names.

Hearing a footfall on the steps, she scanned a property deed under Minnie's name and found that she was the owner of a house in Wilmette. With a scrawling script, she quickly jotted down the address on her notepaper before rolling the top back down, praying it would not crash against the desk. Her hand trembled as she stuffed her pin inside the mechanism and twisted it, locking it before darting across the room to her desk on her tiptoes so her heeled shoes would not give her away, her heart hammering in her chest all the while.

Owens appeared in the doorway, looking quite disheveled from his time in the basement. He wiped each finger on a hand towel, leaving dark smudges on the pristine white surface. "Miss Swan, did you finish your work?"

She looked to the clock, astonished to find that it was nearly twelve o'clock and Owens had been in the basement for half an hour. *It must have taken me a bit longer to open that desk than I thought. I am losing my touch.* "Actually, I still have a little left to do." She lifted the stack on her desk, praying that he did not notice that she had the exact amount of work remaining to do as when he had left her to attend to the stench.

"Save it for Monday," he replied, waving her out of the room. "Auntie Ann gave me a list and I have another hour's work ahead of me on the second floor. Mr. Holmes won't be pleased that I left you alone up here for even a half hour, but for reasons only heaven knows." He shook his head with a laugh. "Seems he should trust the people he hires, but he is a peculiar sort of man. He once had me bring a trunk from the basement to the attic and then back outside in a single day, and when I asked what he had need of it for, he snapped at me, telling me to mind my own business. And last night, he had me move a hefty trunk from the basement to his wagon, and I could've sworn it was the same trunk. It keeps making its rounds,

I guess." He shrugged. "Anyways, sorry for my rambling. You go on and enjoy your Saturday, miss. I'm sure you have things to do."

Too skittish to protest, Winnifred grabbed her hat and slid past him, pausing on the second floor to bid the housekeeper farewell. "Do you know where Mr. Holmes is today, Auntie Ann?" she asked, threading her hatpin through her chapeau.

"He is doing business in Wilmette," she replied, stirring the bubbling saucepot on the stove. "He goes there often, as I'm sure you'll soon notice."

Wilmette. The same town as Minnie Williams's property. I need to see it for myself. The thought of being caught sent shivers down her spine. "Would you mind telling him that I came in today? I left a note for him on his desk, but I wanted to make certain he knows I fulfilled my promise and that I wasn't trying to get out of hours yesterday."

"I'll pass along the message of your dedication to come in on a Saturday. I'm sure he'll appreciate that you got your job done." Auntie Ann snorted, sarcasm exuding with each word as she wiped her beading forehead.

What did I do to earn such aversion? Winnifred shook her head, reminding herself that she needn't worry about what Auntie Ann thought of Cordelia Swan. If her alias was so dislikeable, then she was playing her character well. No one seemed to dislike Winnifred Wylde. . .well, besides Mr. Saunders and his fiancée.

She waved farewell, stepped outside, and blinked against the light, enjoying the fresh air as a warm, gentle breeze rustled her curls against her cheek. She crossed the street and causally glanced about for her protector, but instead of finding Jude, she nearly ran into Percy. In keeping with her cover, she did not greet Percy, but apologized as she might to a stranger and walked a block or two down before turning left, waiting for him to join her. As soon as he rounded the corner, she grabbed his coat sleeve. "Where is Jude? I mean, Detective Thorpe?" Jude would never leave her, not even if he became ill again or there was an emergency, especially after what had happened yesterday. *Surely, Father did not reassign him.* Her heart thudded. *He wouldn't. He promised.* After their time together at the fair yesterday, she was certain that Jude felt something for her, but out of respect to her father's wishes, Jude was remaining silent.

"He was here this morning, but then your father sent me to release him and tell him to return to the precinct on an urgent matter. Apparently, Inspector Wylde trusts me with your safety as much as one of his top detectives." He grinned, offering her his arm.

She pushed down her rising panic. Even after hearing her father's renewed and adamant stance against her marrying a lawman, she was having a difficult time releasing her dreams of a future with Jude. A part of her still held on to the hope that maybe that magical place in her mind called One Day would become a reality.

While she enjoyed Percy's company and thought he was quite handsome, he still lacked the one thing she craved. He wasn't Jude. *But maybe if I honor Father's request to see Percy, I can soften him to the idea of Jude.*

Percy shoved his hands into his pockets and kicked a rock down the sidewalk. "And since I knew you were going to be off this afternoon, I asked your father's permission, which was granted, to have you come to my estate on Lakeshore Drive." He gestured to the clouds. "It is a perfect day and not too hot for a stroll on the grounds and possibly a game or two of badminton?"

The address she had finally procured weighed heavily in her reticule. "That sounds lovely, but I really ought to follow up on this lead." It felt wrong to accept his invitation when she knew her affections lay elsewhere, even if she did promise her father to see Percy. He was kind and mostly thoughtful, but more importantly, expressed an interest in her hobbies, which included his favorite thing, his books. He didn't deserve to have her heart's sloppy seconds. No one did.

"Come on now. I'm sure you can work on it with Jude come

Monday. You need to take your mind off your work for once and enjoy yourself. I should know. I get quite obsessed when I work on a novel. It is literally the only thing that is on my mind from the moment I wake to the moment I sleep, and even then, I dream plots. Until I met you and. . ." He reached for her hand and threaded his fingers through hers.

"And?"

"And now, I have a new dream."

She looked to see if she could catch a hint of teasing in his gaze, but all she saw was stark earnestness. How to tell him that she wanted the man she could never have? Was something wrong with her to not desire the man before her who was on paper her perfect match? Thinking of her father's stipulation, she selfishly relented and allowed him to assist her into his awaiting carriage, the tufted seats smelling of new leather. Next to Percy's flawless attire, she once again felt underdressed, being that she was in her work suit of navy. But, unfastening the ribbon necklace hidden under her collar, she slipped on her mother's pearl ring, knowing it would add a bit of sophistication to any gown.

Percy chatted the whole way up Lakeshore Drive, telling her about his new book, which sounded almost word for word what she had told him of her time with Holmes. Losing herself in the plot that was based on her own adventures, Winnifred couldn't help but be excited to think that she was going to have such a substantial influence on her favorite author's next work.

At the abrupt turn of the carriage, her shoulder was thrown against his, and Percy paused in his talking to smooth back a wisp of her hair, his eyes locking on hers. He leaned toward her, but she cleared her throat and twisted toward the window, thanking the Lord that they were pulling into the drive of a large estate that could only be described as a castle. "Is this your home?" she squawked, feeling awkward at what had almost transpired between them.

"Ah yes, this is White Castle. It has just been completed."

Her breath caught as they drew closer. Having lived in a modest cottage her entire life, the sight of the greenery surrounding his castle made her feel quite small, but something about it reminded her of someplace dear. Upon further examination, she realized that it was a perfect match to the setting of one of her favorite novels. "White Castle. . .isn't this the setting for your first novel?"

He smiled and nodded, helping her down. "That house has haunted me in my dreams for years and I knew that I must have it, so I built this castle with my earnings. My father may not approve of my job, but he appreciates that I earn more than I will ever inherit from him." He held the massive carved mahogany door for her as she stepped into the marble foyer. "I thought we'd take the tour first and have lunch outdoors before selecting a game to play."

Her skirts trailed behind her as she wandered the halls beside him, feeling as if she were Elizabeth Bennett seeing Pemberley for the first time after refusing Darcy. But unlike Elizabeth, it didn't move her to accept Percy's suit. Rather, it widened the cavern between them. She was from a simple home and, as much as she loved the grandeur of the mansions in his novels, she preferred a cozy parlor that was actually lived in with piles of worn books surrounding her.

Percy paused at the large front room that had a net spread from one side of the room to the other over a costly Persian rug. "Have you played a lot of badminton? When I was visiting Morris Montgomery last summer, his sister Danielle, I mean Mrs. Fairfax, told me how she had set up one of these in her parlor. It sounded like such great fun that I thought we might play indoors as well."

Winnifred laughed, remembering well how much trouble she and Danielle had gotten into for that little escapade.

"I haven't played since then, but I'm willing to try my hand at it once again." She swung her arms as if warming up for calisthenics. "Be prepared. I am quite proficient at tennis, and I am prepared to crush your very spirit."

His eyes widened at her threat before he threw his head back and laughed. "That is why I so enjoy your company, Miss Wylde. You are always full of surprises."

Jude was alarmed to be called in to Inspector Wylde's office, especially since he was supposed to be on duty watching the inspector's daughter. Standing outside the open door, he cleared his throat, waiting to be acknowledged and invited inside, but the inspector appeared to be engrossed in the file on his desk. After waiting a few moments, Jude knocked on the doorframe. "Sir? You wanted to see me?"

Without looking up, Inspector Wylde waved him inside. "Yes. Shut the door, will you?"

At the request, a bead of sweat collected on his forehead. Did Inspector Wylde know of his feelings? He was an inspector, after all. The door clicked shut. He moved toward one of the seats opposite the desk, waiting to be invited to sit and be told what was going on. He hoped it didn't have anything to do with Baxter. He wouldn't lie to his captain, no matter what Winnifred preferred.

The inspector folded his hands, resting them on his desk. "My daughter speaks very highly of you." Before Jude could reply, he continued. "Which concerns me."

"Sir?"

"Do you have feelings for my daughter?"

Jude swallowed. This wasn't exactly how he envisioned this conversation. He had wanted to bring it up, but it sounded as if the inspector had already figured it all out when Jude had only just come to the point of admitting his feelings for Winnifred to himself.

"It's a simple question, Detective."

He had taken too long to explain, and now Jude seemed guilty, as if he had been lying to his superior. He cleared his throat. "I was actually going to speak with you on the subject this week, sir."

"Oh Thorpe." Inspector Wylde sighed and looked to the ceiling, rubbing his hand over his face. "Why? Why couldn't you focus on the task at hand instead of getting so emotionally involved? I thought out of all of my men, I could trust you to remain in a professional relationship with my daughter. My *daughter*."

"With all due respect, sir, I was attempting to keep an emotional distance from her, but. . ." He shook his head and lifted his hands up, helpless. "She has a way about her that draws you in, and it is impossible to resist. You should know."

The inspector cracked a smile. "I know you don't expect me to contradict that Winnie is witty or winsome and, not to mention, lovely." He stood, leaning on his knuckles atop his desk. "Nevertheless, I expect my detectives to maintain a level of decorum."

Jude bristled at the insinuation that he had been anything but proper. A thought fluttered into his mind of the crystal cave, but he whisked it away in his anger. "And yet, you placed Baxter as her guardian while I was ill. The man practically shouts his love for her at the mere mention of her name."

"I don't know how things were done in New York, but here, you will address me with respect." The inspector narrowed his gaze at Jude. "However, I will dismiss your tone due to your passion this time. I do not have to explain my reasoning to you. It's true Baxter has always admired Winnie. However, I never once worried about him because she has never shown any interest in the poor fellow."

Winnifred is interested in me? His heart soared. Maybe it wasn't such a lost cause after all. Maybe he could win her heart before that author fellow. He dipped his head. "I'm sorry for my tone, sir. I meant no disrespect, but yes, you are right. I am coming at this from my emotions." He looked his captain directly in the eye. "I would have said something sooner, but I only realized yesterday that I could no longer staunch my feelings for Miss Wylde. I know your preference for whom she should marry, but I would like permission to court your daughter and give her the chance to decide which suitor she would prefer."

Inspector Wylde leaned against the window frame, the dark circles under his eyes betraying a late night. He stuffed his hands in his pockets, his shoulders sagging. "I'm afraid I can't allow that to happen. I do not want my daughter anywhere near a detective for anything other than protection."

Jude's stomach dropped as he gripped his hat. "Are you sure it is the job that you object to, sir, or is it me?"

Inspector Wylde gave him a sad smile. "You are a fine fellow, Thorpe. And if you were in any other vocation besides police work, I'd happily allow you to court my daughter." He must have seen Jude's protest coming, because he lifted his hand and continued. "I saw how worried it made my wife to see me go out day after day, not knowing if I'd come back at night." He lifted the framed portrait on his desk, stroking the rim. "You may have heard that I was injured in the line of duty?"

Jude nodded. "It was because of that injury that you earned your promotion to detective."

"Yes. But on the night I was shot, an officer went to my house and told my wife that I had been taken to the hospital to be treated for a gunshot wound to the chest." His voice grew rough as he set the picture down. "She was so distressed, she suffered an attack of the heart. Even though I recovered, my Eloise did not. Winnifred may have inherited her mother's heart and only time will tell, but I will never allow that to happen to my little girl. While I may allow her to have her adventures, pretending to approve of her sleuthing, I have no intention of allowing her to be in any real danger or to marry someone who is in constant danger."

At the mention of danger, Jude felt a prick of guilt for not informing the inspector about what occurred the day before, but as Winnifred had begged him to be silent until they had proof, he kept it to himself.

"Unless you can suddenly have a new vocation, she will marry Percy."

His words brought Jude's thoughts crashing to a halt. *Winnifred. . .marry someone else?* The thought of her not loving him was painful enough, but the thought of her in some other man's arms, being kissed, being adored, tore at his heart. "Sir, you can't mean that. You know being a detective isn't just a job. For me, it's a calling from the Lord. I cannot—"

Inspector Wylde lifted his hand again. "I know you cannot give up your work, as I could not give up mine. Eloise never once asked me to, for she knew it was my calling as well." He shook his head. "If she had been a girl from my set, it may have been an easier transition. She was from high society, and her other suitors had good, safe vocations. Jobs that would never cause her to worry a day in her life. But, she chose—" He looked out the window and cleared his throat. "Percival will give my daughter a good life, a secure life, yet one filled with the adventure she craves. With an author for a husband, she can use her imagination by helping him in his work."

"But what if she doesn't *want* to marry him?" *What if she wishes to marry me?*

"Winnifred doesn't know what she wants yet, but you can be certain I will heavily influence her decision. When I die, I want to know that she is taken care of. Until then, I don't wish to worry if the man that I am leaving her with will be around to care for her and her children. No, Thorpe. The answer is no."

Jude wanted to argue, but the inspector was still his captain. Short of giving up his calling and finding another means of providing for a family, he could never have Winnifred. He swallowed back his hurt, anger, and confusion. Why would God bring the perfect woman into his life only to take her away? *Lord, I don't think I can bear losing another person I love.*

Chapter Seventeen

"Heart, we will forget him, You and I, tonight!
You must forget the warmth he gave, I will forget the light."
~Emily Dickinson

It had already been the longest Sunday morning in existence when Winnifred received Percy's note, saying that the muse had called and he regrettably must cancel their luncheon once again. Sighing, she crumpled the note and tossed it into the parlor's wastebasket, sick of the inconvenient muse. Pausing, she realized that she had saved room in her calendar for Percy. . .and now she had the entire afternoon free from Aunt Lillian's string of social obligations. Obligations she was forced to keep if she wanted to continue her detective work in the mornings and which left precious little time for her novels. Normally, she would have finished her current novel long ago and already read ten on top of it, but she had been too engrossed in her work to finish.

Since she didn't have Jude with her today, she couldn't go to the Wilmette house, so she tucked her book under her arm, grabbed a picnic blanket, a parasol, her box of emergency chocolates from behind a line of books on the top shelf, and her reticule with the muff pistol. She scribbled down a note to her father, who was working as always, saying that she would be at the park. It made her nervous to know she was alone, but as Holmes's Englewood residence was far from the park, she figured she would be safe enough.

Hat in hand to allow the sunshine to bathe her face, she glanced over her shoulder out of habit before once again remembering that it was Sunday. Jude, of course, had the day off, yet she couldn't help the swell of disappointment in her chest.

The afternoon heat pressed down on her after the coolness of the parlor, and by the time she reached her favorite reading spot, the back and sleeves of her comely pale yellow dress stuck to her skin. Waving her hat in front of her face, she patted her handkerchief over her flaming face before selecting a level spot for spreading her blanket under her favorite black cherry tree, heavy laden with ripening fruit overhead. She opened her box of chocolates and, reclining with her back to the tree, dove into her book to find out what happened to Maid Morwenna and Lord Winston.

Atop the castle, Lord Winston knelt beside the candlelit table and grasped his maiden's hand in his own. "My darling. I think you know what I must ask. With every breath, I think of you. With every sigh, I long for you. With every—"

Winnifred couldn't concentrate. Percy's books *always* drew her in and made her surroundings and thoughts fade into the background, but not even the chocolates were tempting her today. Her father's forbidding a relationship with Jude disheartened her. She had tried to ignore her anger, but it kept bubbling to the surface.

How could her father, who was constantly away working, know her well enough to tell her who she did or did not love? She admitted that he may know what was best for her, but Winnifred ached for him to see beyond a suitor's vocation to his heart and to her own heart. *But, that would require him to leave his precious office for more than a hurried, late dinner at home,* she thought, trying to keep the bitterness of years of lonely meals from bleeding into her rationality. It was difficult to remember why her father worked so diligently in the moments when she desperately needed to take comfort in his arms after Mother's death and in the heartaches since then.

She was tired of following his rules blindly. She wanted something more than staying home and eating a box of bonbons

while reading about adventures. She wanted to *have* adventures…
well, for longer than a mere six weeks. Winnifred laid her head
on the crackled bark of the trunk and sighed as she stared up
at the sunlight filtering through the leaves. She knew her anger
would fade as it always did and she would have to obey, but the
thought of giving up Jude once and for all felt like someone had
reached inside her and was squeezing her heart, attempting to
burst it.

Blinking back her tears, she snapped her book closed and settled back to watch as people passed by, imagining what their lives
were like and making up their conversations in her head to distract
herself from her emotions. She felt quite hidden from the world
under the branches as she observed a gentleman present his lady
friend with a flower. She imagined him commenting on the secret
language of the flower with its hidden meanings of love.

Then, behind them, she spied Jude and his sister strolling toward
her. Her heart beat faster at the sight of him, and she was about to
rise and greet them when she heard his words.

"I'm only saying that I don't think I'm meant to marry. My line
of work is far too volatile to take a wife and have a family."

Winnifred pressed her hand to her mouth, feeling ill, and
watched as Mary frowned. "But what about Father? He had the
exact same occupation as you."

"Exactly." He paused and took her by the shoulders. "As did
your husband. Great men as they were, they each left behind wid-
ows and families, and I see the pain it has caused." He bowed his
head. "As hard as it may be to spend my life without a wife, I cannot, in good conscience, do that to any woman. God has called me
to this work, but unless He presses on my heart that He wishes me
to marry, I will not seek a wife out."

"Oh Jude." Winnifred nearly whimpered, tears stinging her eyes
and wetting her lashes as the dreams hidden in her heart slipped
further out of her reach.

Mary stroked his cheek with the back of a gloved hand. "Are you certain that's what the Lord intended when He called you to this job? Or is it fear that is keeping you from pursuing—"

"I have the Lord, you, Mother, and little Georgie. Who else do I need in life?" He threaded his arm through hers, pulling her close as they strolled away, their words fading with their departure.

The thrumming in her head banished all sound as her hopes burned to ash. Winnifred fought back her sobs that threatened to take over her. Heartbreak was one thing her novels portrayed correctly. Her chest ached with an enduring pain that pulsed through her. *He never proclaimed his love for me. Any affection Jude has shown has always been a farce for the sake of Holmes. It was all me and this stupid book, making me believe Jude could secretly desire me when he's never once told me he has feelings for me. That's what I get for reading between the lines.* She slammed her book down as if it were the culprit, determining to do something she had never done before. She would *not* be finishing the novel.

Gathering her things, she marched blindly through the park. Passing a vagrant man in a threadbare, grimy shirt, she handed him the box of chocolates, and at his unabashed gratefulness, draped her picnic blanket over his shoulders before continuing her journey to the one place besides the church pew that brought her solace. Banning's Bookshop.

The copper bell rang overhead, and she smiled to the owner, who was on a ladder behind the counter. "Hello, Mr. Banning."

"Miss Wylde, it's been far too long." The shopkeeper gave her a little bow from the middle step of his ladder before scrambling down to her. "I set aside a stack of new novels for you I thought you'd enjoy, but since you haven't been here in a few weeks, I was about to restock them with the rest."

She pressed her hand to her lace jabot at his thoughtful gesture. "I'd love to see them. I'm sorry for not coming by sooner to see what you've selected for me. I've been unusually busy of late."

"That's a relief to hear, miss." He stooped and rummaged under the counter where he usually kept the books she requested. "I have to admit, I was a mite bit worried about you, as I don't think there's ever been a week when you haven't come to my shop. Even when you were recovering from pneumonia, you snuck out to come for a new Valentine book. You sure got into a lot of trouble for that little antic." He lifted a stack of books and set them on the counter, giving the top one an affectionate pat. "Now, I'll let you see if anything here sparks your interest." He nodded to the ladder behind him. "I have to reshelve some books, so please take all the time you need."

She cracked open the top book and inhaled. Nothing smelled quite like a new book waiting to be devoured. She felt comforted already, stroking the gold lettering on the spine.

"I'm sorry I don't have any new Valentine books for you. I've heard that his next one will be releasing in a few months," Mr. Banning commented from his ladder, placing the last of his stack into its place. "There was some kind of gossip about him not turning in his book on time and having to get an extension from his publisher." He shook his head as he descended, chuckling. "The ladies are not happy with the delay. You would not believe how many petticoats I have had to turn away. Now, would you like me to wrap up a few of these for you?"

"All of them, please."

Without even a blink of astonishment, he gathered them up as she counted out the correct amount from her reticule.

"All?" Jude's unmistakable voice came from behind her.

Winnifred felt her cheeks warm as her heart began to race, making her feel like a schoolgirl with a crush on the instructor who didn't know of her attraction to him. After what she had overheard, he never would. She would act as if she thought of him as a chum even though everything in her longed to be his. "Detective Thorpe, what a pleasant surprise."

Jude ran his hands over the brim of his hat. He hadn't meant to follow her into the bookshop, only to monitor her from afar until she made it safely home, but seeing the pile of books on the counter through the storefront window, he figured he should come to her aid. "Such formality." He grinned and gave her a bow, pressing his hat over his heart.

"You come to the bookshop often?" she continued in her odd tone as she kept her gaze on the shopkeeper, who appeared to be finishing up wrapping her purchases.

"I saw you leaving the park and, well, I wanted to be sure you returned home safely, but I figured out where you were heading and sent Mary in a hired carriage to where Detective Holt is awaiting her. I thought you might need assistance after such a long dry spell of not going to the bookstore." Jude watched as the man piled the books, one by one, onto the counter, individually wrapped in brown paper and tied with string. He lifted his brow. "You didn't want these bundled together?"

A smile escaped the corner of her pressed lips as if she were embarrassed. "Mr. Banning wraps them individually for me because he knows that I enjoy opening them separately, as if each book is a gift to myself."

He held out his arms. "May I?"

She nodded and stacked the books into his hands as if entrusting him with delicate china rather than sturdy books when she spied a title behind the counter. "Oh! Mr. Banning, could you wrap that one for me too? I've been meaning to read *Lorna Doone* again, but Miss Montgomery never returned my copy."

Mr. Banning rolled his eyes and chuckled. "I should tell you to stop lending to that book thief, but it's good for my business. Give me a moment and I'll have it ready for you."

Jude cleared his throat as Mr. Banning went to the back of the shop. "So, do you think you'll have time to finish these between your investigation and your courtship?" He hated mentioning Percival Covington, but he knew that if he heard Covington's name often enough, he would eventually remember that Winnifred, the only woman he ever desired, was not available.

She laughed and patted his arm. "Never fear, Jude. I should be able to finish these in a few weeks. Besides, Percy is always cancelling, so I need to have plenty of books on hand to fill my long afternoons."

"How did your Saturday morning at Englewood go? I didn't get a chance to ask, since your father called me in to see him." How he wished he could forget his conversation with her father, especially with her looking so pretty in her white hat bedecked with yellow silk flowers matching her gown. His gaze fell on her long lashes and blooming cheeks. *Stop this. It will only hurt more when she weds Covington.* "I need to record anything you found," he added. He set the books back on the counter and reached into his coat pocket for his small notebook.

"I've been anxious to tell you." She turned those bright eyes to him. "I thought I would have to wait until Monday to follow up on my findings, but since you are here. . . I do have a lead." She handed him a scrap of paper from her reticule. "He had the deed for a home on 38 North John Street in Wilmette."

"Wilmette. Isn't that where he is always taking business trips?" Jude memorized the address and handed it back to her.

"Yes, and this is where it gets even more strange. The deed is in a woman's name. Minnie Williams."

"*M. Williams?*" Jude clarified, his pulse hammering in his ears.

"I know. I thought of your mysterious Mr. Williams too, but Jude, there are hundreds of Williamses in Chicago, so the chances are next to none that she is related to your Mr. Williams."

"Nonetheless, I will search under every stone until I've found him. Do you have any information on Miss Williams?"

"She was Holmes's former secretary, who, according to Mr.

Owens, disappeared into thin air. Now why would that be, unless Minnie is that same woman from the symphony and he is keeping her hidden away for some scheme?"

"I'm guessing you want to go to Wilmette and see for yourself instead of sending me?" he conjectured by the eager tilt of her brows and lips.

"Yes. The sooner the better. In fact, we should go now."

"Winnie, you can't up and take the train to Wilmette without leaving word."

"Mr. Banning?" she called. "Could you have your shop boy deliver these to my house along with a note within the hour?"

Mr. Banning returned to the counter and slid a notepad across it to her, reaching for the pencil behind his ear. "Anything for my favorite customer."

Jude watched as she scribbled.

Father,
It's 2:00 now. Ran into Detective Thorpe at the bookshop and am following a lead. Will not be home for dinner. Don't worry unless I'm not home by 8.

Love, Winnie

He grimaced as she folded it up and tucked it into the strings of the top parcel. Her father would not be happy that she was taking off with him, but it was far better that Winnifred had his protection than not. "You do know that the train will take at least two hours *each* way?"

"And that's a problem?" She gave him a grin. "You aren't tired of my company already, are you?" Without waiting for him, she stepped out the door. "We best be off to the train station if we want to be back by a reasonable hour."

Taking in her well-tailored yellow gown that accentuated her golden curls, he felt his heart fall further. Why did she have to be so perfectly wonderful? He attempted to think of an argument to stay her, but she was determined, and if he had learned anything from being with Winnifred Rose Wylde, it was that she was true to her name. She was not like the greenhouse roses of high society. Her spirit was wild. He sighed and tugged on his hat. "Wait for me."

Chapter Eighteen

"I have not broken your heart—you have broken it;
and in breaking it, you have broken mine."
~Emily Brontë, *Wuthering Heights*

The train to Wilmette was so crowded with fairgoers returning that she was beginning to lose hope of finding a seat together. Jude and Winnifred made their way through the cars until they finally happened upon a bench with a small child sitting on the end by the window, her parents across from her. Sitting as closely to the little girl as she possibly could without touching her, Winnifred patted the seat next to her, inviting Jude to join her.

"Sorry. I'll try not to crush your sleeves," he said, attempting to shift away from her as his shoulder pressed up against hers, but there was nowhere to go unless he leaned into the aisle.

"It doesn't matter," she replied, not minding his closeness. She ducked her head at the thought. A lady did not think about a gentleman's arm against her own. She sat as straight as she could manage, shrinking herself by turning her shoulders, but at every jolt and turn of the train, he pressed against her side. The conversation flowed between them as easily and naturally as reading, and it was growing even more difficult to maintain a professional attitude with him. She couldn't help but study his profile as he spoke. He was thoughtful, alert, handsome, and so utterly out of her reach. Her gaze fell on his lips. They seemed to being pulling her forward, calling to her.

"Winnifred?" Jude asked, a question in his gaze as if he had spoken to her before and she had not heard him until now.

"Yes?" She blinked.

"We need to go. Everyone is disembarking."

Flustered at being caught staring, she gathered her parasol and reticule and hurried off the train.

"Have you been here before?" Jude grasped her elbow as they stood on the simple, small platform.

"I never had cause, but let's ask the ticket agent and see if he can point us in the right direction." Approaching the station window, she smiled to the weathered elderly man. "Excuse me, sir. Can you tell me how far it is to North John Street? This is our first time here. Should we hire a carriage?"

"Well, I'd only do that if your legs don't work. It's about a five-minute walk from here, if that." He pointed her around toward the front door. "Go down thataway for a bit and then take a right onto North John Street." He nodded his cap to them. "You two visiting family?"

Jude grasped her by the elbow again and drew her back from the inquisitive man. "Thank you. We're visiting for the evening. Now, what time does the last train leave? We will need to purchase passage back to Chicago."

With their return tickets in hand, they followed the ticket agent's directions and within minutes, they were on the right street.

"I had no idea the house was so close to the station," Winnifred whispered, opening her lace parasol even though it was a cloudy day. "I'm afraid Holmes might be about town and see us," she explained, and propped it over her shoulder so she could still peer through the lace while keeping their faces hidden from view. If Holmes happened to look out his window, he would merely see a couple strolling across the street. She slipped her arm through Jude's, keeping an eye on the house numbers.

Jude tensed. "There it is," he said under his breath as they came upon a large, maroon house. "I don't see him anywhere, but that doesn't mean he isn't just inside or looking through the windows. It's imperative we act as any other couple would and not gawk."

Looking through her parasol, Winnifred saw that the house

had a turret on either side of a large front porch. Directly above the center of the front porch, there was a balcony and still above that was a trio of windows to let the afternoon light into the attic. Right as they were about to pass the house, a little girl came flying around the side yard, giggling. Holmes chased after her, a grin on his face. Winnifred drew upright. She couldn't in good conscience leave the child without knowing she was safe, despite her laughter.

Jude must have felt the same, because he bent to tie his shoe, allowing them to pause long enough to see the front door open. The woman from the night of the symphony appeared, displaying a gold band on her finger that had been hidden the other night by her gloves. Placing her hands on her hips, she called, "Lucy, come now. It's time for dinner. Don't keep your father from his hot food."

"Coming, Myrta!" Holmes called, scooping up Lucy and giving Myrta a kiss before disappearing inside.

"Holmes is married? I thought Minnie Williams owned this house, so why is another woman living here?" Winnifred whispered to Jude as he rose and took her arm again. She hadn't known what she would discover, but she certainly did not expect domestic bliss to be one of her findings. They walked along in silence, only pausing when they came to the end of the block and out of sight of Holmes's house.

"I don't believe it. I just don't believe that Holmes has a wife! All the weeks I have been working at the office, not once has he mentioned a wife. He's mentioned Minnie and Emeline working for him, but Myrta Belknap was only a name on a couple of deeds." She rubbed her temple, trying to make sense of why Myrta was living in a house under Minnie's name. "What is Holmes up to? Why would he keep his wife a secret from me and the rest of the staff?"

"It's only further evidence of his nefarious side and his low moral standards, keeping his wife a secret while flirting with every skirt that comes across his path." Jude scowled. "As much as I'd like us to continue our investigation here, I think we have all we need to explain why a woman's name is on the deed. He's protecting himself, but we don't know yet what from." Jude checked his pocket watch. "Our train will be leaving in a half hour, so let's walk by the house one more time and then maybe find a sandwich to eat on the ride."

Winnifred nodded, realizing that she had forgotten to eat lunch. Passing by the house once again, she could see the little girl and mother eating at the table. However, Holmes was not within sight of the window. A chill stole down her spine as she turned to him, wide-eyed. "Jude. . .you don't think Holmes will be on the same train, do you? He didn't say anything about returning late or being absent from the office on Monday."

Jude ran his hand over his jaw. "What? I thought he was going to be out of town for a few days more. That's what you told me."

"I said he *was* going to be out of town a few days, but I meant that's what I heard on Friday, so it's already been a couple of days." She bit her lip.

Jude grunted. "This is the last train back, and you can bet he will be on it. The cars won't be crowded this time, so we will be hard-pressed to avoid him." He ran his hands through his hair. "Ah, Winnie."

"And I'm sure it would cost a fortune to take a carriage. We cannot return any later than we already are without Father sounding the alarm," Winnifred mumbled, feeling horrible that she had made such a colossal mistake. "But Holmes wouldn't take first class. He is always trying to make a dime, so I don't see why he would spend money unnecessarily, especially since he takes this trip so frequently. If we go now, I can get the ticket agent to upgrade our tickets to first class."

"I can't let you do that." Jude shook his head. "But I think you are right. First class is the only way we can possibly avoid him."

"It's my fault we are having to spend so much more. Please, you must allow me to do this and help me feel a little better about putting the entire mission in jeopardy."

"Very well, but we best make haste. I would hate to run into him on the platform before we board." Jude tugged her arm, picking up the pace to the ticket booth where, after making excuses and small talk, Winnifred paid for the first-class cabin tickets and they rushed aboard the train.

Panting, Winnifred saw that the cabins all had windows that looked out on the train's corridor. That posed a problem in case Holmes walked through their train car, but at least it made sharing the cabin with Jude as proper as it could be under the circumstances. "Maybe once we are seated, we can purchase a sandwich," Winnifred suggested, looking over her shoulder at Jude. She nearly gasped at the figure behind him.

At the terror in her eyes, Jude reached for her hand and whispered, "Where?"

"He's in our car. We need to get into a cabin and *now*." Her voice rasped, her limbs going weak.

Jude's hand found the small of her back and propelled her into the first vacant cabin and closed the door.

"Jude, he's right behind us. He will see us! Jude! What do we do?" She whispered, hating the hysterical tears rising in her throat.

"The one thing that would make any passerby uncomfortable and make them look in the opposite direction." Before Winnifred could even guess what he was about, his left hand was at her waist and the other behind her neck as he turned her back toward the interior windows of the car. Her mouth opened in surprise. "What are you do—"

His lips pressed against hers, silencing her with his passionate, voracious kiss as he tenderly held her to him. Winnifred knew she should protest. She knew. . .nothing but the feel of his lips on hers and the flutter of renewed hope in her heart that Jude cared for her. Her hands trailed up his arms and she encircled his neck, returning his kiss, their breath mingling as he kissed her again and again until, at last, he pulled away, leaving her dizzy. She blinked against the stars in her eyes. *Jude.* "Oh Jude." She rested her head against his chest and sighed.

It felt so right to have her in his arms, her lips against his. At his name on her sweet breath, he bent and rested his forehead on hers, their hats bumping. He wanted to tell Winnifred that he cared for her. That he had spoken with her father. But anything he said would only give her a false impression. *Well, it wouldn't give her any more of a false impression than my kissing her did. Why does she have to be so—* But the inspector did not bless their union, and he could never turn her against her father. He would have to win her hand honorably or not at all.

"What does this mean for us?" she asked a bit breathlessly against his chest.

He pulled back slowly and looked as far as he could through the interior window and down into the hallway of the train before turning back to her. "I'm sorry. I only meant to turn his gaze away from us as he passed by. I didn't mean to get. . ." His words fell flat. He had been dreaming of kissing her from that moment on the Ferris wheel so long ago, but he hadn't intended to ever kiss her before he had permission from her father to court her.

Her rosy cheeks began to deepen in hue as her shy blush turned to that of mortification. "Of course," she whispered, and sank onto the plush red velvet seat. She set to righting her hat before smoothing her skirt. "And did it work?"

He hated that she felt embarrassed when it should have been him feeling that way. "It did. I'm sorry for any distress I caused you. It was all that I could think to do in the moment to keep you safe."

"You can rest easy on that score at least. I feel no distress." Her eyes lifted to meet his as he sat across from her and the train chugged away from the station. "And what if he passes us when the train stops? Do you plan on repeating your act? I dare say you were convincing." Her words turned sharp as she retrieved her beaded reticule that had fallen to the floor.

The hurt in her voice crushed him. "Winnie, I'm so sorry. I didn't mean to make you think—"

"That you were interested in me?" She tilted her chin up, her eyes sparking. "I don't think it. I know it. No man could kiss a woman like that and say he felt nothing. I never took you for a *liar*, Jude Thorpe." She turned away from him and toward the window, her shoulders stiff as she slipped a pocket-sized book from her reticule and set to reading it, intent on ignoring him.

He reached out and lowered her book, taking her chin in his hand. "Winnie, look at me. You know why I can't say what's on my heart. We can't go against your father. You have no idea how much I wish things were different."

"Of course I do," she responded so softly that he barely heard her.

His soul pricked at the thought of the hurt he was inflicting. He could endure the pain his actions caused him for the sake of protecting her, but to cause her pain as well? *I should have never let her convince me to follow that lead today. I should have asked when Holmes was returning. I should have—*

She pulled away from him, pressing a gloved hand to her mouth as she took a deep breath, composing herself. "Sometimes I forget about the mission and that my reality is skewed with my undercover identity. I'm the one who should be sorry. I should have known that your kissing me was only about keeping my cover." Without another word, she lifted her book and hid within its pages.

The next two hours were filled with lonely silence. His arms ached to comfort her, but he knew that any action on his part would only cause them both undue pain. The train halted, and Winnifred leapt out of her seat as if determined to beat Holmes and leave Jude behind in her wake, but Jude lifted a gentle hand to stay her before thrusting his head into the hallway. Holmes was approaching. *God forgive me.* He turned to Winnifred and gave her an apologetic smile. "I'm sorry, but he's coming this way."

Turning her back to the interior windows, she stepped into his arms and lifted her gaze to him. "Jude? Tell me one thing."

Anything, he wished he could say. "And what is that?"

"Do you care for me?"

With every beat of my heart. Jude leaned down and kissed her for the last time. He could swear he heard the sound of his heart cracking.

Chapter Nineteen

"You know that I could as soon forget you as my existence!"
~Emily Brontë, *Wuthering Heights*

Winnifred sat at her desk, bleary-eyed from her sleepless night. All she could think of was Jude's kiss and how wonderful it had been, only to have her world come crashing down seconds afterward.

Mr. Owens plunked a cup onto her desk. "Looked like you could use some coffee, so I took the liberty of getting you a cup, but don't worry. Auntie Ann made it, not me." He winked and stretched his back with a groan.

"Bless you," she whispered, taking an unladylike gulp, pleased with the flavor and thankful for its strength to bolster her through the morning. "Thank you. I couldn't sleep. What has your back hurting? Did you have a sleepless night too?" She wrapped her hand around the mug and propped her elbow on her desk, flipping through the latest stack of papers. She paused at the sight of an envelope addressed to a Mr. H. Howard in a flowing script. *H. Howard. . .as in Henry Howard Holmes?* She turned it over to see that the seal was still intact. *A mistake.* Her hands fairly trembled as she scanned the return address and made out a name. *Georgiana Yoke.*

Owens spied the letter and snatched it out of her hands, tucking it into his pocket. "Sorry, this one is for Mr. Holmes," he mumbled.

"I wonder why Miss Yoke doesn't use Mr. Holmes's correct surname?"

"It's none of my business, but I would think the lady was misinformed from the start and he hasn't corrected her in their correspondence because he doesn't want to embarrass her now that they've been writing for so long." He waved his hand dismissively.

So, he has a wife in Wilmette, flirts with his employees, and corresponds with another woman? She rubbed her hand over her eyes, weary of searching for clues about the disappearances and coming up with nothing that would put Holmes behind bars.

"Anyway, to answer your question about my back, Mr. Holmes came home last night and asked me to move another trunk from the third floor to the basement, and it weighed a ton. Between us, we barely got it down to the basement." He chuckled. "I tell you what, I have no idea how he moves those darn trunks up to the third floor, but he never fails to call me up to the landing to help him take them down."

"Oh? I wonder what he's storing. We haven't had any deliveries for the hotel recently." One trunk wasn't much cause for suspicion, but multiple trunks? It was surely another sign that he was up to something illegal. Ignoring the nearly scalding heat of her coffee, she drained her cup and rose. "This was so delicious. I might go see if I can beg another from Auntie Ann. Can I get you anything while I'm downstairs?"

He shook his head, lifting his cup. "Thank you, but I like to sip mine slowly. You go ahead."

Coughing against her singed throat, Winnifred returned her cup to the kitchen sink, and, as Auntie Ann wasn't in sight, took the stairs down to the basement. The basement door gave an ominous growl, and she was struck by a malodorous smell. She knew Auntie Ann had sent Owens to eradicate it earlier last week. He had found a bag of rotten potatoes and concluded he had found the source. Pressing her sleeve to her nose, Winnifred scanned the dirt-covered floor, her heart nearly stopping at the sight of the trunk in the corner with a rather large, ancient-looking brass padlock securing it.

She bent over the trunk, examining it for any initials, and knocked on each side for a clue as to what it contained. Studying the lock, she was certain there was no way she could pop it open using a hairpin, but she gave a tug anyway, sending the old metal to rattling. The clank made her draw her gaze upward, but when she didn't hear anyone coming to investigate, she tapped the trunk, listening for the hollow sound she knew she wouldn't find, judging from Owens's sore back. She attempted to scoot it a bit to listen for the contents shifting, but found it was far too heavy and would not budge even an inch. At a creak on the top stair, she darted away from the trunk, searching for anywhere that could conceal her, but the basement was too small to offer her any refuge. Thinking quickly, she grabbed a sack of carrots, praying that whoever it was would think she had come down to fetch food for the kitchen.

His eyes met hers, sparking with an anger that struck her as unearthly.

"Mr. Holmes, good to see you, sir." She lifted the sack to her shoulder to draw his attention to it, giving him a bright smile. "Auntie Ann asked me to get her some carrots while she made me a second cup of coffee. She said the stairs are too difficult for her to traipse up and down two flights for every little thing."

"Did she?" He crossed his arms.

He was not satisfied. *How much more will he allow before he fires me. . .or takes me like he did the woman in green and the Conners.* He followed her up the stairs, not even offering to take the sack of carrots from her. His seething anger was nearly tangible, and she could see a darkness in him that she had only guessed he possessed. Surely he was hiding something in that trunk, something that, judging from the look in his eyes, he would kill to protect.

"Miss Swan, wha—"

"I brought you the sack of carrots like you asked." She interrupted Auntie Ann and set her burden on the counter, praying that the housekeeper would protect her lie.

"You asked Miss Swan to fetch you these carrots?" Holmes fairly glared at the cook. "After I told you that no one is to go down there except me or Mr. Owens?"

Auntie Ann must have seen the panic in Winnifred's gaze as she reached for the bag. "Of course I did! Why else would Miss Swan have cause to venture down there? The boarders will be clamoring for their food come dinnertime, and I don't have time to go running up and down the stairs for supplies or wait for you to fetch them or Mr. Owens. Miss Swan had a few moments to spare when she came down to the kitchen for a glass of water, and I thought she could go down in the basement for me this once."

"Water? I thought you were making her coffee?"

"Well, I—" Winnifred fairly stammered as Auntie Ann interjected.

"Sure, she wanted my special coffee, but she will be getting water. It's not fit for a body to drink so much coffee all at once." Auntie Ann put her hands on her hips.

He shook his head and laughed as the cloud surrounding him dissipated. "It's a good thing you're such a good cook, Auntie Ann. Make Miss Swan the coffee and don't send her down there again. As I said before, if you need supplies, ask me or Owens. Now, would you mind stepping over into the hallway, Miss Swan? We need to speak alone for a moment." Mr. Holmes motioned for her to join him.

Her heart pounded as hard and fast as when he had first followed her. *Is this it? Surely he wouldn't try anything with Auntie Ann right down the way.*

"I was sorry to see your note stating that you had a headache last week. I trust you're feeling better?" His brows knitted into a furrowed line, daring her to lie.

"Yes, sir. I'm sorry about leaving early, but I returned, as promised, on Saturday and finished my tasks. I hope it didn't interfere with your schedule."

He shrugged as he clasped his hands behind his back. "I'm not as worried about my schedule, as I am about what I saw."

"Saw?" She steadied her nerves. She couldn't allow him to see how rattled his words made her. *Dear Lord, please let him not have spotted us in Wilmette.*

"I did not wish to bring this up, which is why I waited so long to speak with you on the subject, but it has been bothering me. I was on a walk, and I happened to see you with a young man whom I recognized as the one who lingers nearby here sometimes."

She felt her knees grow weak. *Dear Lord, he's seen Jude.*

"I was puzzled because at the time, I had not received your note, and you seemed well enough. So, I must ask you, did you leave here early with the intention of meeting the gentleman during your scheduled work hours?" Holmes tilted his head, waiting for her to answer.

"Oh no! You can ask the pharmacist downstairs. I took some medicine for my headache and then went for a walk and before I knew it, I found myself at a friend's house and her, uh, cousin happened to be visiting. We had met once before. He asked to escort me on my walk and, as I was feeling a little bit better by this time, I agreed. Since it was after my normal work hours by that time, we ended up at the fair."

He frowned. "I can understand that, but why does he stand around outside my building while you're here?"

Winnifred drew a deep breath. "I think he's been stalking me."

"Stalking you? So, I take it that you do not like him?"

Like? Oh no. I left liking behind long ago. But, feeling that Holmes desired a favorable response for himself, she decided to take a risk and go off script a bit more. "I'll admit that he caught my eye at first, but he was entirely too inquisitive." She gave a little laugh. "I don't fancy being placed on trial every time I step out with a gentleman, so I thanked him and sent him along his way."

A slow smile spread across his features. "Very well. Just as long as you haven't lied to me. If you need me to step in and tell him to leave you be, I will."

She dipped her head, her panic rising at the thought that Jude had been found out. Either he would have to wear a disguise or someone else would have to be placed as her protector. "Thank you, but it is quite all right. He is harmless enough, and soon he will tire of watching for me."

With a bow, Holmes kissed her fingertips. "I would never tire of watching you, Miss Swan. Now, if you'll excuse me, I have something I need to attend to."

At the sound of his steps descending to the basement, she sagged with relief and returned to the kitchen, hands clasped as if she were praying. "Thank you, Auntie Ann. I—"

"I don't want to know what on earth you think you were doing down there." She waved her off with her spoon. "But you should know that Mr. Holmes has fired or evicted every soul who has trespassed down there beside me and Joe. He says he needs some privacy and his boarders don't pay to go down in his basement. I suggest you heed my warning, lest you wish to be fired."

He's fired or evicted every soul. . .or worse?

The grip car ride home was uncomfortable. Instead of Winnifred's usual informative dialogue, they rode together in silence. She kept her gaze averted, seemingly lost in thought, as they passed a throng of people milling to the fair. Jude hoped that it was only exhaustion that was keeping her from speaking to him and not resentment over what had occurred yesterday, but he knew he would be a fool to think it was about anything but the kiss. *Was it really only yesterday?* It seemed like a lifetime ago that he had held her in his arms and created this chasm between them. If only he were free to offer Winnifred all that was in his heart instead of crushing her by saying his kisses were all for the sake of protecting her. He hated that she might think him a cad who went about stealing kisses that didn't belong to him.

In a low voice, he said, "Winnifred, I don't want it to be like this. Can't we at least attempt to move beyond what happened on the train?" *Even though I think of it constantly.* "We have to try or your time at Holmes's building will be for naught."

She clenched her reticule. "I'm fine. What happened on the train is forgotten."

"Please, tell me what happened today."

Clearing her throat, she responded without looking at him and informed him of the letter from Georgiana before relenting and glancing at him. "But, most importantly, Joe Owens mentioned to me that he and Holmes moved another trunk."

"Another one? That makes *three* since you've been there, and he's only been on one business trip."

"Yes. I went down to the basement to see if I could break into it, but the lock is old. I need Father to teach me how to use a lock-picking kit. I can open simple locks with my hairpin, but I need different tools for this one." She slipped off her gloves and fanned her face with them.

"What are you doing tonight?"

She returned her gaze to the street. "Dinner and a book."

Her brief answer proved that she was far from fine. He longed for the ease of old, but he had crossed a line he couldn't uncross. He pulled a small leather roll from his coat and handed it to her. "I can teach you tonight. A good detective should always carry a lock kit."

She held up her hand. "Don't bother. I'll ask Father."

He knew as well as she did that her father lacked the time to teach her. "It's no bother."

She shrugged. "If you insist, Detective Thorpe."

The car reached their stop, and he offered her his hand. She touched it as if it were a snake, briefly, and with veiled disgust. He gently took her by the elbow. "Winnie. We at least need to talk. We cannot keep going like this."

"I can't talk to you. It's too difficult." She jerked her arm away from him, cutting him to the core. "I can't spend every evening with you and pretend like nothing has happened. You kissed me and then apologized for it. It doesn't matter if it was for keeping our cover or not. You still kissed me." She strode faster when her house came into view, as if she could not wait to rid herself of him. "You may be able to lie to yourself, but I cannot." Opening the iron gate, she stepped inside and closed it between them.

"Winnie."

"You best be calling me Miss Wylde from now on, Detective Thorpe," she whispered, gathering her skirts in one hand before climbing the red brick steps.

Her aunt appeared in the window and threw open the door, holding her hand out to Winnifred and nodding to Jude. "Thank goodness. I'm glad you two didn't dally today. Come on inside, Winnifred, a new dress has arrived, and I want you to try it on for dinner tonight. I'll be hosting the Covingtons at my home next week, and I want to be sure you are dressed properly this time."

"Have a good afternoon, Detective Thorpe." And without so much as a glance over her shoulder, Winnifred shut him out of her life.

Chapter Twenty

"All my heart is yours, sir: it belongs to you; and with you it would remain, were fate to exile the rest of me from your presence forever."
~Charlotte Brontë, *Jane Eyre*

Winnifred glanced at the small clock above the carved mantel, counting the minutes until dinner. She shifted in her elegant ivory dinner gown trimmed with yards of extravagant lace and woven with even more pearls than her sapphire damask gown. Aunt Lillian had insisted she wear it for a practice dinner with her and Father and, seeing no reason to argue, Winnifred obliged. With a sigh, she returned her focus to the novel at hand when she heard a *plink* on the windowpane. She drew back the pale blush curtains and fairly pressed her nose against the glass to find Percy below with his hat in one hand and a bouquet in the other. She lifted up the time-worn window with a laugh and leaned out with her hands pressing on the windowsill, the ivy brushing her fingertips. "Why such clandestine behavior when you can knock on the front door?"

He spread his arms wide, and in a dramatic stage whisper replied, "Because this is more romantic." He cleared his throat and began to sing the ever-popular tune, "The Sweetest Story Ever Told."

Winnifred blushed at the tender lyrics as passersby paused at the sound of his baritone filling the evening air, but she couldn't help but be touched by his gesture. After overhearing Jude's declaration to remain single along with his refusal of his feelings toward her, and after her father's warning against her marrying anyone in the field, it was nice to have someone who so openly desired her. To have such a handsome man serenading her acted as a balm to her stinging pride.

" 'Tell me that you love me, for that is the sweetest story ever told,'" he finished and knelt upon the brick sidewalk, holding the bouquet over his heart. "Can you ever forgive me for cancelling our luncheon Sunday, my darling Winnie?"

Winnifred sent him a smile, still aglow from his sweet song. "Of course. Now, won't you come inside and join us for dinner?"

"What kind of suitor would I be if I did not take you out for dinner after being so rude?" Standing, he stuck thumb and forefinger into his mouth and gave a shrill whistle. At his signal, an open barouche draped in a garland of red roses with lit lanterns on all four corners pulled up to her front gate. "My lovely Miss Wylde. Would you do me the honor of joining this lonely heart for dinner?"

She bit her lip, thinking of Jude. Percy was so kind, and she didn't want to lead him on, not when she knew she couldn't give him what he deserved, not yet anyway. Not when her heart was still aching for someone she could never have. "I wish I could, Percy, but I have work tomorrow."

"Please? I will make it worth your while to come with me." He gave her that winsome grin. "I had my chef make your favorite dessert, and your family has already approved, so you say the word and the evening of a lifetime will begin."

She now understood why her aunt had made such a weak excuse to get her to dress so prettily for a simple evening at home. *I can't believe I bought that.* At the hopefulness in his eyes, she was again reminded of Jude's refusal to even contemplate a future with her. She had to try. "Who needs sleep?" She returned his grin, took up her dinner gloves, and headed for the stairs to find Aunt Lillian at the bottom with her hand pressed over her heart.

"Isn't it romantic?" Her eyes glistened. "I remember when one of my beaus sang to me beneath my bedroom window." Draping her own opera cloak about Winnifred's shoulders, she smiled. "Now, I want you to forget all about that Holmes nonsense and have a grand time." She pressed a kiss to each of Winnifred's cheeks, holding her face between her hands. "You look like the picture of your mother."

Winnifred laughed at her aunt's scheming. "What *am* I going to do with you?"

"Thank me, of course, for finding you the perfect man." She pulled a golden curl over Winnifred's shoulder before nudging her out the door. "Go have fun while you're still young."

Picking up her skirt, Winnifred trailed down the steps to where Percy stood holding open the iron gate. Her cheeks flushed at the tableau before her. *This is the exact scene from Percy's novel,* The Bride's Hidden Past. *The scene where Permilia's suitor declares his love in a rose-covered carriage, unaware that he is proposing to a reformed criminal.* She grinned, feeling a bit giddy at the thought that they were acting out the romantic scene.

"Your carriage awaits, my lady." Percival bowed, laying his coat on the sidewalk before the barouche draped in roses. There wasn't a puddle, but the gesture was just as romantic as it was in his books. And yet, she was surprised to feel a bit guilty for stepping on it in her silk dinner slippers. It seemed rather foolish to soil a coat and make unnecessary laundry for the hired help to clean.

Swiping up the coat, he extended his hand to her, assisting her into the carriage. The flames licking the lamps cast a glow in his eyes, causing her starry-eyed heart to flutter at the thought that he was bringing to life scenes she and Danielle had swooned over. She didn't know if it was her nerves or the heat of the evening pressing down on her that made her curls stick to her neck. Whisking out her silk fan, she prayed, *Dear Lord, please don't let him declare anything, not tonight. Not when I'm weak and may say yes for all the wrong reasons.*

Out of habit, she glanced down the street, catching sight of a man standing beneath a streetlight, his gaze directed her way. *Jude.* Straightening her shoulders, she turned from him as the carriage rolled away. Tonight, she would be Percy's heroine. Tonight, she would lay aside all feelings for Jude and never pick them up to examine again. He didn't desire a wife. She wanted an adventure, and maybe Percy would be her new adventure that would last a lifetime.

She studied him in the lamplight, admiring the curve of his jaw, his straight nose, and the ever-present smile beneath that horrid mustache. He was kind and would make a good husband. *Husband.* She had only ever thought of one man in that role as of yet, and that man wasn't the one beside her. Winnifred pressed out a wrinkle in her skirt and determined to enjoy her evening. She turned to Percy and gave him another brilliant smile before asking him a torrent of questions.

In twenty minutes, the carriage pulled into the drive of his castle. Atop the turrets rising on the four corners of the stone estate, she spied lit torches. She smiled in anticipation. "Am I to play Lady Permilia tonight?"

He returned her grin. "I'm so thankful to finally have someone by my side to bring to life these dreams that have only happened in my mind." He hopped down and extended his hand up to her. "Come, my lady. Your dinner is awaiting you atop the world." He quoted the hero and led her inside and up a set of never-ending stairs.

When Winnifred reached the top, the sight before her chased away her remaining breath. Nestled in the rear turret, overlooking Lake Michigan in a glowing pink-and-russet sunset, was a small table draped in the finest of cloths set with her mother's grand china. Winnifred pressed her hand to her mouth, overcome with emotion to finally see the china as it was meant to be used.

He reached for her cloak, slipping it from her shoulders. "I thought that borrowing your mother's china would make you feel at home in a place where I want you to feel at home the most." He reached out and grasped her hand in his as the delicate strings of the quartet she hadn't noticed in the shadows began to caress the night. Percy swayed, gently pulling her into his arms in a waltz. The stars spun overhead, and she felt herself quite giddy over his attention as her white skirts swirled. At the end of the song, he twirled her into her seat with both of them laughing with the ease of it all.

Her hands shook as she sipped her water from her crystal goblet. Even though the quartet was present along with several servants, Winnifred felt quite alone with Percy. She wasn't sure if it was fitting, but she took comfort in the fact that her aunt would have surely halted his plans if she thought it was anything but proper.

Course after course composed of only her favorites flooded the table, and once again she was touched by the preparation that had gone into this meal. Before taking a bite of her meat pie, she asked, "So, how did your afternoon of writing go on Sunday?"

"I am nearly finished. I only need to write the final chapters, which I'm hoping will be inspired by tonight." He set aside his fork, his blue eyes piercing hers.

Her brows wrinkled at his odd statement. "Do you need to discuss possible endings to see which is a better fit?"

Percy gave a nervous laugh and knelt beside the table, popping open a velvet box and revealing a dazzling gold ring with the largest ruby she had ever beheld cushioned between two large pearls. She pressed her hands to her heart, shocked. For all the pride she placed in her powers of deduction, Winnifred had not foreseen an actual proposal coming, not tonight. At most, she thought he would declare his affection for her, but a proposal? She should have seen it, with her father pushing her toward Percy and away from Jude. *Jude.* Any future she had imagined with him had been denied not only by her father but also by Jude himself. *Is this what love is supposed to be like? Serenades and candlelight dinners atop a castle with a quartet playing in the background?*

Percy scooped her hand in his. "Miss Wylde. . .Winnie. I have never met anyone like you before. You inspire me to be better, to be braver. I want nothing more than to spend the rest of my life at your feet, listening to your tales, capturing your light, and writing it down for the world to enjoy. I know we have only been courting for a few weeks and this may seem a bit rushed, but I received word that my proposal for my next work, a Parisian tale, has been accepted. So, the moment I send in this novel to the publisher, I need to travel to Paris to research *The Bride of Notre Dame.* I would be most honored if you would join me...as my wife." He slipped the ring out of the velvet box and held it up, the moonlight catching on the jewels. "Let's start our greatest adventure. Will you marry me, my love?"

Winnifred's hands shook as she closed the front door behind her. The ring box in her reticule weighed heavily on her mind and on her heart.

"There's my girl!" Father greeted her, giving her cheek a tender peck before examining her left hand. "Why, where is your ring?"

"Now, Randolph, we mustn't rush her. She obviously has a lot to think about, and I'm sure she will tell us all about it when she is ready," Aunt Lillian interjected, taking Winnifred's elbow and guiding her up the stairs. "I'll help you undress. You have a long day ahead of you tomorrow with all your work."

Winnifred dreaded Aunt Lillian's cornering her, but there was hardly a polite way to refuse her kind offer even though it oozed with ulterior motives. However, when they reached her room, Aunt Lillian was uncharacteristically silent as Winnifred sank onto her cushioned vanity chair, pulled out her hairpins, and reached for her comb. Aunt Lillian grasped it instead and ran it through Winnifred's waist-length hair.

Winnifred retrieved the box and warily removed the ring, studying the ruby's alluring hue in the candlelight. "It's beautiful, is it not?" she asked, surprising herself by initiating conversation on such a delicate topic. But her heart was warring within her, and she had to speak, else risk imploding.

"Exquisite."

Spying a faraway look in her aunt's eyes in the mirror, Winnifred twisted in her chair and looked up at her. "You mentioned a beau. What happened to him? Why didn't you marry if you had a suitor whom you liked?"

"I should have said yes to the first man who asked me," Aunt Lillian said, running the brush through Winnifred's locks and catching on a wind-tossed curl.

"You had a beau propose?" Winnifred grunted under her aunt's tug through the knot.

She shrugged, a smile playing on her lips. "Two of them, actually, but only one that really mattered...the only one I should have said yes to marrying."

"You were engaged?"

She nodded slowly. "I used to be like you and your mother, always reading to fulfill my thirst for adventure and romance, but those poets and novelists made me chase after the dream of a man I thought I wanted. Someone dangerous, someone who was always surprising me."

"There's nothing wrong with that," Winnifred murmured as her aunt began to plait her hair into a loose braid.

"No, but I gave up the one fellow who truly loved me, who was kind to me. He didn't have much more than his love to offer me, but of course I wanted adventure over the security of his love."

"So you chose the dangerous fellow? What happened to him?" Winnifred's gaze returned to the ring in her hand.

"On the day of our wedding, he left me for another, a Miss King, with a much larger inheritance."

Winnifred teared up and rose, wrapping her aunt in a tender embrace, feeling keenly her aunt's pain from decades past. "I'm so sorry. How could he pass someone as dear as you over, and how could your fortune not be enough?"

She gave Winnifred a sad smile. "There will always be a girl with more fortune, so it is best that you take care and marry the man who does not care for your money, but will rather guard your heart with all his might. Choose the one who will care for you in the years to come and can offer you the security of his steadfastness." She gave her a look and added, "And who has a safe vocation."

"After the jilting, your other beau didn't ask you again?"

"By the time I recovered from the scandal, it was too late. He, as the second son, had already left his home to take a job and had found another and wed her." She rested her hand on Winnifred's shoulder. "Do not abandon a chance at love for the dream of adventure. Percy is a good man and can give you so much. And who knows what adventures lay ahead for the two of you as husband and wife?"

In the shadows on the stoop across the street from the gentlemen's club, Jude checked his pocket watch in the moonlight, waiting. It had taken everything in him to keep from seeking Mr. Saunders out sooner, but now that his family had been assigned a detail and no further threat had surfaced, he'd decided it was time to proceed with caution and had followed Saunders to one of the elite clubs of Chicago.

Leaning against the doorframe and his eyes strained on the front door of the club, Jude attempted to keep his mind off of Winnifred and what he had lost. He groaned against his swirling thoughts and tried to focus on the case he had come to Chicago to solve. At the sight of the lawyer stumbling out the front door and steadying himself with his walking cane, Jude pushed off the wall and strode behind him, following him until they were a block away and caught in a shadow of a building.

"I heard you worked with a Mr. H. A. Williams on his real estate papers."

Starting, Saunders whirled around with his cane lifted, blinking in his stupor as he swayed. Recognition lit his eyes as he slowly lowered his cane. "What's it to you? It was all done quite legally, I assure you."

It's everything to me. "I need his first name and his so-called sister's. The only documents I was able to obtain were signed with initials, and your office was listed for the home address."

"I only ever dealt with them by their initials for their real estate loan. I have one paper with their full names for an insurance policy, but it was so long ago, and I have hundreds of clients that come through my door. You can't possibly expect me to remember them all by name, no matter how pretty the woman."

"So, she was pretty. Can you describe her further, or Mr. Williams?"

Mr. Saunders shrugged. "He was an average man with a thick mustache, but as I said, many come through the office, and I doubt I could give an accurate description since it's been so long. But even then, I'm not supposed to give out my clients' names unless you have a warrant."

Jude stepped toward him, fists clenched. He was so close to solving the mystery, and this man was toying with him. "I don't think you want me to get a warrant, for fear I will uncover something far worse hidden in your files, do you?"

Mr. Saunders gulped. "Come by my office Sunday afternoon when we are closed so as to not raise suspicions. I don't want it going around that a lawman was sniffing about my business. I'd hate to give people the wrong idea."

Chapter Twenty-One

> *"She was one of those, who, having once begun,*
> *would be always in love."*
> ~Jane Austen, *Emma*

Aunt Lillian's story weighed heavily on Winnifred's shoulders as she readied herself for the day of work ahead of her. Not wishing to discuss Percy's proposal with her father, she skirted downstairs before he had finished dressing and avoided the breakfast table in case Aunt Lillian happened to be there, deciding instead to find a bite along the way.

"You are quite the early bird this morning." Jude greeted her with that brilliant smile, folding his newspaper before tipping his hat to her.

She dropped her gaze and tugged on her gloves, feeling strange after all that had transpired since they last spoke. "I can't be late this morning. Holmes has me working on a large project, but I don't feel like taking the grip car. I need to clear my mind with a walk and a cup of coffee from one of the cafés along the way."

"It's an hour walk," Jude chuckled, nodding to her heeled boots.

"Then we best get started. I can walk farther in heeled boots than any dandy with his walking cane." She brushed past him, heading in the direction of South Wallace Street and praying for a coffeehouse to appear as the click of her heels on the sidewalk magnified the silence between them.

"So, did you start reading your books?" He gave her a tentative look as if he were almost afraid to speak with her for fear of over-stepping the bounds he had so carelessly broken.

"Oh yes, I'm halfway through the second one." *My speed in reading has returned thanks to my need to escape the memories of your lips against mine.* Her stomach rumbled, calling to her to feed it. She pressed a hand to her corseted waist. "Do you know of anywhere we can stop for a quick cup of coffee and maybe a baked good or a quick breakfast?"

He nodded, gesturing down the street. "Two more blocks and we will be at one of my favorites. Most mornings I hop off the grip car here so I can have some of Mrs. Sheppard's cherry pastries before meeting you for the day."

She couldn't help but warm at the thought that Jude was taking her to a place he frequented. He paused in front of a small storefront and held the blue door open for her, sending the small copper bell overhead jingling as he waved to the kindly looking woman behind the counter. He helped Winnifred onto the tall wooden stool at the counter and, placing his hat on the seat beside him, glanced at the glass domes of pastries. "Two cups of hot coffee and two of my favorite pastries please, Mrs. Sheppard."

Her hazel eyes sparkled as she pulled two thick porcelain cups from under the counter before reaching for her pot. "Cream and sugar, miss?" she asked, looking Winnifred up and down as she poured.

Winnifred laughed softly. "Always, and lots of it, please. Thank you." She wrapped her fingers around the hot mug, inhaling the bittersweet scent as she waited for the cream and sugar. Jude sipped his black, his dark eyes meeting hers over the brim, sending her cheeks to warming. It was natural being with him, so much more so than Percy. After Percy's sweet actions last night, she felt almost guilty that she still had to fight her affection for Jude, but as much as she wished to, she would never go against her father. She loved him too much to hurt him by running away to marry. But she also loved Jude, and looking into his inviting gaze, she knew he loved her in return. *How can I marry Percy while Jude lives and breathes?* She sighed and accepted the cream and sugar with a nod of thanks, plunking four lumps of sugar into her coffee and following it with a generous amount of cream.

"Long night? I'm guessing your book was riveting? Or did something happen with Percy?" Jude's gaze dropped to his cherry pastry, dripping with thick vanilla icing.

She stirred her coffee, the spoon clinking against the heavy porcelain cup. She didn't wish to divulge the tenderness Percy had shown her. It was too sweet, too genuine to speak about with another. "It was an extremely long night. I stayed up until two o'clock reading because I couldn't fall asleep."

"I see." He gripped his coffee cup in both hands, his jaw tightening as if he knew that Winnifred received a proposal last night. "You had a lot on your mind, I gather?"

She rested her head in her hands. "Aunt Lillian and Father are pressuring me, and I just want to be left alone for a few more weeks until this case has been solved. It's too important to be distracted by other things."

"Pressuring you to do what?" Jude asked, but with one look into his eyes, she knew that he had already guessed.

"To leave this so-called nonsense behind." *And settle down by marrying Percy.* Checking her watch pin, she gulped the remainder of her coffee, wrapped her pastry in her handkerchief, and dug some coins out of her reticule, leaving them on the counter. "Breakfast is on me. Come, we have lingered too long already, so we best take that grip car after all." She straightened her shoulders and set aside the events of last night, attempting to focus on the task at hand as she rode on to South Wallace Street.

Winnifred buried herself in her work, determined to get through the entire pile of new receipts when Mr. Holmes popped into the office and called for Owens to join him in the basement. She gave Holmes a smile, hoping they were beyond their awkwardness after the basement incident, but he barely even acknowledged her. *This won't do.* She twisted her hands and waited for Joe to return before slipping out of her chair to find her employer. Following his voice, she passed a dozen doors before spying him in the hallway just outside another room with the same large trunk from the basement beside him.

"Good afternoon, Mr. Holmes," she called causally, walking up to him, a smile at the ready.

He jumped at her voice, closing the door before she could reach him and see inside. He fumbled with the keys and quickly locked it before his gaze fell to the trunk. "Afternoon," he replied with a warm smile that caught her off guard.

She nodded toward the trunk. "Going somewhere?"

His hands patted his waistcoat as if feeling for something before answering with a flustered *humph*. He withdrew a polished brass key with a decorative grip and dropped it into his coat pocket. "Yes, but not with this trunk. I'm only moving some things from the basement that I was about to put in this room for, uh, storage."

But then you locked it before putting the trunk inside to keep me from seeing? Knowing she had rattled him, she pretended to ignore the obvious. "I wish you safe travels. Oh, and I wanted to let you know that I am almost through the stack on my desk. Is there anything else you wish for me to work on before the week's end?"

He tugged on the lock of the trunk. Satisfied, he turned his full attention to her. "Why yes, thank you for asking. I have some paperwork I marked for you that I left on my desk, but it's not much, I'm afraid. I'm sure Owens will tell you about the need to reduce hours, but. . ." He opened his pocket watch before grunting and snapping it shut. "Is that really the hour? I must be on my way. Can't miss the train. Owens!"

"Sir?" Joe's head popped out the office doorway, and Holmes motioned for Owens to join him.

"I've decided to take this trunk with me along with one more trunk from the basement, so I need your help getting them out to the wagon. I just need to fetch one more item." Riffling through his keychain, he lifted the correct room key to the door, but paused, looking pointedly at Winnifred, obviously wishing for her to leave before he opened the door again. "Please have all the paperwork finished by the time I return."

Winnifred knew that if she was going to find out anything, she needed to take more risks. She was certain that erring on the side of caution had not earned her father the position of inspector. Crossing to her office window, she peered out to see Holmes and Owens struggling to load the heavy trunk in the back of a wagon. *This is it. It's now or never.* She must throw caution to the wind and make something happen. She was out of time.

Not wanting to be caught by Auntie Ann, Winnifred unlaced her shoes and, in her stockings, left the only room on the third floor she was allowed access to and began to explore, making her way to the locked room. The hallway twisted and turned, revealing room upon room that went from small to medium with a few windowless ones that housed overstuffed chairs, rugs, and basins, ready for an occupant, with the exception of a bed. She found it odd that Mr. Holmes would decorate a windowless room. Judging from the debt lining the ledgers from top to bottom, all the rooms were going to have to go for quite the rate, but she couldn't imagine anyone renting a windowless room for a long period of time even if it was so close to the world's fair.

Pausing at the farthest door down the hall, she knelt and tried first to use her hairpin on the lock Holmes had secured earlier, twisting the pin this way and that until she heard a faint click. The door swung open as she rose. Beside an overstuffed armchair and on top of a faded Persian rug, sat a crate. The lid gave an ominous creak as she lifted it and shifted through the straw to find some of the blue-and-white pottery left over from the time she heard about from Owens when Holmes attempted to hide it from his creditors. But, as the papers had already covered the story, she knew a crate full of pottery wasn't enough to have Holmes arrested. If the creditors had already descended upon him and he still evaded arrest, she had to find something else, something that would stick. There was a reason he had locked this room, and she was going to find it. She knocked on the walls and gently tapped floors in a way that she hoped would sound like a bird had gotten through the window. Listening for hollow noises, she prayed no one would become curious and come upstairs to investigate.

Not finding anything, she wound through the halls, opening and closing doors until she found a room that was bare except for a single throw rug in the center. Walking over the rug, her footfalls sounded hollow.

That's strange. Getting on her knees, she rolled up the carpet, her heart pounding at the sight of a ring on the floor. *A trapdoor?* Heaving it open, she poked her head through and saw that it led to the bathroom downstairs. She blanched. *What kind of person has a trap door leading to the bathroom?* Not wanting to be found by someone walking into the bathroom below, she quietly lowered the door. It was not against the law to have a trap door, and she was fairly certain the papers had mentioned something about that or a storage space in the floor between the levels in that first raid so long ago.

She continued knocking on the walls of the empty room, but didn't find any hollow spots filled with anything nefarious. With a sigh, she rolled her eyes, lamenting that her romantic novels had filled her head with false walls. She headed for the closet even though it was far too obvious a place to conceal any evidence. She opened the small closet and stepped inside, only to find yet another door inside. She turned the knob and, to her surprise, it was unlocked.

Taking a deep breath, she entered another windowless room, stepping lightly for fear that she would inadvertently find another trap door in this maze of a house. In the corner of the room, she spied a lump on the floor. She tentatively stepped toward it before bending down to make out that the shape was a woman's brooch. Taking out her handkerchief, she scooped it up, and upon examining it found a hint of green fabric caught in the bent head of the pin as if it had been ripped from a bodice. Her heart hammered in her chest. Had the woman in green been kept a prisoner in this very room?

"Miss Swan?" Auntie Ann called from downstairs.

Winnifred tucked the pin up her cuff into her sleeve and raced out of the room, closing the doors behind her as she went, only pausing to quickly lock the room with the crate. Whisking the dust from her hem, she hurried downstairs to find not only Auntie Ann in the kitchen, but Holmes, along with a lady dressed in a stylish pink gown with white flowers embroidered on her puffed sleeves, brazenly hanging on his arm as she smiled up at him.

"Mr. Holmes! I thought you'd decided to leave." The pin in her sleeve weighed like lead, and she feared any movement would cause it to clatter to the floor.

He shrugged. "I decided to put off my travels until Sunday evening. I ran into this young lady at the station, and she said that she was in need of a room for the night. I thought, why not show her the soon-to-be finest hotel in Chicago?" He grinned down at the girl. "We haven't officially opened for business yet, but how could I turn away such a sweet lady when my unopened hotel has rooms aplenty?" He looked to Winnifred. "Since Auntie Ann is busy with dinner, will you show her to the green room on the second floor? I've recently converted it back into a bedroom, and I'm anxious for it to be used."

Winnifred nodded and gestured for the girl to follow her, their every footstep echoing in her mind. *Doomed. Doomed*, their steps seemed to say. Something would happen to this girl. She could feel it in her bones. *Lord, help me get through to her.* She took the satchel from the girl who couldn't be much older than she was and led her to the now tidy room, devoid of the Conners' possessions. Her gaze moved to the corner where she had found the rust-colored stains on the floor. Scrubbed clean. "Are you here by yourself, Miss. . . ?"

"Miss Lance." She turned to her and smiled as she looked about. "I didn't have anyone to bring me to the fair, so I brought myself." She sat on the bed, spreading her hands on the coverlet. "Any words of advice on what to see and what I should not bother seeing?"

"Advice? You shouldn't trust everyone you happen to meet, not even hotel owners. Just because a man may own a hotel does not mean he is trustworthy. The White City is a dangerous place to roam about unescorted. If you prefer to see any of the sights, please, ask me to go with you." Pausing at the door, she whispered, "There are thieves and worse running about. Enjoy the fair, but please be on your guard, and do not trust strangers."

Stepping into the hall, she nearly fainted at Holmes standing there with her hat in his hand.

"I hate to ask, but something came up and I need you to come in on Sunday morning, if possible. There is a project I need your assistance with that cannot wait until Monday."

Her father would not be happy with her skipping service, but for this once, she knew it would be acceptable. "Of course, sir. I'll see you the day after tomorrow." She took her hat and lingered with her hand on his arm as she gazed up at him through her lashes. "I look forward to it."

Winnifred fairly trotted to the grip car line in her excitement. Her hand went to her sleeve to feel for the lump, but felt *nothing*. Gasping, she stopped so short that the man behind her on the sidewalk rammed into her, knocking her hat askew.

"I'm so sorry, miss!" The man, who turned out to be Jude, examined her face. "Are you quite all right?"

"I lost it," she murmured, nearly in tears.

"Lost what?" He glanced about the sidewalk as if whatever she had misplaced would appear.

"The evidence. After all these weeks, I finally had something to show my father, and now I've gone and lost it between the time I was in the kitchen and when I was in Miss Lance's room!"

"Slow down," he whispered, taking her by the elbow. "I'm sure it can't be all that bad. Tell me what happened."

Jude watched from his desk as Percival Covington opened the door of the inspector's office before turning to bid the inspector farewell with a grin on his face. Jude set aside his sandwich, all appetite gone, and moved as quickly as he could to avoid being caught by the author. The office was no place to get work done with Covington chatting up the inspector, much less Officer Baxter and his relentless babbling. He would finish writing his case notes in the comfort and quiet of his own apartment in half the time it took here. Jude was nearly to the bottom of the stairs when Percival called to him. *Blast.* He turned to Percival and gave him an obligatory nod.

"Detective Thorpe, wait." Percival trotted down the steps to catch up with him. "I wanted to ask how Miss Wylde's work went today since I wasn't able to join you." He followed Jude out the door. "Where are you heading in such a rush?"

Jude tugged his hat over his eyes. "Home," he replied, ignoring Percival's first question. He recounted what Winnifred had briefly mentioned to him of a Miss Lance taking a room and of her finding and misplacing a brooch, which had been evidence toward her sighting of the woman in green.

Percival let out a low whistle. "Sounds like we both have had quite the day. Do you mind if I walk with you?"

Seems to me you already are. "You don't live anywhere near me."

"I know, but I could use the walk. I have entirely too much on my mind. This waiting is nearly unbearable. This morning when I awoke to no news, I began thinking that my building anxiety might be the end of me."

Jude grunted, the pain in his chest needing an outlet. As much as he wanted to make his excuses and bolt, he had to know for sure what had happened. After seeing them ride off in a carriage trimmed with roses, he knew in his heart what had occurred. But when he had seen Winnifred this morning, she didn't have a ring on her finger. That gave him a shred of hope before remembering that she may have been wearing it on a necklace to keep her cover as she had been doing with that pearl ring of her mother's that never left her skin.

He cringed, hating the idea of Percival proposing even though he knew he had no right to as he had no claim on her affection. If his love was unselfish, he would want her to move on with her life and find happiness, but thinking of her kissing Percival set Jude's teeth on edge. "Waiting on an answer, eh? Does that mean you've asked Miss Wylde for her hand?"

Percival cleared his throat. "I didn't mean to let on to all of that, but I suppose that's what I get for having a detective for a friend."

A friend? He wouldn't go that far. Possibly forced acquaintances. But friend? If Winnifred hadn't been in the picture and maybe, just maybe, if Percy didn't talk quite so much about his books, Jude could see them getting along. "So, that is a yes."

Percival grinned at him. "I know it is a bit rushed, but I have my reasons. Please don't say anything to anyone. I would hate to break the news before even having an official answer from the lady."

Jude forced himself to extend his hand. "Congratulations. I wish you both the best." The words sounded perfectly normal, but inside he was roiling with turmoil. He had lost her. For all of Winnifred's declarations of not wanting a suitor, he knew that Percy had been her favorite and, as her father and aunt wished her to marry Percival, she wouldn't say no, not after what Jude had told her.

Percival made small talk to which Jude attempted to respond until he reached his apartment, and as he did not invite Percival up, they parted ways. Climbing the three flights, Jude fished his keys from his pocket. The two keys jangled together, sounding quite lonely. One for his apartment and one for his sister's house. He opened the door to his apartment and was greeted by no one. The emptiness of the days before him seemed daunting, and the passion of his calling waned.

He tossed the keys onto the kitchen counter and opened the small icebox, finding a bottle of milk and an apple. It was hardly enough to call dinner, but it would have to do for now. Chomping into the apple, he sank into his old overstuffed chair in front of the fireplace and squinted over his paperwork. He had forgotten to open the faded calico curtains that had been left by the previous tenants.

Sighing, he lifted his gaze to the cracked ceiling as his discontentment threatened to overwhelm him. The evenings that he had so enjoyed before meeting Winnifred now spread out before him in an endless, meaningless eternity without her. *Lord, help me bear it as she becomes another man's bride.*

Chapter Twenty-Two

"Hope is the thing with feathers that perches in the soul."
~Emily Dickinson

After a long Saturday of combing the world's fair for any sight of Miss Lance that had yielded nothing, Winnifred's limbs ached as she climbed the stairs of the Englewood building Sunday morning. The scent of cinnamon rolls wafting down the stairwell was making her mouth water and her stomach rumble. Surrendering her resolve to go straight upstairs to the office, Winnifred made her way to the kitchen. "Good morning!" She looked expectantly to the cooling rack with the cinnamon rolls dripping with thick vanilla icing. "Have all the boarders had their breakfast?"

Auntie Ann laughed and set a roll on a plate, handing it to her. "Not all of them, but knowing your sweet tooth, I had the foresight to make an extra one for you."

"You are wonderful!" She bit into the roll and, holding her hand over her mouth, she asked around her mouthful, "Did you happen to see our latest boarder this morning on her way to the fair?"

"Seems that she isn't going to the fair after all. She departed this morning at dawn."

Winnifred nearly choked on the roll. "She *left*? Did you see her go?"

Auntie Ann set to washing her mixing bowl. "No, but Mr. Holmes said that she decided to go home. She packed her things and left before I was even out of bed."

That's mighty early, if Auntie Ann wasn't even up. She swallowed her bite that had turned to dust. "I might step outside and eat this in the fresh morning air before going back upstairs," she said, thanking Auntie Ann. She took the back stairs, not bothering to even fetch her hat from the rack. She had to find Jude.

Jude jumped to his feet as their eyes met from across the street. Winnifred dropped her gaze, remembering that she might easily be spotted from the window above. She rushed down the sidewalk, away from the first-floor shops and around back to the alley, to the meeting place that Jude had told her would be safe in a pinch. She slipped into the shadows, wrapping her shaking hands around the plate in an attempt to keep from dropping it.

Jude ran up to her, set the plate atop a closed trash bin, and gathered her hands in his, looking her over for an injury. "Winnie," he breathed. "Winnie, are you all right? Did he hurt you?"

She crumpled into his arms, sobbing. "I should have gotten Miss Lance out when I had the chance. I should have—"

He lifted her chin to look at him. "What happened? If you don't tell me this instant, I'll go in there and confront Holmes myself."

She wiped at her cheeks with the back of her hand. "Holmes has taken Miss Lance. I'm sure of it. He's taken her and hidden her away somewhere." She poured out what Auntie Ann had told her, heartbroken.

"She may yet still be alive." He grasped her by the shoulders. "You must search the third floor, and if you don't find anything there, check the basement again. I don't know how you will be able to manage it with Holmes about, but we will pray the Lord gives you the opportunity. If you do not find her by tomorrow, we will submit a missing person report and you will not be returning to his employment. One day of her not showing up and the hotel being the last place she was seen is all your father will need for a warrant, which will catch Holmes off guard."

"The warrant will take too long. I have to find her. I'm confident she did not leave the building." Realizing that she was still gripping his forearms, her cheeks warmed and she dropped her hands.

Jude pulled a handkerchief from his pocket and dabbed her eyes before tucking a loose curl behind her ear. "Take care of yourself, Miss Wylde. I couldn't bear it if anything should happen to you."

Under his tender touch, she stilled and gazed up into his warm, amber eyes, losing herself in their golden depths before her focus settled on his full lips. She longed to kiss him again, and Jude stepped toward her as if he too felt the pull. He drew her into his arms, his hand caressing the base of her neck.

"Miss Swan?" Holmes's voice called from around the corner, stopping them.

Her eyes widened. "What do I do?"

"Go," he replied, ducking into the shadows.

She grabbed the plate, accidentally dropping the roll, and dodged around the corner, plastering a smile onto her face. "Mr. Holmes! I—"

"Where were you off to again?" He frowned. "One minute you were upstairs and the next, Auntie Ann said you stepped out for fresh air. I thought you had become ill again."

"I'm sorry, I did feel rather sick to my stomach, and I didn't wish to become ill on Auntie Ann's floor and make her think her cinnamon roll was to blame." She ran her handkerchief over her neck, wiping away the sweat. "Even though I think it was."

"Ah, well, I'm sorry to hear that, and I'll be sure to avoid them." His gaze trailed her neck. "Are you better now?"

Her neck burned from his brazen gaze as she joined him in walking back to the building. "Yes, sir. The fresh air and an alleyway to drop off the roll was all I needed, but *please* don't tell Auntie Ann, for I'd hate to hurt her feelings when she works so hard to please us."

"That's kind of you. I knew you had a sweet heart to match your beauty." He stepped closer and pulled the wisp of hair from behind her ear that Jude had tucked only moments before, allowing the tendril to dance across her face in the humid breeze. "What would you think about going on a business trip with me? I used to take my last secretary every month to a special client I had a few towns away."

Knowing she wouldn't be around beyond tomorrow if they didn't locate Miss Lance, she returned his audacious grin and nodded. "I would be honored to accompany you."

His eyes sparked with what seemed to be surprise as a slow smile lit his features. "Marvelous. I'll plan a trip for next week if that is agreeable."

She dipped her head. "Anything to help you, Mr. Holmes."

He smiled and reached into his coat pocket, retrieving a folded paper and handing it to her. "Though I am loath to talk of business, I need your assistance pulling some items from upstairs. We need to make sure that nothing on this list is left behind. Owens and I will handle the heavier items, of course."

She unfolded it and read over his instructions on removing porcelain basins, a bathtub, and various home goods from the third floor. She frowned. "Are you selling the hotel, sir?"

His brow crooked as his tender expression vanished in a flash. "No. I just want it done, and without any more silly questions, if you please, Miss Swan. None of the other secretaries disappeared so much on the job or questioned my methods near as much as you. Am I going to have to find myself a new secretary, or are you going to comply without questioning every little thing?"

She barely kept herself from shrinking back at his erratic, almost violent reaction to her innocent question. *If I'm ever going to have the chance to find Miss Lance, I'm going to have to convince him to keep me.* "Forgive me. I am so sorry. I forgot my place and will do this at once. Would you like me to see to hiring a couple of men to move the tub for you and Mr. Owens?" She allowed her gaze to fall on his arm as she gave him a smile. "But then, I'm sure you don't even need Mr. Owens to help you."

A grin lightened his features as he held the door for her. "I know I may look like I can manage, but I'll have Joe assist me just in case. I'd hate to break the porcelain tub for pride's sake. Now, let's get to work. I'm going out of town this evening, so we need to have this done by this afternoon."

Winnifred began following the list, starting with the farthest room down the hall, noticing that the room that Holmes had locked was not listed. She had never before been given leave to explore the third floor with everyone's knowledge, and she wasn't about to squander her chance. She couldn't help but feel amazed at the swift answer to their prayers. *Thank You, Lord. Guide me to Miss Lance,* she prayed as the men walked by carrying down crates full of paperwork from the office, grunting from the weight.

Alone at last, she darted to the locked door and gently knocked, whispering, "Miss Lance? Miss Lance if you can hear me, knock on something." She didn't have time to use her hairpin, so she pressed her ear to the door, listening for any signs of life inside.

Footsteps sounded on the stair. Winnifred darted away from the door and into one of the nearby rooms on the list, grabbing a table lamp to carry down to the kitchen where they were sorting things, nodding nonchalantly to Owens and winking to Holmes in passing. *I've got to find a way to get into that room. There is a reason it is still locked.*

Even though Miss Lance had roomed on the second floor with the other boarders and she strongly suspected the locked room to be holding the answers, Winnifred still searched for anything that could help locate Miss Lance as she ticked off her list. Scooting an overstuffed chair out into the hallway and toward the stairs, Winnifred wondered if Holmes was intending to do something with all this furniture or if he was returning it to his creditors. She mopped her forehead and nearly laughed at the thought. Most likely, he was having the staff hide the items before the creditors came to collect them. She had seen how he gave the creditors the run around. Men came to him constantly, ready to take away everything, but after a few drinks with Mr. Holmes and his gregarious manner, they left without their money, feeling as though they had acquired a chum.

Breathless, she left the chair at the top of the stairs for Joe and returned to the windowless room for the porcelain basin. She carefully carried it down to the kitchen table, nearly panting with the effort. With each load of dusty items that entered her pristine kitchen, Auntie Ann exclaimed over the mess and waved her hands, not happy with the chaos at her table as Holmes, Owens, and Winnifred deposited doorknobs and basins to sort through and pack away.

Winnifred trudged up and down the stairs so often that her feet began to ache and she sorely regretted wearing her heeled shoes. However, the pain helped to distract her from the thought of Miss Lance's disappearance or Percy's looming proposal. She was fetching the last basin from one of the larger corner rooms when she noticed a couple of pails and a paintbrush sitting by the room's single, dusty window.

"Thank you for your hard work today. I hope your evening is restful and your limbs aren't too sore," Holmes said from behind her, taking the basin from her and gesturing for her to follow him to the kitchen. "I gave everyone the rest of the afternoon off and the whole of tomorrow because I will be away. I don't think it's right for people to continue working when the boss is off on vacation."

Hearing the tail end of their conversation, Auntie Ann sighed. "After what my kitchen has been through today, I'm going to need everyone off so I can set the house to rights again."

Holmes ignored the agitated housekeeper, took Winnifred's hand in his, and gently pressed a kiss atop it, his whiskered upper lip brushing against her skin, sending suppressed shivers down her spine. "I'm looking forward to our business trip with only the two of us and to becoming better acquainted with you."

Shocked with his boldness, she couldn't even answer as Miss Swan. "I thought Owens would be joining us?"

Auntie Ann sent her a scowl, mumbling something under her

breath about Emeline and the impropriety of it all.

At this, Holmes's eyes saddened only for a moment before a darkness set behind his pupils. "I *told* you, Auntie Ann, Emeline ran off to be with her new husband. You saw her announcement card. And it was strictly a business trip that Miss Cigrand and I took. That burning passion you thought she had for me was nothing more than an infatuation. She is happily married and will never return here. And I would like it if you would refrain from mentioning her, as it is too painful to remember the kind spirit that will never again fill these halls, *unless,* of course, her husband returns with her." Clearing his throat, he nodded to Winnifred. "Enjoy your time off, Miss Swan."

Jude watched as Winnifred pinned on her hat then let her arms fall limp as she stretched her neck from side to side. She paid her fare and boarded the grip car, lifting her normally pristine skirts that were now marred with gray streaks. She sank into her seat and leaned her head against the pole, staring at nothing as he slipped into the seat next to her. He snapped open the paper to read until they had traveled a safe distance from Holmes. From behind the pages, he counted the blocks until he finally was able to turn to her as she yawned and noticed him watching her. She laughed at being caught and held up her hand, blocking her yawn, her pretty hands red from working. *What did Holmes have her doing?*

"Sorry. I'm exhausted from today."

"From searching? Did you find anything of Miss Lance?"

Her amusement faded at once. "No, but it wasn't from lack of searching. I'm praying that Holmes is telling the truth and that she simply left by her own volition. Holmes had Owens and me doing the oddest things. He had me carrying down the basins from all the third-floor rooms while he and Owens moved all the furnishings to the second floor and then set to work removing most of the doorknobs from the third floor. He's up to something devious, but for the life of me, I know not what." She ran her handkerchief over her face. "He will be out of town this evening and has given every-one the rest of the afternoon off as well as tomorrow. I've made up my mind that I need to seize this opportunity, break into that locked room, and search the place one last time. If I am ever going to find my evidence, tonight is the night, so I will go home for a bite to eat, make my plans, and then return."

Jude loathed the idea of her returning to the Englewood build-ing, especially at night. He rubbed his hand over his jaw and shook his head, desperate to protect her. "Inspector Wylde told me at the very beginning of all this that he doesn't want you to be in any danger, and with Miss Lance's disappearance, it sounds like this is getting far, far too dangerous for you to do alone. I'm sure he will be confident enough in your findings now."

"I need this evening." She said as they hopped off the car.

"You can't—"

"I must. Detective Thorpe—Jude. If I have the chance to save Miss Lance, I must take it. I will go tonight, with or without you."

With a relenting sigh, Jude showed her to the door before tak-ing another grip car to Saunders's law office. Going around to the back door, he knocked lightly and waited. *If he does not show up, I will hunt him down to whatever lunch party that peacock is prancing around and grab him by the scruff—*

Jude's train of thought was interrupted as Saunders jerked open the door and fairly pulled him into a dark back room, file in hand. "You have something for me?" Jude asked, straightening to his full height as he looked down on the man.

"Yes. As I said, they only placed initials on the loan papers, but for the life insurance policy, which I didn't recall until after your departure, they were required to use their names."

"And?" Jude nearly growled.

"The man's name is Horace A. Williams."

Jude jotted the name down unnecessarily. He would never

forget it. He would search the city until he found his Horace Williams. "And the sister's name?"

"Minnie Williams."

Jude gripped the edge of the desk, feeling as though Saunders had punched him in the chest. *Minnie Williams. The same name of the woman on the deed of Holmes's Wilmette property.* He swallowed, processing what it meant. "Do you know where Minnie Williams is living now?"

"Living? Can't say. Since you caught me outside the club, I've been doing some checking on Miss Williams's policy, and apparently there was a claim on her life insurance not too long ago. I made a note of it here." He slid a notepad across his desktop and pointed to the claim date.

Two weeks before Victor's death. Jude raked his hands through his hair and groaned. If Holmes had used an alias and paraded Minnie, his so-called lover, as his sister, and she had disappeared right before an insurance policy had been claimed. . .Winnifred was in grave danger.

Chapter Twenty-Three

"You have been the last dream of my soul."
~Charles Dickens, *A Tale of Two Cities*

To get out of going to a neighbor's ball with her aunt and father, Winnifred did the only thing she could in the situation. Come down with an abrupt stomachache. After reassuring her family that she would be fine without their care, she slowly climbed the stairs, the train of her favorite ivory evening gown trailing behind her as she bid them farewell with a hand to her stomach and a groan. At the click of the front door, she rushed to her bedroom's window seat.

The russet sky dripped down onto each windowpane as she gazed out to the street below and watched her father and aunt leave in the carriage, thankful they would be busy dancing until long after midnight. Wringing her hands, Winnifred paced to the mantel clock and back to the window. *Where is Jude?* She didn't have time to change as she had to be at the Englewood building and back before her father returned. She would give Jude three minutes to appear. Then she would leave without him.

Two minutes ticked by and a hired carriage rolled to a stop under the streetlamp on Lakeshore Drive. Knowing it was Jude, she raced down the stairs in her dinner slippers. If she were to sneak upstairs to the third floor unnoticed by the boarders, she would need to have stealth on her side. *Lord, help me.* Wrapping her shawl about her shoulders, she stepped outside, the warm, damp air enfolding her in its dark embrace.

Jude hopped out of the carriage, his brows rising as his gaze fell to her attire. "You might be new to this whole detective business, but wearing an ivory dinner gown isn't exactly the most surreptitious choice."

She laughed and clutched the fetching powder-blue silk shawl closer. "I was trying to be convincing in my efforts to attend a dinner with my father and aunt. If I dressed in a navy gown meant for working hours, they would know something was amiss, and I didn't have time to change. So, you could say it is a *very* surreptitious choice." Her lips quirked, mocking him, when her stomach rumbled so loudly she would have laughed if she weren't so stressed over the evening before her. She pressed a hand to her waist before looking up to him, heat spreading across her cheeks.

He held out a hand to her, but instead of opening the carriage door, he stood in front of it. "Before we go one more step, there is something you need to know. While Holmes is out of town, I still want you to be on guard. I believe Holmes is responsible for the disappearance. . .and, most likely, the death of Minnie Williams, who is the so-called relation of the very Mr. Williams I have been seeking all these months."

She pressed her hand to her mouth, tears filling her eyes as she grasped his hand. "Your Mr. Williams was Holmes all this time? He—he really is a killer?"

"I can't prove it yet with the paper trail that I have, so I'll have to get a warrant to search his house, but I believe Victor must have found out about Holmes filing a claim on Minnie William's life insurance policy and was ready to make an arrest when Holmes murdered him to keep the secret."

Her stomach roiled. "And now I am positive that Miss Lance is still in the Englewood building. You may need a warrant to search, but I fortunately do not."

"Miss Wylde!" A voice called before Jude could even respond to Winnifred.

Jude released her hand. He didn't need to turn to know Percy was running up to them. He glanced at Winnifred and noticed her cheeks pale at the sight of him, sending a spasm of hope jolting through his chest. Surely that was not a sign of an eager bride.

Percival trotted up to them dressed in black coattails and swiped off his top hat, his full attention on her. "Miss Wylde, please, don't think I have come to press for an answer."

An answer. Jude's hungry gaze met hers, and in that instant, he was certain that she knew his secret, that he would have proposed to her if her father had not intervened. Her eyes widened and her lips parted, but Percival continued on, not realizing the quake that had rumbled to life between the pair. Jude dropped his gaze to give them the semblance of privacy.

"Percy, I'm afraid I can't talk right now." Winnifred interrupted him and motioned to the carriage. "I have to go."

His eyes sparked. "I figured when you didn't arrive with your family to the ball that tonight's the night?"

She nodded, a hint of impatience in her tense shoulders. "I need to find a woman, a Miss Lance. Jude will begin his search of the building in the morning, but by then, it may be too late."

"I knew it." He grinned, stuffing his hands into his pockets and fishing out a small notebook and pencil. "If you don't mind, I will come along then and see you through your last mission."

Jude scowled. He didn't need to have the author hanging about, distracting him from the task at hand. He needed every moment devoted to watching and listening for Winnifred, should she have need of him, and the thought that she might need him put a fear in his soul that had never been there before. He wished she would turn back even now, but in his heart, he knew that if Miss Lance was in danger, Winnifred was her only hope of being rescued before it was too late. He tried to take comfort in the fact that Holmes was out of town. She would not be in danger on that count at least.

Winnifred gave Percival what seemed to be a tentative smile. "Of course, but we need to leave now, and I can't discuss—"

"I understand completely. There will be no more talking of Paris," he whispered, taking her hand to assist her inside.

Jude stepped in before Percival, ensuring that he would be on the seat next to Winnifred, keeping her safely nestled beside him. If he could not act as her escort tonight, he would at least be near her during these last moments when she was not promised to another and he could still imagine a future with her, futile though it may be.

Winnifred remained uncharacteristically silent on the ride to the Englewood building, her hands knit together on her lap, turning her knuckles white.

He bumped her with his shoulder, startling her out of her reverie as Percival stepped out first, leaving them alone at long last. "This is it. We need to walk the last few blocks. Though I know it is pointless to say this yet again, I wish you would allow me to go in your stead."

"And what if you run in to Auntie Ann or any of the boarders? Dinner may be over for them, but it's only nine o'clock, and nearly all will be awake. I can more easily explain myself than you can." She pressed her hand over his. "Jude. I want to thank you for all you've done for me. No one else has ever believed in me the way you have. No one else—" Her voice caught, and she paused to swallow and smile up at him, tears filling her enchanting eyes. "Has ever treated me as an intellectual equal." She shook her head. "My father loves me, but he thinks of me as a little girl whom he must protect, not a responsible woman. You could have turned me over to my father tonight, but instead, you respected me and trusted my judgment."

He grinned at her, hoping to break the tension. "The night is only getting started. I may turn you in yet, Miss Wylde."

She squeezed his forearm before taking Percival's hand to descend from the carriage. One block before they reached the Holmes building, she paused and gave them a shaky smile. "Thank you both for coming along with me on this adventure."

"I wouldn't have missed it for the world. This was just what I needed to finish my novel, Miss Wylde." Percy bent and kissed her hand.

Pulling back, she stepped toward the building, but Jude grabbed her by the wrist and pulled her into a fierce hug, whispering into her ear. "Do not take any unnecessary risks. Your cover is not worth imperiling your life. If you feel in danger, run and scream for me, and I will come."

Winnifred let herself in through the side door and took a moment for her sight to adjust to the darkness before taking the staircase to the third floor, her slippers silent on the wood. Reaching the third-floor landing, she let out a sigh of relief that she had made it so far without encountering an obstacle. Usually, by this time, the heroine in Percy's novels would have been met by someone with a butcher knife, but she had made it. She heard a creak and glanced over her shoulder and listened, but besides that one noise, the house was abnormally still. It was so quiet that it seemed as if all had miraculously gone to bed early. She shook her head. *Calm down and focus.*

Winnifred made straight for the room Holmes had lingered at earlier, the one locked room that the staff had not been allowed admittance to and one of the few rooms with the doorknob still in place. With a quick check, she found that it was, of course, still locked. She slipped a hairpin from the intricate coiffure that her aunt's maid had fashioned and, kneeling down, worked it into the mechanism until she heard that faint click. She grinned and tucked the pin back into place and slowly stepped into the room, mindful of the floorboards groaning over Auntie Ann's or some boarder's head.

Devoid of curtains, the window let in a hazy stream of moonlight that, in the darkness, looked like an opera house spotlight. It gave her just enough light so she could make out the shape of a trunk, the same one Holmes had been lugging up and down from the basement. Moving across the room toward the trunk, something glistening in the moonlight caught her eye. There, in the corner of the room, was the polished brass key from Holmes's pocket lying, forgotten, on the floor next to the trunk. Winnifred had played this moment so often in her mind that she could hardly believe it was truly happening. *In Holmes's haste to leave the house, he must have dropped it. Dear Lord, thank You.*

Scooping up the key, she flipped it over in her hand in disbelief as she knelt beside the trunk, a stench burning her nose. She resisted the urge to press a handkerchief over her nose and reached to insert the key but paused, puzzled by the strange mixture coating the trunk and keyhole, leaving a pool at the base of it. *What in the world?* She looked for the source and found that the black substance was dripping down the corners of the windowsill as well. She touched it lightly and rubbed it between her thumb and forefinger. *Pitch. Why on earth is there pitch everywhere? If a candle gets anywhere near. . .* Her heart hammered in her chest and she twisted about, trying to see if there was any immediate danger. She spied nothing but a couple of pails of pitch in the corner of the room. Undeterred, she took a deep breath and inserted the key into the padlock and turned it. The lock burst open, making her jump at the sound.

Straightening her shoulders, Winnifred jerked on the lid of the trunk, but it didn't budge. *The pitch must have glued it shut.* She bit her lip, trying to figure out how to pry it open when she discovered something was caught in the lid of the trunk—an emerald-green tattered ribbon. Gasping, she fell onto her backside and scrambled away from the makeshift coffin. "Dear Lord, no," she cried, recognizing the vivid hue from that day at the fair so long ago as the creak of a door came from behind her.

Turning to the noise, Winnifred's body tensed at the looming figure in the doorway. She clutched the key in her fist and hid it behind her skirts in a desperate attempt to save herself one last time. Spying the paintbrush dripping with tar in his grip, she realized Holmes was in the midst of setting the stage for a fire. He would never let her leave the building alive.

"It's a pity." Holmes sighed, set aside his pail, and brushed off his hands, approaching her. "You were quite a pretty little thing, and I was growing fond of you even though you are involved with a detective."

"Wh–what are you talking about, Mr. Holmes? I was only up here looking for a stray cat that I saw—"

"No sense in pretending and weaving more lies, Miss Swan. I know who your detective really is and why he is here. I just wasn't entirely sure you were aware of his scheming until now. A stray, Miss Swan? Surely you could come up with something better than that." He reached in his pocket, but she did not wait to see what he was retrieving.

"Jude!" Winnifred screamed, praying her voice would carry through the window. "Jude! Help me!"

Holmes shook his head and smiled as he twisted his hands around the neckcloth he had taken from his pocket. "No need to call for your beau. This room has one of the thickest walls in the place, and he won't hear you."

"Stay back, or else." Winnifred's hand went for her pistol, but to her horror, she found that in her haste to leave the house this evening, and in her confidence that Holmes would be out of town, she'd left her reticule, her precious reticule, with her pistol inside. She scrambled to her feet and ran to the window, slamming her fists against the glass, screaming, but the glass did not break. *Why aren't the boarders hearing me?* She smashed her fists on the glass again and again.

He gave her a smile as if amused at her antics. "That is one of my show pieces from my glass company that I started a couple of years back. It's unusually thick, so it will not break under a weak feminine hand."

"Help! Someone help me!" Winnifred screamed, ramming the window with her shoulder.

He strode toward her, a demonic flame in his gaze. "And don't bother screaming, because the others won't hear you either. I put some of my special sleeping serum into their soup. They won't wake unless physically stirred, which I intend to do when I finish up here, but they will be so drowsy, they won't recall it was I who woke them."

Winnifred charged past him, ready for a fight, but he let her by and laughed.

"Run my little bird, run!" He called, trotting after her.

She turned the corner and found herself at a dead end with one last room beside her, doorknob in place. Not bothering to check to see if it was still locked, she slammed her shoulder into the door, the weak lock breaking at once to reveal a room with what she hoped to find, a second exit. "Jude! Help me, Jude!" she screamed over and over as she clutched her skirts and ran through the maze of rooms, desperate for an escape. But everywhere she turned, he was there with that infernal grin and harrowing, cross-eyed gaze, haunting her as he laughed at her attempts to escape.

Thinking of the trap door leading to the downstairs bathroom, she bolted for the room, praying that she might have a chance, when he appeared again, blocking her exodus. Her knees weakened, and seeing that outrunning him was impossible at this point, she lifted her hands to him as if keeping a bull at bay. "Mr. Holmes, Henry, please don't do this. You won't get away with killing—"

"I don't know what you mean. I've been getting away with quite a bit since I came to this town."

She could hear her heart pounding in her ears. "What do you mean? What did you do with that woman in green? What did you do with Miss Lance? Where is she?"

"Would you like to see her?" he asked, wickedness lighting his eyes as he took a step closer to her. She darted backward, forgetting her flowing skirts, and tripped over them in her haste to get away from him. Seizing her by her hair, he wrenched her head back, the pain nearly blinding her. "If you are quiet, I will make this as pain-less as possible. If you scream. . . Well, let's just say that my days of dissecting cadavers at the academy will come in handy."

Her body tremored at his threats, but all of her father's instructions of fighting off a predator returned to her. She was *not* the weak heroine. Slamming her fist up his nose, she jerked herself back to escape him as he groaned in pain, but he only gripped her in his arms tighter, pulling her inside the room with the trunk as she struggled against him. Screaming, Winnifred elbowed him in the ribs, digging her fingernails into the exposed flesh at his collar. With a growl, he threw her over his shoulder, but, twisting her body, she managed to knee him in the chin, causing him to drop her on the floor.

He cupped his hand under his bleeding nose. With a devilish laugh, he gave her a crimson grin that sent shivers down her spine. He drew his hand back and slammed the back of his fist against her face, knocking her down and banging her head against the floorboards.

She groaned as darkness enveloped her. In a fog, she watched as he threw open a hatch. *Dear Lord, he has another trap door.* She couldn't run. She couldn't even walk if she wanted to. *What did Father say to do if force didn't work?* Winnifred blinked against the warm liquid dripping down her forehead. She lifted her fingers, wiping the blood from her eyes as her dim thoughts pieced together that she must have cut herself in her fall. *Use reason. Speak.* "H–Henry, please. I'm begging you. Please. I have money. Spare me, and I can give you anything you want, along with my silence of this night."

He squatted on the floor next to her and lifted a finger to her cheek, stroking it. "Aw, sweetheart. Do you think me a fool? You are a working girl. What do you have that you could possibly offer me? Your insurance money will be more than enough to tempt me. I doubt you have ten thousand dollars to take the place of your life insurance policy. I would lose if I let you live. Besides, I would never trust you to remain silent even if you had the funds. Insurance fraud is most frowned upon, you know." He grabbed both of her wrists in one hand and with the other, held the hatch open. "You should have minded your own business, Miss Swan."

"I will. I promise, I won't breathe a word about the arson," she whimpered, frantic. "Please—"

"I'm out of time and, quite frankly, so are you, my dear." He shoved her backward.

Winnifred screamed, groping the air in a vain hope that she could catch hold of something to keep her from falling. But she caught nothing and fell into the black hole, landing hard on her ankle and side as he locked the door, leaving her in pitch blackness. "You cannot leave me in here! Please. Have mercy." She banged on the floor, praying that someone on the second floor would wake and hear her. *Where is Jude? Why hasn't he come?*

Tears traveled down her face as she cried out again and again, but heard nothing in return except a faint crackling. The heavy scent of smoke wafted through the cracks in the floorboards. "Dear Lord, the pitch." *I am going to be burnt alive.* Crawling on her hands and knees, she searched blindly for a way out when her hands touched something cold. She let her hands trail the object, trying to decipher what it was until she touched a coldness that could only be that of death. Scrambling back, she lifted her trembling hands over her head and sobbed, feeling like an abandoned little girl again. A scripture pressed on her heart, wrapping her in God's embrace as she recalled His Word. *Fear not: for I have redeemed thee, I have called thee by thy name; thou art mine. . .when thou walkest through the fire, thou shalt not be burned.*

Her sobs quieting to a gentle flow, she whispered the same phrase she had for years. "I will not be afraid, for I am Yours, Lord. I am Yours. I am never alone." *And if my time has come, Lord, thank You for giving me a chance to have found love.* Closing her eyes, she curled around her knees and pictured Jude's face one last time.

Chapter Twenty-Four

"I was made and meant to look for you and wait for you
and become yours forever."
~Robert Browning

I f Percival did not stop talking soon, Jude would stuff his tie down
his throat. Scowling, he stepped away from the writer, whose
scratching pencil was driving him to distraction. *Is this all a game
to him? Everything he talks about refers to his blasted story. He seems
to only see Winnifred as a means of gaining inspiration and does not
comprehend that she is in real danger.* To keep himself from knocking
the man unconscious, Jude checked his watch for the tenth time,
his eyes widening. She had been in there for nearly three hours, but
he would have to keep waiting. She'd told him if she wasn't out by
midnight to come in after her, but not before. He would give her
ten minutes, but not a second longer.

The dog in the alleyway began barking again as viciously as he
had for the entirety of Winnifred's time in the building, drawing
Jude's gaze from the third story toward an alley, where he saw a cat
with its back arching as it hissed at the yelping dog.

"They are causing such a din, it's surprising that the whole of
Englewood isn't awake by now chasing the culprits down." Percival chuckled as he dug a paper bag out of his pocket and popped
something into his mouth before offering the sack to Jude. "Pep-
permint? Helps keep me awake and curb my need to snack while
writing."

"No, thank you." Jude waved him away. Even though he was
hungry, the thought of joining in Percival's camaraderie while Winnifred was in danger made his insides turn.

Percival began scribbling away again. "I'm almost done with

this book. I can't wait to show it to Winnie."

Winnie? He cringed at the familiarity. Jude returned his attention to the building when he spied puffs of smoke seeping out of one of the top-floor windows. His heart thudded. *Dear Lord in heaven.* He sprinted toward the building and slammed his shoulder into the door Winnifred had gone through, breaking the lock with the single blow. Not knowing what he would encounter, he drew his revolver and raced up the stairs, bumping into a staggering man who was rubbing his face.

"Who in tarnation are you?" the man mumbled, lifting his fists in an attempt to strike Jude even in his stupor.

"Police. Get everyone out. The top floor is on fire!" Jude sprinted past him and up to the third floor. "Winnie? Winnifred! Where are you?" He shouted her name over and over, praying for direction. Remembering her descriptions, he opened the fourth door on his left where the trap door was located. Flinging open the hatch, he saw nothing but the second-floor bathroom and heard the boarders below crying out.

Blast it all. "Winnifred!" He called out again, racing out into the hallway. He ran from room to room, searching for her, to no avail. Closing each door he encountered to keep the flames from spreading faster, he rubbed his hands over his face. "Lord, where is she?" His voice grew rough. "Oh my love. My darling, where are you?"

Jude felt an unmistakable pull toward the room that was nearly engulfed in flames. Throwing the door open, he stepped inside and crouched low, covering his mouth with his handkerchief against the billows of smoke greeting him. "Winnie!"

Something large near the window was ablaze. Jude stepped closer and found what seemed to be a trunk, and then he heard a faint cry. He spun around. "Winnie! Winnie! I can hear you. Call again!" He coughed into his handkerchief and began to pound on the walls, searching for a false wall when he heard her call again.

He looked down. *A second trap door?* He lunged for the corner of the flaming rug and, dragging it back, flung it aside to find a latch. With one tug, he knew it was locked. Glancing at the blazing walls and floorboards, Jude saw he only had moments before the third story was nothing more than ruins. "Winnifred! It's Jude. If you can hear me, stay in a corner if you can. I need to shoot off the lock, and it might penetrate the wood and ricochet." He aimed his firearm and pulled the trigger, blasting the lock to bits. He threw open the door and there, far below him, were two crumpled figures huddled in the corner. *Lord let them be alive.* "Winnifred!"

She flinched at the blast from above, but at the wrench of the door, smoke filled the small space and she coughed against the gray cloud that engulfed her. Blinking, she lifted her head. "Jude?" She sobbed his name, lifting a hand toward him, her head throbbing. *Thank You, Lord.* She crawled to her knees, her vision blurring, but she had to warn him. "Holmes," she whispered. "Holmes is here. And Miss Lance, she's—"

"Are you hurt?" Jude's voice cracked as he sprawled on the floor, reaching down into the cavern, the flames above him casting a glow about him in the haze of smoke. "Can you stand? I need to grab your wrists. We have to get out of here."

"Miss Lance is alive, but only just." From the light of the flames, she was finally able to make out that she was in a windowless, doorless room with eight-foot ceilings. "It's too high. You have to get her out too, but if you come down here, I doubt you will be able to climb out with Miss Lance and me weighing you down."

"Can you lift her enough for me to grab her?"

Gritting her teeth against the pain in her ankle, Winnifred gripped Miss Lance under her arms and heaved her up then managed to lift the girl's arm enough for Jude to snatch her by a wrist and draw her up as easily as he would a rag doll.

Her strength gone, she balanced herself on one foot as she lifted her arms to him like a child. His fingers encircled her wrists, and with a groan of pain, her vision blackened for a moment as she found herself drawn into his arms. "Jude, oh Jude," she cried over and over into his shirt. She had thought she would never see him again, never feel the strength of his arms surrounding her. She buried her face in his shirt, inhaling his scent beyond the smoke.

"I've got you, Winnie." He spoke as if calming a frightened animal.

"Take Miss Lance down first and come back for me," she whispered despite the tears streaking down her cheeks at the thought of being left again.

"Not a chance. I can take you both." He tossed Miss Lance over his shoulder, holding her in place with one arm and encircling Winnifred's waist with the other. "Hold on."

Winnifred wrapped her arms about his neck and hopped on her good foot, and the three of them fled from the room as the rest of the floor crackled into flames. Halfway down the second flight of stairs, Winnifred's ankle gave out, and with a cry of pain, she sagged against Jude. "Get her to safety and come back for me."

Jude's gaze tore from the flames on the third floor to where Winnifred sat on the steps. He gripped her behind the neck and pressed his forehead to her own, his lips a hairsbreadth from hers. "I will come back for you."

He bolted down the stairs as the floor above her cracked. Spying the flames licking the top step, she scooted down the steps then heard a groan from a beam. Her gaze tore upward. "Jude!" she screamed, lifting her hands above her head to block the falling debris when she felt strong arms encircle her, sweeping her away from danger.

"Hold on!" Jude shouted, bolting down the stairs, not stopping until they were safely outside. His chest heaved beneath her as he paused beside Miss Lance's unconscious form on the sidewalk across the street from the burning building where the rest of the tenants stood shivering, huddled in their blankets as they stared up at the flames. "That was too close. I should have carried you both, but I thought it would be faster—"

She turned her head away from the sight, crying. "Oh Jude. I thought I was going to die." He enveloped her in his arms and pressed a kiss atop her hair that had spilled to her waist. Surprised at the action, she lifted her face to him, the moonlight filling her gaze. She ached to kiss him. "I'm so sorry for avoiding you after that day on the train. I never should have acted so hurt when you were only doing what you thought was best. I didn't want to die with how we left things between us. I—" She dipped her head, unable to form the words that were spilling over her heart and instead whispered, "I'm so sorry for the way I acted."

"I was a fool to let you go without a fight, Winnifred Wylde." He pressed his forehead to hers again as if he couldn't bear to be apart from her. "When I thought I'd lost you. . ." He shook his head, his amber eyes brimming. "I never want to lose you again, Winnifred. You are the very heartbeat within me, and I love you with every breath in my body."

"Oh Jude." Her heart felt near to bursting at the words she had given up all hope of ever hearing, but grimaced as his chin touched her sore cheek.

Jude's face twisted as his fingers traced the side of her face. "What happened? Did you cut yourself in the fall?"

Her hand shook as she touched the tender spot, shivering at the memory. "Holmes struck me, and I hit my head when I fell."

Jude's jaw tightened, but his grip on her was gentle as he shifted her in his arms, moving as if to help her sit down on the sidewalk. The action frightened her. She felt that if he released her, she would fall into that cavern, never to see the light of day again. She entwined her arms about his neck and tucked her head against him.

"No. Please," she whimpered. "Don't. Not yet."

His chest rumbled beneath her in a groan as if her agony caused him pain as well. She felt his lips press atop her head again as he whispered, "I've got you, my love."

Giving into the darkness, she murmured, "Don't ever leave me again."

Chapter Twenty-Five

"Think now and then that there is a man who would
give his life, to keep a life you love beside you."
~Charles Dickens, *A Tale of Two Cities*

With his arm about Winnifred's waist, Jude knelt beside Miss Lance, anxiously trying to assess her state while keeping Winnifred from fainting again.

Auntie Ann ran over to them. "Miss Swan! Are you well? What on earth were you doing inside—" Her jaw dropped at the sight of the figure before them. "Miss Lance? What is she doing here? I thought Mr. Holmes said she left. We didn't know she was still inside." Tears filled her eyes as she pressed a hand to her mouth.

Jude pressed two fingers to Miss Lance's neck to feel for her pulse. "He lied, but she is breathing still."

"Thank the Lord." Holding her worn pink robe to her chest, she sank down beside them, her shaking hand on Miss Lance's forehead. "I don't understand. Why would Mr. Holmes lie about her leaving?"

The bell of the fire wagon rang out as it careened around the corner, rolling to a halt in front of the building. Firemen began pouring out, hose at the ready to extinguish the flames. Beyond the fire wagon, Jude spied the police wagon speeding toward them with a hospital wagon not far behind. "Would you mind staying with Miss Lance while I fetch a nurse?"

"Of course," she replied, her hands wrapping protectively around the girl's.

"Jude?" Winnifred's voice cracked, her hand reaching for his.

Scooping her up in his arms, he cradled her against his chest and carried her to the hospital wagon and away from the gathering crowd.

"Do you need assistance?" A female nurse ran to them, bag in hand as she reached for Winnifred's wrist.

"Yes, but there is another in more need at present." He nodded to where Miss Lance lay on the ground. "She is barely breathing and is unresponsive."

"Keep an eye on this young lady, and I will be back to check on her," the nurse replied, already running.

Winnifred's stillness frightened him, but not wanting to break his word and set her down, he shifted her in his arms and took in her bruised face. The cut on her cheek had left a crusty line of blood from her upper temple to her jawline, the purple hue on her cheek already deepening. Anger bubbled in his chest. *Lord, let us find Holmes at once and bring him to justice for what he's done to Winnifred, Victor, Miss Lance, and all his other victims.*

"Jude!" Winnifred sat bolt upright in her bed, spreading her arms about in search of him. Someone grasped her hand, tethering her to reality as the morning light filtered through the heavy curtains.

"Winnifred." The soft reply of her aunt came to her. "Oh, thank the Lord you are awake. I was beginning to worry that you'd—" Her voice cracked.

"Aunt Lillian?" She felt the tears cascade down her cheeks as she blinked away her panic to focus on her aunt who was still in her finery from the ball.

"Yes, my sweet girl." Aunt Lillian sat on the bed and brushed back Winnifred's curls from her damp, hot cheeks. "Would you like some water?"

At the clink of metal against glass, her gaze flicked to the darkened corner of her room where Doctor Reynolds was stirring a concoction. "She needs some medicine first. This will help ease the pain in her leg." He handed the glass to her aunt.

My leg? Her gaze settled on her raised foot, swathed in a tight bandage. She tested it and muffled a groan.

"Don't move it," her aunt scolded.

"Where's Father?" Winnifred croaked, her eyes widening as she wrapped a hand about her throat. Her voice sounded like it had when she had that severe cold last year.

"With all the smoke you inhaled, you will sound quite hoarse for a few days." The doctor clicked his black leather bag closed. "You were very lucky to have been found when you were. Any more time in that smoke and. . ." He left off his words and shook his head. "Keep an eye on her, Lillian. Please inform the staff of her needs, and I will be back later in the day to check on her."

"Thank you, Doctor." Aunt Lillian lifted a glass to Winnifred's lips. "Your father wouldn't leave your side all night. I finally sent him to bed for fear he would take ill."

Her throat burning, Winnifred drained the glass and wiped a drop from her mouth with the lace cuff of her white nightgown. "Father was here? He didn't rush out into the field to catch Holmes?"

Aunt Lillian moved to fill the glass again. "Of course not. He can barely function for all his worry. I haven't seen him in such a state since Eloise. . ." She let her sentence drift into silence.

Winnifred's throat swelled, but not because of the smoke. "And Miss Lance?" She blinked back her rising tears and whispered, afraid of the answer. "Is she. . . ?"

The morning light spilled into the room as her father's form filled the doorway. "Safe, thanks to you and Detective Thorpe," he answered as Aunt Lillian moved past him to show the doctor out.

Winnifred looked to her father, wanting, needing to ask about Jude, but knowing his feelings about Jude, she wasn't sure how she could broach the topic. "Have you seen—" Her voice tripped, and she began coughing in earnest.

Her father handed her the glass of water and patted her on the back. "Yes, Percy came by early this morning."

Percy. The glass shook so in her hands that she feared she would spill it. She set it aside on the cane-back chair. She hadn't even thought about Percy while she was in that room, facing death. All of her thoughts were with Jude and always would be. She had known it in her heart all along, and she was fooling herself into thinking she could accept Percy's hand while Jude was breathing. She would wait until the Lord showed her father that she and Jude belonged together. As long as it took, she would wait. "I meant Detective Thorpe. . .Jude."

He sighed and removed the glass and wiped the wood with a pristine handkerchief before it left a ring on the antique chair. "I knew you did. I'm afraid that after his rescuing you from certain death, you will have little place in your heart for a man who did not run into the fire for you."

Winnifred wrung the comforter between her fists, remaining silent as Father took a seat on the bed beside her.

He grasped her hand, drawing it onto his lap and stroking it. "When faced with losing you, it put things in perspective for me, and I've decided that whatever your decision is regarding Percy, I will respect it. I will not force you into a marriage with a man you do not love."

She was so taken aback by her father's change of heart that all she could do was embrace him. The movement jarred her ankle, causing her to moan, but even so, her heart felt much lighter know-ing that she was no longer expected to accept Percy's proposal. "Thank you," she whispered as he kissed her cheek.

"You know I've only ever wanted what was best for you. I love you, Winnie girl. Your mother and I always called you our greatest treasure. When she died, I wanted to protect you so badly that I'm afraid I might have given you the impression that I didn't care, but I did and I do." He bowed his head. "It's rather difficult for me to express myself. Your mother was always the one who had a way with words. I would just listen." He lifted his gaze to hers. "You do know I love you with all of my heart?"

She waited for the years of hurt to rise up and claim the joy her father's words gave her, but instead, she felt something in her break, and the anger she had always just pushed to the side finally vanished. Closing her eyes, she laid her head on his shoulder and absorbed his strength. Inspector Wylde was finally her father again. "I love you too."

He sighed and wrapped his arms around her before kissing the top of her head and clearing his throat. "Well then, I think you should get some rest. Would you care for one of your books from the library downstairs?"

"I've read them all." She attempted to laugh, but it came out sounding like a cackle. "But having lived the part of a heroine and surviving death's fatal blow, I think I will never again read Percival Valentine's work. His novels take over one's imagination so. No, I think I will have to learn to be content with your book of sermons and a cup of strong coffee to keep me awake to read them."

"I'm sure your aunt will be relieved to hear that." Father laughed softly and shook his head. "But, I give it a week. Good night, darling."

Jude paced the sidewalk in front of Winnifred's ivy-covered cottage, looking up at her window at every turn, eager for news. The doctor had left an hour ago, but Inspector Wylde had yet to fetch him. *What could possibly be taking so long?* He ran his fingers around and around the brim of his hat, and at the click of the front door opening, he strode forward. "Please, sir, I have to speak with her. Is Winnifred, Miss Wylde, well? The doctor was in there so long, and he wouldn't tell me how she was doing. I thought that there may be something wrong. Is she all right?"

Inspector Wylde squeezed Jude's shoulder, halting his questions. "I'm sorry for keeping you in suspense. I went up to check on her right before the doctor left, and she was resting comfortably. The doctor was thorough and concluded that despite minor smoke inhalation, bruising, cuts, and a twisted ankle, she is fine and will make a full recovery within the week."

Thank the Lord. Jude sagged with relief. "May I see her?" He knew he was being bold to ask to call on her after his conversation with the inspector, but a deadly situation tended to make people bold, refining thoughts that were confused or silent before. There was no confusion left in him. Winnifred Wylde was meant for him and he for her.

Inspector Wylde sighed and ran his fingers through his hair. "A responding officer spoke with some eyewitnesses, and they relayed what you did." He stared directly at Jude. "While Mr. Covington stayed safely away, a figure was seen sprinting into the flaming building. Is it true that when you spotted the fire, you ran into the building and remained searching for Winnifred after every other person had poured out onto the sidewalk?"

Jude looked away from the inspector for a moment, trying to gather his thoughts. While everything in him wanted to cast Percival in a bad light, he knew it would not be the fair way of winning Winnifred's hand. He shrugged. "It's true I ran for the building, but I'm sure I heard Covington yell that he would fetch the fire department. If he had not gotten to them so quickly, much more than the third floor would have burned. We each had our part in keeping Winnifred and other civilians safe."

Inspector Wylde cleared his throat. "I know what I said to you was harsh. It still would not be my first choice for my daughter to wed someone with a dangerous position. But, I realize she is *my* daughter, and I feel that danger will never be far away from her. If anyone can protect her, it is you, a man who—" His voice seized. Pausing, he ran his hand over his mouth and gathered himself. "Who will run, without hesitation, into the fire for her, risking his life."

Jude's heart thudded. *Is he saying. . . ?*

"I will never be able to repay you for what you have done for me." The inspector squeezed Jude's shoulder again. "You have my permission to approach my daughter with courtship. However, you cannot see her right now. I don't want her to make a rash decision while she is caught up in the romance of it all and refuse Mr. Covington's hand because you were the one who carried her from a burning building like some damsel in distress in one of her thousands of novels." He waved his hand over his head and rolled his eyes.

Jude's throat closed with emotion, and he stuck his hand out to the inspector. "Thank you, sir. I will make it my mission in life to keep your daughter safe and happy."

He clasped Jude's hand. "If she is happy, then I am happy." Clearing his throat, he stepped back. "Now, to the business at hand. Since Holmes is still on the loose, I want you to continue to act as Winnifred's guard until we are certain he is not in the city anymore. As per your suggestion, I have officers on their way to the Wilmette house." He lifted Jude's small, black leather notebook. "I'll read over your case notes, and hopefully there will be something that will lead us to his location sooner rather than later."

Chapter Twenty-Six

"I love you not only for what you are,
but for what I am when I am with you."
~Elizabeth Barrett Browning

Winnifred awoke to a single candle burning beside her bed. She blinked, confused as to why the room was so dark. Her gaze flitted to the mantel clock. *Eight o'clock? Did I sleep the day away?* She rose on her elbows, panic setting in at being alone at night. Her forehead beaded with sweat as she watched the candlelight dance, casting a sinister shadow on the wall and bringing to life the memory of the crackling floorboards and smoke descending into the dark pit.

She scrambled to her feet, but the moment she set the slightest bit of weight on her left ankle, she cried out in pain. She gripped the bedpost and leaned heavily against the wood, taking a breath to steady herself and attempting to gain her thoughts. *You are not going to die in that hole. Jude found you. The Lord sent you Jude.*

Her gaze fell to her open Bible, resting on the chair beside her. She didn't remember putting it there. She reached for it, held the pages up to the candle, and read, "The Lord is my light and my salvation; whom shall I fear? The Lord is the strength of my life; of whom shall I be afraid? When the wicked, even mine enemies and my foes, came upon me to eat up my flesh, they stumbled and fell." She closed her eyes and allowed the psalm to bathe her in peace. In spite of all the evil that Holmes had intended for her, the Lord had other plans and had led her to find Miss Lance and had sent her Jude in her moment of need.

Oh Jude. Winnifred ached to feel his arms about her once again, protecting her from harm. She was gripped with the need to see him. If she could only see Jude's face, she could return to sleep, certain he was well. Slipping on her coral dressing robe, she slid off the mattress, knowing without a doubt that he would be below her window, protecting her as he'd promised. She grasped the bedpost, reaching for the chair in a slow, labored movement to get to the window seat. Hopping on one foot, she crossed the room, grabbing whatever she could manage. She sank onto the seat with a grunt, sweat dripping down her neck from the effort.

Winnifred pressed her hands against the glass and absorbed its coolness and rested her forehead against the windowpane. She didn't care that she looked like someone trying to escape as she searched the street below until she found him standing under the lamppost. She threw open the window. "Jude," she called in a loud, hoarse whisper, nearly cringing at the thought of her father hearing her from the parlor. "Jude!"

He trotted over to her window and looked up at her, concern edging his every feature. "Winnie! Is something wrong?"

I'm being held captive in the name of resting, so it wouldn't necessarily be a lie to hint that something is amiss. Satisfied with her reasoning, she waved him up. "I need you." *There, that wasn't a lie.*

Climbing the latticework, Jude was up the side of the house before she could even think of her excuse for calling him up. He grasped the ivy-covered windowsill and without effort, slipped inside, his feet landing on her floor with a light thud. He scanned the room, his gaze pausing on the open door. "Is someone out there?" he whispered, pointing toward the hall.

Her plan had seemed flawless at the time, but when she gazed up into his golden eyes, she lost all train of thought.

"Winnie? What's wrong?"

"I'm afraid there's lots wrong. But it's not because of someone roaming about the house." She sank onto the window seat, hoping that if she did not look at him, she could gather herself enough to say what was on her heart.

He gently cupped her chin in his palm and lifted her gaze, questions in his eyes. "Winnie?"

She sighed and gave a half-hearted shrug. "I'm afraid I'm all out of books and there's no one here who can save me. They all think I need rest, but what I need is more books."

His concerned brow smoothed. "So, you need to be rescued?"

"I'm afraid so." She rose, mindfully tucking her injured foot up under her, and hopped toward him, nearly losing her balance. "I'm quite the damsel in distress, really."

He shook his head, laughing as he grabbed her elbows, steadying her. "If there is one thing you are not, it is a damsel in distress." He stroked an escaped curl behind her ear. "I wish I could stay, but. . ." His gaze flicked to the doorway, his meaning clear. "I'm afraid that in a novel, a hero might attend a damsel in distress in her chambers, but if it's not an emergency, *I* had better take my leave before your father has me thrown in jail. Then you will have to do the rescuing."

Her cheeks burned at his gentle admonishment. She grasped her dressing robe's collar and pulled it against her neck, suddenly aware at how the situation would appear to anyone who had not just been delivered from a burning building in the arms of the man she loved.

"But may I come call on you in the morning?" he asked.

Her heart soared. *Call on me?* She knew he could have said visit or check on her, but he'd deliberately said *call.* "I would love that. Yes." *A thousand times, yes!*

He grinned as if he could hear her thoughts. "I really want to kiss you right now, but—"

"But you are aware that her father, who is an inspector, heard you enter through the window and might catch you?" Her father's voice sounded behind them, making her start and lose her footing again.

Jude grabbed hold of her waist and eased her back down onto

her cushioned window seat. "Sir, I'm sorry. I didn't mean—I thought she was in danger."

He lifted his hand, staying Jude's explanation. "I heard Winnie call for you. Well, Daughter, since you are awake and seem far too excited to sleep, perhaps we can all adjourn to the parlor where we can discuss the case at length." Without waiting for their reply, he scooped her up and marched them downstairs, placing Winnifred on the settee and propping her ankle upon his favorite tufted footstool. He then draped a blanket over her for added modesty before joining her on the settee with Jude's case notes in hand.

"Have you spoken with Miss Lance?" Her heart hammered in her chest, eager for any news.

"She is awake and on the mend, thank the Lord. However, she doesn't remember how she got into the room under the trap door."

"What? How could she *not* remember?" It took everything for Winnifred to block the vivid memories.

"The doctors think she has amnesia, which was brought on by the traumatic events of her ordeal. She could remember within days, years, or never. There was one thing on her person that she did not recall." He withdrew a brooch from his waistcoat. "This was in her pocket."

Winnifred gasped, pressing her hands to her chest.

"Is that—" Jude asked, his gaze flitting between her and the piece of jewelry.

"Yes." Winnifred took it from her father and turned it over to find that hint of green caught in the pin. "I'm fairly certain this belonged to the woman at the fair I saw all those weeks ago. I must have dropped it by accident in Miss Lance's room and she found it and brought it to Holmes." She blanched. "He must have panicked and wanted to get her out of the way. Miss Lance almost died because of *me*."

Jude shot to his feet and crossed the room, kneeling in front of her. "Do not place that on your shoulders. It is because of you that

Miss Lance is alive. Holmes most likely marked her as his next victim anyway."

Father grasped her hand. "Jude is right. There is too much blame being passed about when it is *one* man who was the cause of all this evil. Holmes was the one who attempted to murder her and you are a witness. That alone will be enough to detain him until his trial."

"That does bring me a small measure of comfort. And of course, there is always the charges of arson and insurance fraud," she added.

Father's brows rose. "I thought he'd just completed that building?"

"I have been in that building for the past month, and I can tell you that the third floor is slapped together." She tapped the notebook. "If you read further, you will read about when Jude went to different contractors, following up on the leads I found in the ledgers. Except for his primary lawyer, Holmes has never paid a single one of them for their work. It was worth it to him to burn the third floor for the insurance."

Jude nodded. "It's true. He owes so much on the building that the insurance would be the quickest way for him to make money and not have to pay off creditors."

"So you have no doubt that he was burning his building for the insurance money?" Father asked, looking to Winnifred.

"Positive. Before he threw me into that secret room, I saw him with the pitch in his hands that he was using to coat the third story to light it ablaze. Holmes has always been upfront about his insurance policies with his employees and requires all of his staff and boarders to fill out an insurance form. If you look into his policies for Emeline Cigrand and Minnie Williams, I'm certain you will see they have been claimed. He said that after I perished in the fire, he would gain ten thousand dollars from my insurance policy."

Jude pressed his lips into a grim line. "I can attest to that, sir. It is not the first time he's tried to fake someone's death to claim insurance money. . .a fact that Victor paid with his life upon learning."

Father groaned and leaned his head into his hands, betraying his pain at this news. "The depth of this man's depravity is astounding. We will open Officer Victor Wallace's case again and see that he has justice. Even without any evidence for attempted murder, we can, at the least, book Holmes with insurance fraud based on his actions tonight."

"Have the men found Holmes yet, Father?"

"He's disappeared into thin air. I'm sure he's going to lay low for a very long time. But know this." Father reached for her hand, squeezing it. "We *will* find him. And when we do, he will be charged to the full extent of the law for the death of Officer Wallace and be put where he will no longer hurt anyone. Until then"—he tapped Jude's case notes—"we will open a missing person investigation on Mrs. Conner, her daughter Pearl Conner, Miss Cigrand, and Miss Williams, with Holmes as the prime suspect in their disappearances."

"Disappearances? I can only hope they have disappeared and he did not do something to them." Winnifred twisted her hands in her lap as memories haunted her. "When I first checked the Conners' room, Mrs. Conner's trunks were abandoned along with Pearl's favorite doll, and I found stains on the floor that looked like dried blood."

Father jotted down her comment before closing the notebook, and rose. "We will check on that as well. I had best be on my way to prepare the detectives. Tomorrow, we are going to question the staff and all the boarders to get to the bottom of this." He looked at Jude. "You may keep Winnie company for one hour, but then my daughter needs to rest." His eyes sparked with a hint of mischief. "For I believe she will have a caller coming tomorrow morning."

Chapter Twenty-Seven

"We were together. I forget the rest."
~Walt Whitman

October 1893

Strolling toward the grip car line to see the fair one last time before it closed, Winnifred couldn't keep the smile off her face as she listened to Jude recount his day, giving her all the delicious details that he knew she enjoyed. Having Jude court her was so unlike having him as her protector. He was less guarded in his attentiveness to her, affectionate and tender. His heart was hers, and his adoration proclaimed it to the world.

"What on earth?" He paused in his story, breaking her reverie as he paused across the street from her beloved Banning's Bookshop. The doorway was positively bursting with women.

Approaching the storefront, Winnifred found it more crowded inside than she'd ever seen in her entire life. "There must be some sort of author event?" she guessed, weaving through the crowd to see for herself.

Women were dressed in their finest visiting gowns, their hair perfectly curled, coiled, and pinned. Their fans fluttered in the heat of so many bodies, and all carried a copy of Percival's latest work that had released only two weeks ago, causing one of the greatest stirs among her circle. Being so absorbed with Jude, she had missed her chance to place her name on the request list for the first shipment and had not been able to procure a copy for herself. Whenever someone began discussing it over tea, she fairly ran away with her fingers in her ears, not wishing to hear even the tiniest point of the plot for fear it would spoil the novel before the next shipment arrived at Banning's.

The flustered owner waved to her, but did not come to greet her as was his usual custom. She looked to where the crowd of women were pressing and saw that a small platform with a desk had been set up at the front of the store. She gasped at the sight of Percival sitting behind the desk, pen in hand, signing copies left and right with a poster next to him that read, *"Meet the famous Percival Valentine, author of* His Secret Wife *and his latest success,* The Swan in the Murder Castle.*"

Her mouth dropped, and she grabbed Jude's forearm. "Percy is exposing that he is the author."

Jude's own jaw dropped. "And he titled his book after you?"

Her cheeks reddened, but she couldn't deny it. "Seems so."

Upon seeing them, Percy rose from his desk, lifting his arms to quiet the buzz in the store. "Ladies and gentlemen," he began, though upon Winnifred's glance about, she saw that the only gentlemen present were Jude, the owner, and himself, "I would like to introduce you to the *real* Cordelia Swan from my latest work, *The Swan in the Murder Castle!*"

The women gasped and turned, shock in their gazes, and a few with jealousy lining their thin smiles.

"You are Cordelia?" The woman next to Winnifred gaped, pressing her copy that was already showing signs of wear to her ample chest. "How romantic!"

The ladies surrounding Winnifred looked her up and down as if finding her lacking while others murmured with joy upon meeting the real heroine. "Oh, how wonderful to have two men vying for your hand," the rotund lady next to her cried, her fan all aflutter.

"And beside her is the *real* detective who stole the heart of Cordelia Swan, Detective Jude Thorpe!" At this announcement, Winnifred was completely eclipsed. Jude attempted to step away, but the women pressed on him from all sides, begging for an autograph from the hero they declared the handsomest man they had ever beheld.

Seeing Jude's dismay, Winnifred couldn't help but laugh. She couldn't argue with their frantic assessment. Women practically swooned as they pressed their pencils into his hand. "Can you sign it, 'To Jane, my damsel.'"

"No." He gave Winnifred a look, begging for help. "I don't even know what I would be signing, and who is Jane?"

The pretty girl laughed. "*I'm* Jane, of course, and this is the book about you and Cordelia Swan and the Murder Castle."

Winnifred lifted her brow at the name. *Murder Castle. . .sadly accurate.*

Jude flipped the cover open, his brows rising as he tilted the page for Winnifred to read the dedication.

She read aloud, " 'To the real Cordelia Swan, the one who got away.'" She looked up at Jude, hoping that the uncomfortable situation did not just get worse. From the way it sounded, Percival had grown fonder of her since their parting ways. Before she could apologize, another avid reader grasped Jude's sleeve, begging for his signature.

"Darling Winnie!" A familiar pair of arms embraced her.

"Danielle?" Winnifred squealed with excitement. "I thought you still had a week of your honeymoon left."

"Business brought us home last night. I was going to stop by your house this morning with a signed copy for you as a present, but then I received *all* of your letters to discover that you know the author!" She grabbed her by the arm and giggled. "I'm sure you melted when you discovered it was Percy. I know I did! You must come to my new home to tell me all about your time with him and about you-know-who." She grinned and nodded toward Jude, who waved Winnifred over to him, desperation in his eyes as the women clamored for his autograph.

"I will, and I want to hear all about your own adventures," she replied, giving her best friend a kiss on the cheek. "I'd better go help him, but I'll see you tomorrow?"

"Absolutely." Danielle laughed and squeezed her arm. "Now go. I don't want to lose my place in line."

Winnifred began to weave through the mass that had formed between her and Jude. She felt someone grab her by the elbow and turned to find Percy. He tilted his head, motioning for her to follow him a few feet away to the corner of the store. The ladies near them quieted in what Winnifred was certain was an attempt to overhear the conversation between a former beau and his lost lady.

"Miss Wylde, I'm so sorry about all this. I hadn't meant to expose you today, but it felt as if it was a divine moment. I had to acknowledge the woman who inspired me to claim my work. *You* made me proud of what I wrote. While it may not be as grand as being a lawyer to some, *I* am finally proud of it." He pressed a book into her hand. "I was going to send this to you with a note telling you about publicly claiming my pseudonym." His gaze met hers, and he gave her a small, knowing smile. "I heard from my mother that you and Jude are courting, and I wish you every happiness."

"And I you, Mr. *Valentine*." She lifted the book. "Thank you. This is only the beginning of your fame. I can feel it."

He grinned. "I hope so, but my greatest hope is that we can still be friends? And that I might be able to run a plot point by you if I have a question or need some advice?"

She smiled at him and stroked the book's rich red cover. "It would be an honor." She turned, looking for Jude, who was waving her over again. "Now, you'd best get back to your adoring followers so I can rescue my hero."

He gave her elbow a squeeze and returned to the platform as Winnifred grasped Jude's arm and drew him away from the crowd. "Excuse me, ladies, I'm afraid this hero is already taken."

Escaping outside, Jude removed his hat, wiping at his forehead with his sleeve. "I have never felt so overwhelmed, not even when I was in the middle of an angry crowd in New York." He looked at her, brows lifted, "You book enthusiasts are insane!"

She laughed and grabbed his hand, pulling him toward the grip car line. "Come on, let's get you to the fair."

After dining at the Louisiana building's café for the last time, they promenaded in the court of honor, admiring the electric lights twinkling in the evening sky. "I'm going to miss this." She paused, resting her head against his shoulder. "I can't believe that in two weeks, everything will be gone."

"Well, not everything." Jude grasped her hand, turning her to him.

Winnifred gazed up at him, the stars beginning to shine above, casting a glow on his tousled brown hair. "I'll never forget our first day here together."

"Shall we take one final Ferris wheel ride and say good-bye to the fair in style?" Jude threaded her hand through his strong arm.

Smiling, she allowed him to pull her toward the Midway and onto the Ferris wheel. Surprisingly, no one else boarded the last car with them. They stood by the panoramic window as they rose in the night sky, and she observed the fair with Jude's hand wrapped around hers in silent contentment. At the very top, she felt him move away and turned to find him kneeling. Her heart thudded as he reached into his pocket and retrieved a gold ring with a small amethyst nestled between two gold roses.

"Winnifred Rose Wylde, this summer has been the best of my life. And for once, the summer does not have to come to an end. I love you with every breath of my body. Will you be my Wylde summer rose forever?"

"I was yours the moment I met you, and I will love you for

always." Winnifred grasped his face between her hands and delicately, tentatively drew her lips to his in a sweet, gentle kiss that promised their happily ever after was only just beginning.

Acknowledgments

To the reader: Thank you for getting to know Winnifred Wylde and Jude Thorpe. I hope you loved them as much as I do!

To my husband, Dakota: You are and always will be my inspiration for all heroes. Thank you for your constant encouragement and support in my writing. I could not write without you, especially now that we have our sweet baby boy. I love you!

To my little treasure, Liam, my baby: Thank you for your snuggles of support and for showing me a new side of the Lord's unconditional love for His children.

To my family, Dad, Mama, Charlie, Molly, Sam, Eli, Aunt Maureen, and Amelie: Thank you for babysitting all those hours to help me meet my deadline. And for all of your encouragement! Isn't there a saying about it takes a village to help write a book?

To my wonderful betas, Theresa and McKenna: Thank you for your guidance, reassurance, and cheering.

To my wonderful agent Tamela Hancock Murray: Thank you so much for your encouragement over the years and for always believing in me and my writing. Your support and dedication made this novel possible!

To Becky and Ellen and the Barbour Publishing team: Thank you for your countless hours of hard work to bring Winnifred and Jude's story to life! Y'all are wonderful!

And to the Lord for His steadfastness and constant, overwhelming love.

Author's Note

While Winnifred Wylde is a fictional character, Doctor H. H. Holmes was very real and became infamously known as America's first serial killer.

True to the story, Holmes used many aliases. Although his birth name was Herman W. Mudgett, he most often went by Henry Howard Holmes, or simply H. H. Holmes. He actually did use the name H. A. Williams to obtain a real estate loan for his so-called sister, Minnie Williams, who was believed to be his lover at the time. Along with loan frauds, Holmes also dealt heavily in life insurance fraud.

Not mentioned in the book was Holmes's first and only legal marriage to Clara A. Lovering. The couple never divorced, but as you can guess from Holmes's character, he was not faithful to his first wife when he "married" Myrta and had a daughter, Lucy. This second family lived, unbeknownst to Myrta, in a house under Minnie Williams's name.

It is believed that Holmes's secretaries, Miss Cigrand and Miss Williams, and his former boarder and friend's wife, a Mrs. Conner, all at one point fancied themselves in love with Holmes and later became his victims, along with Mrs. Conner's young daughter, Pearl. Miss Williams's younger sister was last seen with Holmes, and it was her mysterious disappearance that inspired the kidnapping of "the woman in green" in my story.

Upon his arrest, newspapers across the country dubbed Holmes's building the "Murder Castle" and depicted it with varying designs. For the most part I relied on sketches from an article in the *Chicago Tribune* for my description of the maze of rooms that Holmes designed for killing without detection. To keep his nefarious activities secret, Holmes would continually hire and fire contractors so that no one could fully grasp what he was up to. The Murder Castle really did have a trap door, windowless rooms, and spaces between floors. I added the second trap door and changed a location of a room or two for the purposes of the story.

The article written in the *Chicago Tribune* about Holmes's strange castle was quickly forgotten in the excitement of the world's fair since Holmes had not been caught committing any crime worth an arrest. The Murder Castle was merely considered another curiosity in the news.

The fire scene is also based on fact. Holmes owed so many contractors, investors, furniture suppliers, and laborers from the construction of his building that collecting the insurance payout is believed to have been the reason he coated the third floor in tar and set it ablaze. The burning of the trunk of evidence was a fictional addition.

After the fire, Holmes fled Chicago and "married" Georgiana Yoke, the beautiful, young teacher with whom he had been corresponding. Thus he became a bigamist twice over, as he was still married to both Clara and Myrta.

Holmes was eventually caught, tried, and executed for his crimes, but it was a long, gruesome path to the gallows, along which many innocents tragically died at his hand.

Grace Hitchcock is the author of three novellas in *The Second Chance Brides*, *The Southern Belle Brides*, and the *Thimbles and Threads* collections with Barbour Publishing. *The White City* is her debut novel. She holds a Masters in Creative Writing and a Bachelor of Arts in English with a minor in History. Grace lives in southern Louisiana with her husband, Dakota, and son. Visit her online at GraceHitchcock.com.

True Colors. True Crime.

The Pink Bonnet (June 2019)
by Liz Tolsma

A new series of books for fans of real history that is stranger than fiction continues with a stop in Memphis during 1932. In trying to protect her three-year-old daughter, Cecile Dowd unwittingly puts her into the clutches of Georgia Tann, corrupt Memphis Tennessee Children's Home Society director suspected of the disappearance of hundreds of children.

Paperback / 978-1-64352-045-2 / $12.99

The Yellow Lantern (August 2019)
by Angie Dicken

When a doctor's assistant is forced to be a spy for grave robbers, she must await the next funeral while working at a cotton mill. But what price will she pay when she falls in love with the manager of the mill and her secrets begin to unravel?

Paperback / 978-1-64352-083-4 / $12.99